Justice Denied

Judge Wilhelmina Carson Series

Justice Denied

M. Diane Vogt

Writer's Showcase
presented by *Writer's Digest*
San Jose New York Lincoln Shanghai

Justice Denied

Writer's Showcase
presented by *Writer's Digest*
an imprint of iUniverse.com, Inc.

For information address:
iUniverse.com, Inc.
620 North 48th Street, Suite 201
Lincoln, NE 68504-3467
www.iuniverse.com

ISBN: 0-595-12897-1

Printed in the United States of America

For Robert.

Acknowledgements

Every book is a community project and this one is no exception. For insights into the military mind, I thank my friend and neighbor, Lt. Colonel Robert H. Barrow, USMC, as well as my friend, William G.K. Smoak and countless other fine men and women who were so generous with their time. My colleagues at the Bar, and the many excellent judges I have had the good fortune to know, give Willa her realism without the burden of her quirks and eccentricities. Tom and Katie Hill, the most experienced police officers I know, read the early drafts and helped with technical issues.

JUSTICE DENIED would not have been written without the enthusiastic support and advice of my reading group: Michelle Bearden, Kate Caldwell, Betty Cohen, Laura Howard, Allison Jennewein, Deborah Jordan, Rochelle Reback, Robin Rosenberg, Wendy Cousins Savage, and Amy Sharitt Leobold. As always, my great friend and business partner, Lori-Ann Rickard, provided the cheering section every author needs, along with the all important critical eye.

My gratitude as well to Carolyn Cain, Doug Sahlin, John Taylor, Margaret Maron, Larry Block, Elaine Viets, Barbara Parker, Jim Norman, and other members of the Florida Chapter of Mystery Writers of America, who listen to my rants, offer editorial service and web design, and just generally, support mystery writers in Florida and everywhere. Thanks to the members of DorothyL, probably the best web address out there, SILICONE SOLUTION found an audience that made JUSTICE DENIED possible.

My readers, family, friends, neighbors and co-workers who have encouraged me to keep going. Without you, none of this would have happened.

Perhaps most importantly, to Robert, my partner in everything.

1

The day John Hamilton was shot was the last normal day of my life. I didn't know that at the time, of course, but it was obvious with the clarity of perfect hind sight. Things had been changing around me without my participation, permission or perception for several weeks. That Friday morning, I was half watching the final testimony in the Senate confirmation hearings from my chambers in Tampa's Old Federal Courthouse while I tried to catch up on my orders.

My name is Willa Carson and like other United States District Court judges here in the Tampa Division of the Middle District of Florida, I have a constant, never ending, boat load of work that threatens to bury me long before I have a chance to die a natural death. A new Supreme Court Justice is more important to me than a lot of other news since General Andrews would control my life in many ways if he was confirmed and I wasn't overly happy about that.

Not since President Bush had appointed Clarence Thomas to the Supreme Court in 1991 had there been such a public display of outrage at a President's choice as we'd been subjected to since General Albert Randall Andrews, Tampa's highest ranking Army officer, was nominated to join Thomas on the bench. Today, the crowd outside the Capitol building in Washington, D.C. was larger than on the first days of the hearings. I felt sorry for the protesters. It's not easy to have the courage of your convictions after standing outside for nine days of January ice showers.

At the beginning of the march, the protesters had been neatly organized, with the right-to-lifers on the left, the gays and lesbians on the right, and the anti-military group in the center, flowing out to the back, but the factions had mingled into a single, huddled mass. The homemade signs they carried were soaked. Blue magic marker ink running off onto the hands and heads of the sign carriers gave them an even more bedraggled look. Fires in old barrels were the gathering places for anyone who could get near them. I barely registered the scene while I was working at my desk, but the commentators shivered while ice water dripped off their umbrellas in the cold and made me glad I live in Florida. It so rarely rains here in January that I leave the top down on my car for weeks at a time. I'm self indulgent that way. Or maybe, just lazy.

Despite the horrid weather, the protesters came and waited and every day their numbers grew. They chanted, picketed, sang songs. Whenever a member of the media came by, they raised their faces and their voices, hoping to be recorded, seen, and heard on the constant coverage by MSNBC. This time, unlike the weak- principled liberals who opposed Judge Thomas, they vowed, they would win. To have that level of determination was a wondrous thing, indeed. I like to think I'd had it once, when I was young and idealistic. Not anymore.

Things change, of course. I know that. I've lived almost 40 years and I've learned a few things. To do what these protesters were doing required the kind of conviction I no longer possess. Why not? Before I was appointed to the bench, I practiced law long enough to learn that there are always thirteen sides to every story. There is no black and white; no right and wrong. And it's always "what have you done for me lately?" General Andrews was finding that out now. It must have been a hard lesson for a popular war hero to learn.

For an hour, the television commentators rehashed the course of the hearings. No one had a crystal ball and predictions of the outcome ranged from a complete victory to total loss—for both sides. Whether the nominee would be confirmed was alternately feared or cheered, depending on the speaker's point of view.

I had the television on, but I hadn't really started watching the coverage when, about ten minutes before the hearings were set to begin, the Supreme Court nominee's limousine pulled up to the curb. The Capitol Hill Police personnel assigned to assure his safety surrounded the car and the passenger door opened. I glanced up from my work to see the first man step out. It was the nominee's personal secretary, John Hamilton. As he straightened up and rose to his full height of five feet, he looked around at the crowd. Hamilton took an opened black umbrella from one of the officers standing to his right while I was barely paying attention, waiting for the real story to start. Then, Hamilton stood to the side to let the nominee, General Albert Randall Andrews, out of the car. I jerked my head up when I heard a loud pop, pop, pop over the noise of the chanting crowd. I watched the chaos, horrified and impotent. Screaming and falling bodies were everywhere. Hamilton went down, almost like a cartoon, flat on his face. On international television. It reminded me of news clips I'd seen when Jack Ruby shot Lee Harvey Oswald, right in front of God and everybody. Americans have a long history of shooting political figures they don't agree with. Look at Lincoln, both Kennedys, King, Ford, Reagan. Sometimes, like Jim Brady in the Reagan shooting, someone else gets in the way.

I picked up the remote and turned up the sound on the television. My eyes were glued to the set now as the camera panned the front lines of the crowd and quickly spotted a man with a gun making his way up to the curb. The instant replay showed Hamilton step out of the car and the shooter raise his arms while holding a hunting rifle. The rifle's recoil reflected three shots to Hamilton's chest. The shooter was wrestled to the ground and taken away in handcuffs in a matter of seconds, as Hamilton was quickly put on a stretcher and moved to the waiting helicopter.

The television picture had my full attention as General and Mrs. Andrews stayed in the car, almost invisible in the crush of the crowd, until the paramedics arrived. As both a judge and the wife of a highly placed Republican, I'm accustomed to seeing people I know personally on television. But to view people I know being shot and trapped in a car by an angry mob was surreal, a familiar scene grotesquely formed. I knew the General's famous temper would make him want to get out of that car and beat the shooter to a bloody pulp. Apparently, his handlers knew better than to let him do that. So they waited inside the car until the D.C. police marched into the street, up to the car and surrounded the passenger doors.

Madeline Andrews would be terrified. She was a gentle soul, not meant for the line of fire. When Madeline chose Andy, did she think she'd be subjected to the glare of media scrutiny, pummeled by questions, even shot at? How could she have known? None of us can predict the future and how well can we ever really know another person? Especially when, like Andy and Madeline, we marry young.

I thought about my own marriage and knew I'd be no better suited as a human target than Madeline was. But my husband, George, would never put me in that situation or any other situation that might hurt me, physically or otherwise. George viewed it as one of his missions in life to take care of me. He would be furious that even a potential judicial candidate could be gunned down in the full daylight with half the country watching. Not that I was all that keen on the idea, either.

"George is perfect," all my friends tell me. George was a banker when I married him. But now, he owns and operates Tampa's finest five star restaurant and handles our investments. He says it's the perfect job: it pays well, you're your own boss and you can spend most of the day in your pajamas. George is tall, dark and handsome–at least to me. But I do admit, he can be a little stuffy sometimes. He might be the only man on the planet who still carries a pressed linen monogrammed handkerchief every day. All the women love George, but they don't have to live with him. I imagined Madeline Andrews thinking something close to the same thing right now. All the country loved a war hero, but they don't have to live with him. Not for the first time, I wondered why she'd want to.

I watched as General and Mrs. Andrews were hustled out into the corridor formed by uniformed police officers holding open, black umbrellas. They walked up the Capitol steps and into the building to continue the hearing. General Andrews was virtually invisible inside the protective parallel columns of policemen. And no one else shot at him.

Inside, the Senate Judiciary Committee was already seated, Democrats on the left. Appropriately, George, would say. His politics are more than a little bit right of center, which is one of the few things we disagree about. The questioning of a Supreme Court nominee is done by seniority, alternating between the parties. After days of questions, it was a good thing someone was keeping track of who was next. Those of us watching the hearings could only try to keep up.

This morning, Senator Sheldon Warwick, another Tampa resident who wasn't on my list of favorite people, opened the hearings as he had each of the last nine days. Warwick was the powerful Chairman of the Senate Judiciary Committee and the senior senator from Florida. Today, he expressed his condolences to Hamilton's family and to the General whom, we all presumed, narrowly missed losing a close personal friend just now. As he always does, Warwick sounded more than a little insincere to me when he asked, "Would you like to delay today's questioning, General? We would certainly understand."

General Andrews was appointed by the current Democratic President. Whatever Senator Warwick's personal feelings, often plain throughout the past few days, Warwick—a Democrat—was not going to be faulted for lack of decorum or apparent respect for a war hero and one of the former Joint Chiefs.

For his part, Andrews could have been carved on Mount Rushmore. He was six feet of tall, cool, granite sitting there, waiting for another round from his own personal firing squad, dodging bullets without moving. He appeared completely unfazed by what happened outside. Andrews' demeanor was the same straight-ahead, unflinching look he'd been giving all of the committee members for hours of testimony. The look that's bred into every senior military man. The one designed to quell fears and coerce submission from all in its path. "Thank you, Senator," he said as if he'd been offered tea and toast. "No."

I wondered, not for the first time, how a man like that could have compassion for those less fortunate and why the President had ever appointed such an inexperienced, unyielding man to the Court. I could think of a dozen more qualified, less controversial candidates. George's theory is that General Andrews must have dirty pictures on the President, or something equally vile. But George is a very active, influential, conservative Republican. He would disapprove of anyone the Democrats chose, regardless of his suitability. Like a winning football team in the final minutes of the Super Bowl, the Republicans were in control of the Congress and they were trying to run out the clock on the Democratic President whose term ends in less than a year. Republicans want none of this President's judicial appointments confirmed, hoping to stall until they again control the White House and the appointment process.

Today was the last day of the hearings before the Committee took its vote. There had been acrid, bitter and vicious testimony given by high-ranking and influential witnesses for six days. He could not be compelled to do so, but General Andrews had consented to testify. So far, that seemed like a huge mistake in judgment to me. The television coverage had been constant, the Committee working well into the night and through the weekends. For most of it, I was glued to the set. I wasn't about to miss the grand finale. Everyone in Tampa's Old Federal Courthouse was watching, anyway. No hearings would get held today in my courtroom or in any other.

Senator Warwick passed the questioning to Senator Houston, the reigning senior Democrat from Alabama. Senator Houston was ten years older than God. He'd been through all this many times before. He was smooth and had a way of sneaking up on witnesses without them even knowing it. Verbally, of course. In this case, Houston was supposed to be supporting his party's nominee. Why he hadn't been doing that gave the commentators countless hours of on-air speculation time.

"General," Houston said, in his long, slow drawl, giving the word about four more minutes, "Why do you think some fellow out front would want to kill you?"

Without so much as a flinch or a pause, General Andrews said, "Why do you think he wanted to kill *me*? He shot my secretary. I haven't any idea why he did that. Do you?"

The conversation in the room buzzed at louder decibels. It wasn't like General Andrews to sidestep any issue. Usually he confronted everything head on, loudly and with opinionated obstinacy. In fact, that was what had been getting him into trouble with the crowds so far. It seemed General Andrews had an opinion on everything. Not unusual for a general, but likely to get a Supreme Court nominee rejected. The thing the public fears most, and his opposition hopes for, is a nominee with an opinion. Sandra Day O'Connor got confirmed even after she testified that she personally deplored abortion, but would not let her personal views influence her vote. Of course, she was a Republican, George said. To him, that meant you could trust her word.

During these hearings, the General went out of his way to state his opinions as controversially as possible. Almost as if in challenge. Although he kept saying "I have no personal agenda to take to the Court," every time he was asked a direct question on a controversial issue, he didn't hesitate to state his views.

He was for abortion. "Why should any more unwanted children be brought into the world?" He was against gun control. "Why not let the drug dealers kill each other? Save us all some money." He opposed prayer and supported corporal punishment in the schools. "We need prayer at home, where it belongs," he said. "Hitting children gets their attention." He opposed gays in the military and the volunteer army. "It's every man's patriotic duty to serve, but we don't need the morale problems coming with sexual experimentation programs in the military." He favored the death penalty. "Prison doesn't deter crime, but death makes damn sure that particular felon won't commit another crime." He opposed welfare and any support for the homeless. "Those people would be fine if they'd just get a job and support themselves." And perhaps the biggest sin to conservatives, Andrews thought the Supreme Court should make the law, not just interpret the Constitution. "This country needs help. The founding fathers died over two hundred years ago. And if they lived here now, they'd be making some changes, too."

General Andrews had not heeded Benjamin Franklin's advice that it is better to keep one's mouth shut and be thought a fool than to open it and remove all doubt. Andrews managed to offend Democrats and Republicans, conservatives and liberals, men, women, children, scholars, clerics, radicals, gay and straight alike. The pundits had dubbed him the Archie Bunker of the Supreme Court. He was becoming a laughing stock, but the possibility that he might actually be confirmed was not a joke. Polls showed that Andrews was very popular with most voters and a war hero besides.

Americans have had a long love affair with military men. We hadn't had an opportunity to put one in high office since Eisenhower. Some people thought it was time to do it again. If General Andrews ran for President, even George thought he would win. The wonder wasn't that someone tried to kill Andrews today, but that more than one person hadn't tried it before now. And the bigger mystery, to every thinking person in the country, was why in the hell President Benson had appointed such an obviously unsuitable candidate to replace the ultraconservative Chief Justice when he retired, even if Andy was a popular general. George's dirty pictures theory was looking better all the time.

Senator Houston continued, just as unruffled as Andrews, but considerably more rumpled. Not many big older men can stay crisp under the glare of hot lights. Strictly speaking, General Andrews wasn't entitled to wear his uniform now that he'd retired, but he had it on anyway. Almost in deliberate contrast, Senator Houston's uniform was the businessman's suit, a symbol of the civilian authority Andrews was attempting to join. It was January in Washington, but the cold outside was heated to boiling by hot lights, hot tempers and hot air inside. Senator Houston's bald head gleamed with sweat, but he was not deterred.

"General, just a few minutes ago one member of that very large, angry crowd of Americans outside walked up to the curb and shot the first man to get out of your car. Are you trying to tell this committee that you believe you were not the target of that crime?"

"Not at all, Senator. I'm saying I don't know that. And neither do you. Why should we assume it? I'm very sorry for John Hamilton, and I'll be going to the hospital to see him as soon as I'm released here. I'm pleased that the man who shot him has already been apprehended. Since he committed his crime on television for the world to see, I expect a speedy conviction and an appropriate punishment. I don't see it as relevant to our purpose here today."

The buzz of the crowd grew louder. Someone gasped. Senator Houston just smiled. He said "General, I take it you don't believe a Supreme Court Justice should be elected by popular vote?" Houston looked over his half-glasses at the crowd and they laughed appreciatively.

"Senator, I have defended democracy and representative government on the front lines of three wars and several peace keeping missions. I don't think my patriotism can be seriously questioned. When I returned from the third Gulf War, I received a hero's welcome. Are you suggesting I'm not popular with the people, or just with some right-wing nut case who wants me to change my stand on abortion?"

Touche', Andy, I murmured to myself. *Touche'*. The nomination was controversial from the start. Although Andy has a law degree, he's never practiced law and never served as a judge in any jurisdiction. That doesn't disqualify him from any federal appointment. After all, I'd never been a judge before my appointment, either. But at least I'd been a lawyer. Andy had never done that much. If the hearings demonstrated nothing else, they proved again that General Andrews is cool under pressure. That wasn't enough to make him a good justice and I knew from talking to George and Jason that many of the senators from both parties on the judiciary committee disapproved of him.

The hearing went on for two more hours and then concluded. Perhaps the committee felt no more damage could be done. Or maybe, like Andrews and Warwick, they all had Friday afternoon planes to catch. Andrews was hosting a benefit golf tournament tomorrow and I was signed up to play.

Senator Warwick announced the close of the committee's business, thanked the General for coming and said deliberations would begin in closed session Monday.

I turned off the television when the commentators began to rehash what I'd spent the day watching. I figured my take on it was as valid as theirs. I wasn't sure how the vote would go; how could they know? The committee would make a recommendation to the full Senate and we'd all just have to wait to see whether Andrews would get confirmed.

I asked my secretary to order grilled chicken and cole slaw from Gladstone's and worked straight through lunch time. I wanted to come in to the office tomorrow to clean up some of my cases and review the file for the trial that would start Monday, but I'd promised several weeks ago to play golf with my friend and former law partner in the annual General Andrews Blue Coat Golf Tournament this Saturday. It would be a long Sunday to get ready for the trial and I wasn't looking forward to it. If I didn't get these orders done today, I'd be putting in over ten hours on the Lord's day of rest.

I tried to concentrate on my work, but my thoughts returned to Andrews. For the first time in my married life, I dreaded going home.

George had become so obsessed with the Andrews nomination that my home had become a cold and lonely place. George's vehemence caused me to consider Andrews once again.

Like Norman Schwartzkopf, General Andrews is a Tampa treasure. He's lived here since he worked out of McDill air force base as a part of the joint command that directed the course of the third Gulf War. He lives at Tampa Green, an upscale golf resort on Lake Thonotosassa, now that he's retired. Two local schools were named after him and he lent his name to several charitable events. The General had my support, just for all the good works he'd done here in Tampa.

George feels very, very different about it. First, General Andrews is a Democrat. To George, that's just short of saying he's an ax murderer. There is only one party: the GOP, the Party of Lincoln, the Republicans. Conservative and capitalist. But George's GOP is big, inclusive, supportive and fiercely independent of big government. George agrees with Thomas Jefferson that self-discipline is the best discipline and there's no need for the government to take care of its citizens because the citizens can take care of themselves, if they're just allowed to do so. General Andrews' brand of liberalism is, to George, worse than anarchy.

Like I said, George is very active in Republican politics. He is very close to the Chairman of the Republican Party here in Florida, the fourth largest state in the Union. George doesn't hold any office in the Party, but only because he doesn't want to. Which is to say George is a very highly placed Republican, even if most voters have never heard of him. George has no patience for bureaucracy of any kind. He wants to be free to pick his battles, and he's picked this one.

George and I know General Andrews personally. George doesn't like him. If the committee recommends the nomination, the full Senate will endorse the recommendation. George had been lobbying with my brother, Jason, and anyone else who would talk to him, to be sure that didn't happen. He was royally angry that he hadn't seen it coming, but no one had. George was watching the hearings today. Either the house would be empty while George was out politicking tonight, or he'd have his team at home, strategizing the defeat of the nominee. I was weary of the whole mess, so I just kept working here where I had complete control of my environment.

When the security guard came by on his eight o'clock rounds at the courthouse, I gathered three volumes of the file for my Monday trial, *Newton v. The Whitman Esquire Review*, and left the office. Both the plaintiff and the defendant in the case left a lot to be desired, but I don't get to pick the cases that get assigned to me. The plaintiff was a notorious local lawyer with political aspirations and the defendant was a radical alternative scandal sheet that, but for the First Amendment, would have been put out of business long ago. I had trouble not only with what *The Review* chose to say, but also with their right to say it. Everyone is entitled to some privacy, in my view. And we should get to decide what gets shared. Airing their dispute over the extremely radical practice of gay "outing" in the public forum of my courtroom was not designed to protect anyone's privacy.

As I waited for the ancient elevator, I planned my strategy to avoid discussing the nomination with George when I got home.

Our private conversations, few as they were lately, revolved around Andrews. George spent every available waking moment with party members, senators we know, volunteers—in short, anyone who shared his opinion that General Andrews should never, under any circumstances, sit on the Supreme Court. Not for the first time, I wondered why George was so passionate about this. His interest had gone beyond influencing the process. He had a personal stake of some kind in the outcome that I just did not comprehend.

And he wasn't the only one. Senator Warwick, too, was obsessed with Andrews' nomination. He and George, normally polar opposites on political issues, joined forces on this one, although few people knew that. If they hadn't met several times in our home, I wouldn't have known it. When I asked George about it, he brushed me off. What was going on here?

Preoccupied with my concerns for George and a little jealous of the fascination this nomination seemed to have for him, I walked through to the parking garage, dumped the file on the passenger seat of the black opal Mercedes CLK I call Greta, put the top down and got in.

I tried to leave my reverie and really experience the short drive west on Bayshore Boulevard toward Plant Key. It was a new exercise called "mindfulness" I've been working on lately to satisfy my soul mother, Kate. The idea is to be completely aware and involved with the present moment, whatever you're doing. I've been practicing it faithfully on the drive home every day, but I can't say I'm getting any better at it. Kate assures me I'll get it eventually and when I do, she says it'll be a real awakening. Maybe. All I'm getting out of it so far is a reminder of the beautiful view of blue sky, winding tarmac, palm trees and water that surrounds my home. I guess that's not so bad either. Kate's a lot smarter than we all give her credit for. Too bad she's not clairvoyant. The ability to predict the future, changing only a few small things, would have saved us all.

2

Ten minutes later, I walked through the front door at Minaret, our nineteenth century home. Our flat is on the second floor. George's five star restaurant is on the main floor. Minaret is named after the bright steel onion dome on the top. Our house was built by Henry B. Plant, a local railroad baron who also built The Tampa Bay Hotel, now The University of Tampa. The dining room was the ballroom when the house was first built and today it comfortably holds about thirty round tables.

When I walked in, all the tables were full and prospective diners were waiting in the lobby. I hate coming home after six o'clock on Friday night because I can't get up the stairs without stopping to play hostess to whoever might be waiting for a table. Tonight, to my surprise, General Andrews and his entire family were waiting to be seated. If it bothered him that he'd just missed fatal lead poisoning this morning, he didn't show it.

I welcomed Andy and Madeline to George's. "Willa, what a pleasure to see you," Andy said, as he took my hand and kissed my cheek. Madeline gave me a little hug, too.

"You know our children, don't you?" Andy asked. Then he introduced them all to me again, the mark of a gracious man who has more than a little trouble remembering names of people he doesn't see regularly.

Andrews' sons were identical twins, Randy and Bobby. I'd met them years before but they didn't live in Tampa. They were both in the army, as their Dad had been until he retired. They looked a lot like their father: tall, dark and slight. Their brown hair and cornflower blue eyes were striking, but that seemed to be the full extent of their mother's contribution to their appearance.

The General's daughter, Robbie Andrews and her husband John Williamson, lived here in South Tampa and were also members at Great Oaks, where I play golf every Saturday. Actually, it was the only place to play golf that didn't require a twenty-minute drive, so most golfers in South Tampa were members there. Great Oaks has a very liberal admissions policy: anyone who applies gets in. Which was a good thing for me. A federal judge can't belong to any discriminatory societies, but that's another story.

Robbie had her broad back to her family, admiring the antique sideboard George's Aunt Minnie had left us with the house. She was opening the drawers, examining the brass pulls, just generally being nosy. Robbie turned and gave me a thin smile when her father said, "And you know Robbie and Jack, of course." I nodded in their direction while Robbie nodded back.

John was charming, as always. The pronounced white streak on the left of his widow's peak kept him from being blindingly handsome, although John was good looking in a rugged way. Not perfect, but he was one of those men that turned heads when he walked by. Everyone noticed John, men and women alike. His charming demeanor only added to his allure.

"What brings you all to George's tonight?" I asked Madeline and Andy, who were standing close together holding hands, as if they were young lovers, not a couple who had been married over thirty years.

"It's Andy's birthday today. There's no better restaurant in Tampa than George's," Madeline said with her typical soft southern sincerity. Madeline Andrews is a quiet woman, born and bred in south Georgia, a real southern belle. Her soft drawl is hard to hear and if she's ever said a negative word about anyone, it was not repeated to me. Madeline is every southern boy's fantasy wife, if the boy is of a certain age. She is without flaw as far as I can tell. Except her hair style, a page boy parted on one side and held in place by an unobtrusive beret, which looked exactly as it must have been styled by her mother at age six. I've begged my friends to tell me if I ever get so stuck in my glory days that I look like a caricature of a "nineties woman," whatever that is.

"We also thought we'd celebrate the end of those damn committee hearings," Andy said to me, smoothing his red striped tie over his flat stomach and closing the middle button of his navy sport coat. "I'm glad to be through with that inquisition. Next week they'll vote and then it'll go to the full senate. I should be on the job in no time at all. We'll have a chance to work together, Willa." Great. I can't wait, I thought.

John Hamilton's shooting proved that the "lunatic fringe" believed Andrews was about to be the next Supreme Court Justice, but based on the amount of behind-the-scenes work George had been doing, Andrews' nomination was far from certain to be confirmed. Then again, the commentators gave him a better than fifty percent chance of winning.

"I'm sure you're right, Andy," I told him as I said my goodbyes while the hostess seated them in the main dining room. Heads turned as polite diners sneaked covert glances at the man who might be the next Supreme Court Justice. Pondering the quantity of Andy's self-deception while completely oblivious to my own, I transferred my weighty files to my other arm and walked up the winding, open stairs to our flat before I could get stopped by someone else.

Pushing open the heavy oak door with my hip, walking into our living room and on through to my study, I dropped the heavy files onto the floral needle-pointed seat cushion of one of Aunt Minnie's harp-back chairs. I wouldn't lift those files again tonight and glared at them for being there.

I resented spending my Sunday on a case that, to my mind, never should have been filed in the first place. I tried every way I could think of to settle the case. Mr. Newton didn't need the money and was interested in clearing his name. Litigants who believe "it's the principle of the thing" are the bane of my existence. American jurisprudence today is not the principle of the thing. It's overworked, overcrowded and overcommitted to handling cases that are about real injustice and real damages. We don't have time for the principle of the thing. The principle of the thing is to settle your own grievances and stay out of court.

Harry and Bess, our two Labrador retrievers, were laying on the kitchen floor, not even bothering to raise their heads when I came through the door. "Can you tell by my footfalls that I'm not a burglar, or what?" I chastised them. Harry looked at me with one yellow eyebrow raised. Bess started to get up, but then she thought better of it and lay back down again. "Nice to see you all, too," I said, opening the freezer for the Bombay Sapphire to go with cold tonic and sliced lemons. I added ice and took my drink out to the veranda along with my first Partagas of the day to see the remnants of the sunset on the waters of Hillsborough Bay. The Partagas was the last of the limited reserves George bought me for Christmas and I'd been saving it for a special occasion.

I looked at the cigar, smelled it, tasted it and wondered not for the first time whether fifteen dollars was just too extravagant for something that would intentionally go up in smoke. According to the propaganda, Partagas cigars come from the Dominican Republic and are made from tobacco originally from Cuba. Hand rolled, of course, and aged until just the right flavor was to be experienced. It was the aging, along with the Cuban tobacco, that made the limited reserves special. I held the cigar between my thumb and forefinger, sipped my drink and thought about whether I really wanted to smoke this last one. I've been thinking I should quit, but I long ago gave up trying to overcome my vices. How many vices I have depends on who you ask. Before I could make up my mind, George came up behind me and gently put one hand over each of my eyes.

Sounding more like speedy Gonzales, he said, "Ah, my leetle one. How can one so beeyouteeful be so alone?" George's fun-loving side has faded in the last seventeen years, but a couple of martinis still bring out the best in him. Apparently he'd started happy hour without me.

"I used to have a lover, but he left me for a Democrat," I told him, not so tongue-in-cheek. Lately, George had been so preoccupied with defeating General Andrews' appointment that I'd hardly seen him. Since he's usually home at the restaurant every night, I'm not used to spending my evenings alone and I don't like it.

George bent down to kiss me. "Hitting below the belt, Willa. You of all people should know how important this appointment is. The Democrats have had too many Supreme Court appointments in the past few years. Even suggesting that flaming liberal 'Randy Andy' can replace such a great conservative is just an outrage."

His Glenfiddich on the rocks firmly in hand, he sat down in the wicker rocker next to mine. He was dressed in a suit and tie and which meant my fantasy of a quiet evening at home was going up in smoke faster than the Partagas. George leaned over with a lighter and I put the cigar to my mouth. If I couldn't relax tonight, I really deserved this special treat, I decided. He'd just have to buy me some more.

"Did you see the hearings today?" I asked him after a silence punctuated with a good deal of puffing.

"I saw John Hamilton get shot, if that's what you're asking. And I'm really sorry, but I don't for a minute feel any responsibility for that. If the nuts are excited to violence by these hearings, you can imagine what they might do if Andy's actually confirmed."

"What are you conservatives doing to make sure that nothing worse will happen?"

"What are we supposed to do? Give speeches telling people to write their senators instead of shooting the guy?"

I didn't have the energy to debate the issues right then, but I did believe the Republicans had been whipping up the fringe, not trying to assure them that the process would work without resorting to violence.

Saving that debate for later in the weekend, I asked instead, "Why are you all dressed up?" Might as well get the bad news now.

"I'm meeting Jason downstairs for dinner in a few minutes. You might want to join us. You don't see Jason very often and I don't know when he'll be in town again."

Jason Austin is the closest thing to a big brother I've ever had or will have. His mother, Kate, took me in when my own mother died and my stepfather couldn't face life without Mom. I was only sixteen then. It's true that I don't see Jason often, and I do enjoy his company, but he is just so much work. Jason's brilliant. An intellectual, you see.

Jason also happens to be the chief counsel to the Senate Judiciary Committee–the committee responsible for Andrews' confirmation hearings. Earlier today, I'd seen him on television, sitting at the right hand of his boss, Senator Sheldon Warwick.

Jason's conversations are about important matters; his work is important; the trivial has no place in Jason Austin's life. Even trivial things like family. Jason lives in Jason's world. The rest of the 270 million people in this country live somewhere else.

If he wasn't my brother, I don't think I'd be able to stand him. But Jason is exciting to be around and I've always had a special bond with him that I don't have with anyone else. So I did want to see him.

No wonder men don't understand women. I don't understand us, either. I savored my cigar, finished my drink and told George I'd shower and join them downstairs.

As I undressed and headed into the shower, I looked longingly at my oversized bath tub. When we renovated Aunt Minnie's house, we expanded the closets, the bathrooms and the bedrooms. I agreed to replace the plumbing, but I insisted on keeping the mammoth, claw-footed tub. If I got into the tub tonight, I'd never get out. So I took an invigorating ginseng gel shower instead and tried to convince myself that I still had some energy left. I dried my hair (two minutes), put on my face (three minutes) and slipped into a wine silk pantsuit with a cream chemise and low heeled sandals (one minute). No jewelry. George says I'm fast, for a girl.

You wouldn't think deep wine would be a good color on me, that it would clash with my auburn hair, and maybe it does. But I like it. As I looked at my reflection in the full length mirror, I noticed I could have used a little more concealer for the shadows under my eyes. But then I gave it up. It was just barely nine o'clock. Maybe I'd get to bed before midnight, with any luck.

I stopped on the landing to lock the door and then turned around to look into the foyer of the restaurant below. Peter, George's Matre d', was standing near the door, chatting with a departing couple. Peter appeared enraptured by whatever the portly gentleman was saying while he simultaneously shared his attention with the man's equally well-fed wife. Both looked like they wanted to take Peter home to fatten him up and seemed genuinely pained at not being able to do so.

It's no wonder Peter's constantly receiving gifts from George's diners as well as offers to move to other restaurants. Tampa's oldest five star restaurant has been trying to woo Peter away from George for years. A Kentucky restaurant even sent Peter a racehorse for Christmas last year. If Peter wasn't such a good friend, and didn't love Minaret so much, I'm sure he'd have headed for greener pastures by now, along with the horse he kept. Of course, I think Peter is already working in the epitome of his chosen field. Not that I'm biased.

I walked slowly down the stairs, watching the guests, looking again at Aunt Minnie's tastefully decorated foyer. When Aunt Minnie lived here, the house was a private home and these were her secretaries, breakfronts and sideboards. Even the small butler's table between the upholstered camel-back sofas in the center were Aunt Minnie's pieces. The soft blue fleur de lis wallpaper had been restored to match its former gilded excellence. Would she be pleased to have her beautiful things returned to usefulness or horrified that strangers came into her home for lunch and dinner seven days a week?

As I passed through to the main dining room, I wiggled my fingers in a wave to Peter over the heads of the departing guests. I stood in the doorway for a few minutes, dreading the gauntlet of diners I'd have to run before I could reach George and Jason at their far corner table. The restaurant owner's wife has certain obligations that I'd prefer to ignore sometimes.

I passed the Andrews' table where no one seemed to be having a very good time. I nodded to Senator and Victoria Warwick, who were eating alone at a window table overlooking the garden. Mrs. Warwick had on one of the red, low-cut dresses she's favored since she got breast implants a few months ago. The Senator looked very GQ in a grey cashmere suit, pink Hermes tie and the black, reverse calf, bench made shoes that are his trademark. They look like Hush Puppies to me, but Jason tells me there's a huge difference. I suspect most of the voters think they look like Hush Puppies, too, which may be the point. The fact is you have to be rich to be able to afford the job of civil servant, but all the politicians act like they're champions of the poor and average income people because there are a lot more middle income folks who vote.

I passed a few more tables and only had to stop to speak to one couple briefly before I finally made my way over to George and Jason. I felt like I'd just crossed Times Square on New Year's Eve, or Ybor City's Seventh Avenue in front of The Green Iguana on any given Saturday night.

Jason stood up and leaned over so he could give me a light, polite, southern hug. Kind of a lean across the body and a small pat on the upper back. It took me the longest time to get used to it when I moved here from Detroit years ago. This pseudo hug is the southern equivalent of the New York cheek to air kiss, I guess. Jason is no more southern than I am. Maybe now that a southern Democrat controls the White House, the hug is a politically correct Washington thing.

"Hey, Willa, you look great, as always," he lied.

"You look tired, Jason. Don't you ever get break?" Jason is a solid, dependable-looking man. He's average: average height (5'10"), average coloring (brown hair, hazel eyes) and an average dresser (Brooks Brothers). Actually, on the dressing thing, he could get the same suits at Stein Mart for half the price, if he had more imagination. Tonight, he looked as if he hadn't slept in weeks, which I guessed to be the case based on the amount of sleep George had been getting.

"When I accepted the job, the title sounded so good, I just thought it would look good on my resume." More lies. Jason had never leapt without looking in his life and I knew he hadn't done so when he accepted the job of chief counsel to the senate judiciary committee at Senator Sheldon Warwick's request. Jason had worked as Warwick's aide for the previous ten years. The chief counsel position was a promotion, of sorts, and for a politically ambitious man like Jason, a very powerful post. His ability to participate in and influence the selection of men and women who might serve on the courts of the United States for over twenty years was more than just a resume builder. I wondered when Jason had learned to lie so smoothly and why he was lying to me now. I thought I knew Jason well. Maybe not. Maybe none of us really knows another. Or ourselves for that matter. I should have reflected on that thought at the time, but I didn't.

Before we could sit down again, the local NBC anchorman, Frank Bendler, walked up to our table and George invited him to join us.

"How'd you get the night off, Frank?" Jason asked him. "It sure wasn't a slow news day." Everyone groaned at Jason's less than rapier wit.

Frank responded, "I covered all that at six. Gayle Sierens gets to cover the President's trip to Tampa tonight, so I thought if I came over here, you or George might give me something new for the eleven o'clock news. It was just luck to find all the main players in the same dining room." Washington-based Tampans were taking the weekend break in the long hearings to come home for the charity golf tournament tomorrow, but Frank finding them all here was more than just luck. So much for polite southern diners; someone had called and tipped him off.

"Wait a second," I said. "Why is the President in town? Didn't anybody stay in Washington this weekend?"

"Apparently not. They just moved the committee here, I'd say." He glanced around the room and let his gaze rest pointedly on General Andrews' table and then the Warwicks'.

George and Jason exchanged a look I couldn't decipher and George said, "You'd better not have a camera in here, Frank," with the sternness he usually reserves for misbehaving Labradors.

"Of course not." Frank managed to sound wounded before he grinned. "I got the footage when everyone arrived and the camera is outside, waiting for their departures. Where we can bombard them with questions. We wouldn't *think* of doing that in here."

"This is private property, Frank," I told him.

"Is it? I thought it was a public restaurant." Frank said too sweetly, before he turned to Jason. "Hasn't anyone told your boss that he and the nominee are on the same team? Warwick and the other Democrats seem to be going out of their way to make George's team the winner here."

Jason looked down at his heavy Waterford wine glass, studying the circles the red wine had made on the cream damask table cloth. He seemed to be considering the question, but probably was only considering the answer. Senator Warwick and the other Democrats on the Judiciary Committee had been almost openly hostile to Andrews' nomination on national television for the past three weeks. Today's questioning was the topper. Every news reporter from Tom Brokaw to Frank himself had made more than one comment about it on every newscast, news magazine or teaser since the televised hearings began. The curious thing was that it hadn't dented Andrews' popularity in the daily and weekly polls that controlled everything in political America now.

Like everything else "inside the belt-way" as they say, I viewed this as one great political game that usually made me yawn. If Andy "got Borked," the insiders' euphemism for a nominee being attacked and rejected, it wouldn't be the first time. And it was all old ground between George and Jason. They'd discussed it endlessly for weeks now.

Frank was still looking for his sound bite. The trick to dealing with the media is to ignore what they ask you and answer their questions with what you want them to repeat. Jason had lots of experience at this and gave Frank something he could air. "Senator Warwick supports the President, Frank. What the President wants, we aim to deliver," Jason said.

Both Frank and George seemed satisfied with that, which was curious, I thought at the time. And I was right. Everything's obvious, once you know the answer.

After Frank left us, stopping briefly at the Warwicks' table and then the General's, George said, "Why don't we talk about something besides business? Jason, anything new on the romance front?"

Jason smiled wanly. "Way to go, George. Choose a comfortable, non-controversial topic, why don't you?" We all laughed. Jason's bad luck in the women department was a family joke. He seemed to always be choosing the wrong woman, one way or another. He kept us laughing with his self-deprecating accounts of failed relationships for the next hour while we consumed the heavenly cuisine for which diners are willing to pay George's exorbitant prices.

George and Jason ordered the night's special Grilled Beef Tenderloin with Marsala-Mushroom Sauce, and I had Roasted Garlic and Brie Soup with the chef's signature dill bread. By the time we got to the Coconut-Cardamon Custard Tart with Oven-roasted Bananas, our fatigue and all bad humor had completely dissipated. Anger just can't survive around such heavenly food.

We decided to take our coffee and cigars out on the veranda of the Sunset Bar where it would be quieter. There was a full moon tonight casting a long shimmering shadow over the water. We started toward the door, right behind Senator Sheldon Warwick and his wife, Tory. The Warwicks didn't see us, thank you God, and we were about to pass safely on the right when they made a tactical error and walked within six feet of the Andrews' dinner table.

General Andrews raised his voice almost to the shouting point. "I'd sneak on by if I were you, too, Sheldon. I can't remember the last time I've been so skewered by my own side."

All heads turned toward the Andrews table. Senator Warwick, always cognizant of his public image, said, "Andy, now is neither the time nor place to discuss this. Why don't you come by the house in the morning and we'll talk about it." That was the wrong tone to take with a general, even a retired one, and apparently the wrong thing to say as well.

"Sure, Sheldon. Then you can lie to me in private instead of saying whatever it is you have to say in front of everyone here." The General got up from his chair, threw his napkin down on the table by his plate and started to move toward Warwick, who was now almost all the way past the end of the table. "It hasn't bothered you to attack me in front of the entire country in those damn hearings you're heading up. Why should it bother you to have it out here and now?"

Madeline Andrews placed a restraining hand on her husband's arm, but he shook it off, angrily. "This doesn't concern you, Madeline. Do you want to step outside, Senator, and settle it right now?" General Andrews challenged, his chin high, with the air of a man accustomed to fighting his battles with his fists.

By this time, we had reached the table and both George and Jason tried to calm things down. George walked toward the General and Jason approached the Senator. "Gentlemen, please. You're upsetting my guests. Why don't we just—"

Before George could work his magic, Tory Warwick had had more than enough. I saw Frank Bendler standing in the door way, taking it all in, when Tory Warwick reached over, picked up a heavy, full lead crystal water glass, drew back and threw it with all her strength at General Andrews. If she'd hit him, it would have knocked him down, she'd thrown it with such force. Unfortunately, her aim wasn't improved by her alcohol consumption and she missed. The next thing I knew, I was flat on my butt on the floor and my first thought after I got there was how this would get reported on the eleven o'clock news. At least it wasn't on film.

Tory didn't knock me out, but I definitely felt dazed. I reached up and felt the tender spot on my forehead, just in front of my right temple. It was swelling rapidly and someone handed me a towel filled with ice. I couldn't open my eyes because the subdued light in the dining room was blinding. There was nothing wrong with my ears, though. George was shouting. In public. Angrier than I'd ever witnessed. He gave Andrews a push toward the door that landed Andrews against Warwick and nearly knocked them both over.

"Get out! Get out right now and don't any of you attempt to come back here! Andrews, Warwick, I'm disgusted with both of you! Forget the checks, just leave. And do not try to make a reservation here again. Peter, these people are leaving and they are not to be permitted to return. Ever."

George bent down to me, asking me if I was alright. I tried to assure him it was an accident, that Tory Warwick had meant to hit the General. This made George even angrier. I guess it would have been okay if she'd been *trying* to hit me. Go figure.

Peter was ushering the Andrews and the Warwicks out, Frank Bendler following them for further news. Tory was trying to reach me to apologize and Jason just kept moving her toward the door. Peter came back and began his Henry Kissinger routine with the other diners who were openly staring now. I heard him offer his apologies and a dessert of their choice, compliments of the house.

After a while, I could stand up without feeling too dizzy. We walked over to the Sunset Bar, me with a big white ice filled towel held up to my forehead, Jason holding one elbow and George holding the other.

"I cannot believe that woman," George was still sputtering.

"George, you know she wasn't herself," Jason soothed.

"So when she's herself, I suppose her aim is better? Then she could have beaned the next justice of the Supreme Court? That's just great, Jason. Just great."

"What do you want Sheldon to do? He can't stay home with her every night he's in Tampa and he stays in Washington as much as he can," Jason retorted. His defense of Warwick was nothing if not consistent.

"Well, they can both go somewhere else to eat from now on. And I don't need that hothead Andrews in here, either. Tory wouldn't have thrown the glass at him if he hadn't started a fight. I meant it when I said neither one of them are welcome here again. If Willa's seriously hurt, it'll be worse than that. For both of them." George was really pissed. He was close to violence and it scared me. I'm not used to seeing him with a temper. George is the most civilized man I know. To my George, violence is a bad thunderstorm. Who was this testosterone-laden, protective male sitting next to me, anyway?

"Look," I said. "You two need to calm down. Everybody's gone now. I'm still living. And I'm thirsty. Where's that after dinner drink and cigar you promised me? I have a feeling we're all going to need it about eleven-oh-five."

They gave it up because they knew I was right, but they wanted to keep at it. The tension they'd been living with over Andrews' confirmation needed a release. The steam had blown past their control here tonight, but the controversy was still boiling under the lid. I was getting a sizeable lump on my forehead which would look just great in the morning. George and Jason managed to calm down but they couldn't pretend to be interested in anything else now. They took up the political discussion they'd wanted to have at dinner but wouldn't risk being overheard.

"How is the committee vote going to go? Any idea?" George asked.

"Some of the senators have declared themselves already. Some did it in their opening statements and others have formed their opinions during the questioning. There are still enough that are at least undeclared to make it a horse race. Right now, I'm not sure how it will go."

"What does Warwick think? He's the chair of the judiciary committee. He has some influence," George said dryly.

"He has a lot of influence. But the Democrats are not the majority party in congress, you know. Nor are we a majority on the committee," Jason reminded him.

"You can't seriously think any elected Republican would cast a vote for that ignoramus," George declared.

I was feeling a little like a spectator at a tennis match. Jason must have known more than he was willing to share with George, and George was determined to find out. For me, nothing was being served by this volley and my head was really starting to throb. I was hoping that eventually this, too, would pass. Nor did I want to miss golf tomorrow over a headache, so I decided to call it a night and left them deep in their plotting. When I went up to bed, they didn't even notice.

I should have stayed up for the late news, just to see how bad it really was, but bad news usually gets worse in the night, so I fell into sleep. It would all be repeated ad nauseum tomorrow anyway. I found out much later what it was that Jason knew and George didn't. I should have stayed at the table, although it might not have mattered. I've gone over all this so many times, trying to figure out if I could have done something to stop the events that followed. But all the alternatives I can think of wouldn't have made any difference. I hate thinking I'm powerless over events, even though I know I can't control everything and especially can't control every one. If George had wanted me to know what was going on, he'd have told me long before that Friday. I may not understand women, but I sure as hell don't understand men. Not at all.

3

The alarm went off at six o'clock but it took me a few minutes to realize what it was. When I rolled over to turn it off and snuggle up to George for a few more winks, I realized he wasn't in the bed. George never gets up before six o'clock. We're both owls. We detest those bright-eyed larks with their worm fetish. I was only slightly awake, but I knew this was not right. Maybe he just couldn't sleep and had gone into the kitchen to make coffee. He does that sometimes. Harry and Bess were waiting at the end of the bed when I managed to open my eyes, so I gave up and faced the day.

I went into the bathroom, washed my face, examined the big purple egg on my forehead where Victoria Warwick's glass missile had hit me, and put on my running clothes. I walked through to the kitchen with Harry and Bess at my heels, thinking I would tell George where I was going. But he wasn't there. I asked Harry and Bess where he went, but they weren't talking. I was on a tighter than average schedule because of the golf tournament today, so the dogs and I went down the back stairs to the beach.

I wasn't awake enough to throw sticks into the water to tire them out first, so Harry and Bess ran way ahead of me. When I'm in good form, I do an entire lap around our island. Sometimes two laps. Other days, I just do half a lap and take a golf cart back. Today would be a complete lap day if it killed me.

A lot of people run just for exercise, hating every minute of it. For me, though, it's a spiritual experience. I love the sand, the water, the sunshine and the companionship I get from Harry and Bess. After years of running, I'm able to get to the runner's high in about fifteen minutes and it carries me the remainder of the run. Sometimes, I have to consciously bring myself to stop. During the summer I feel like I'm melting.

By the time I got back to the house, huffing and puffing, I was sweating like an NBA player in the final two minutes. I went out to the water and jumped in with Harry and Bess, who were already there. This is the part they like the best because they get to submerge me and each other ten or twenty times before I'm completely exhausted and give up. We got out, rinsed off at the outdoor shower, and I put them in their screened sun porch to dry off while I trudged up the back stairs. Now, they would wait patiently until after my shower for their breakfast.

Harry and Bess are litter mates, even though Harry's yellow and Bess is black. They were very cute puppies, obnoxious adolescents and now, the equivalent of twenty-something adults. They are a joy to be around and I love them both in place of children: I don't have to pay for college and I'd likely get arrested for putting kids in a cage.

George was still nowhere to be found, so I had to make my own Cuban coffee before I headed to the shower. When I came out, dressed in purple and jade plaid Bermuda shorts and a jade golf shirt, thinking I didn't want my clothes to detract from the lovely color on my forehead, my coffee was ready. I called the dogs to eat, filled a travel cup, let myself out of the house and went down to Greta.

It was still early enough that dew on the St. Augustine grass and bright pink, red, purple, white and melon colored impatiens gave everything a crystalline shimmer. As I drove out from the circle in front of Minaret, the sun was lighting the sky over the Port of Tampa and Harbour Island to the east. Why would anyone live in Florida without a convertible? In a convertible, you experience all of the gloriousness Florida weather has to offer. I have discussed this, over wine of course, with a number of native Floridians. Sometimes they say they never had a desire for a convertible until they owned one, or rented one, or took a ride with a friend. Once exposed, they're all hooked.

But how could you not know that being outside, able to see all around and feel the warmth that we live in would be glorious? Oh, convertibles can be noisy. The tops get worn and have to be replaced periodically. In the old days, they used to leak. But now the only real drawback is that you can't have rain gutters over the windows. Given the amount of rain we get in Florida in the summer, that can be a serious drawback for people who frequent drive-through windows. But otherwise, is there any choice really between a stodgy old Rolls Royce and the least expensive Miata? Sport utility vehicles? Give me a break.

By the time I started across the Plant Key Bridge toward the Bayshore, the sun sparkled on Hillsborough Bay while two dolphins, swimming side by side, raced Greta and me the length of the bridge. They won. It was glorious. I've always loved morning. It's just that I usually sleep through it.

The short drive from Plant Key to Great Oaks golf course takes me east on Bayshore Boulevard and into the old Palma Ceia section of town. As I approached the large, plantation style club house, I realized, as I always do, how amazing it is that such a beautiful thirty-six hole golf course is nestled right in the center of South Tampa. The sun had been just over the horizon when I got back from running the dogs and now it was in full form.

In another month, it would be just about the right temperature to play golf in the early morning. But in January, the temperature was just a little cool. My tee time was seven thirty-two, so I should finish up my eighteen holes before noon. This tournament is for charity and we play a scramble. All four golfers hit every hole and then you choose the best ball. In theory it speeds up play and everyone gets a good score. Why not? But in reality, four golfers have to have a conference over every hole and the decisions that eventually get made are not always quick, to say the least.

The event was already in full swing when I arrived and let the valet park my car. I went into the locker room for my shoes and met my friend and playing partner, Mitch Crosby, outside. Mitch and a few other golfers had gathered around waiting for General Andrews, the guest of honor, to give the kickoff speech. Our group would be the fifth foursome off, after the General, his son-in-law, John Williamson, Senator Warwick and the Mayor's foursomes.

As I joined the waiting group of golfers, one of the men said to me, "Where's George, Willa? I thought he'd come out for the opening ceremonies. He's usually here."

I responded, "I don't know where he is at the moment. When I got up, I found a note saying he'd gone jogging." Everybody laughed at that.

"Sure," one of the guys joked. "What's her name and how long has George been seeing her?" They got a good laugh out of that one and the teasing continued until someone else raised a topic that turned the conversation.

Mitch and I were playing today with Dr. Marilee Aymes, one of my personal favorites. The fourth member of our group was Christian Grover, a local lawyer who just happens to be dating my little sister, causing me an everlasting stomach ache. "I can't believe I agreed to team up with those two today, Mitch. What was I drinking when you got me to consent to this?" I said. I continued to sip the coffee I'd brought from home, which was just now cool enough not to burn the hair off my tongue.

"I thought maybe your consent had something to do with that pretty blue egg on your forehead. Like you were deranged or something. What happened to you?" Mitch responded.

"I had the misfortune to be near the infamous Tory Warwick's flying Waterford last night," I said, as I gently fingered the lump. "And it's purple."

"That's a natural hazard around here, all right. I should have recognized the imprinted pattern. Lismore, isn't it?"

"Smart ass."

"Yep. That's me." We kept up like this as we checked our bags and cart, found our specially marked balls and prepared to tee off. Finally, the chairman of the committee went up to the microphone and said we'd be starting without the opening remarks today because General Andrews hadn't yet arrived. They moved the General's foursome back in line and the second group teed off. Rumors that General Andrews was with President Benson and the President might be joining us quickly buzzed through the group. But by the time our group was set to tee off, neither General Andrews nor the President had arrived.

Marilee Aymes, a sixty-something cardiologist here in town, was in rare form as we sat waiting for our turn at the first tee. I could hear her lighting in to Grover before we even got started. Whatever bad karma had given me these two as playing partners, it was worse for both of them, having to be together. Unlike oil and water, it didn't appear they could be mixed into suspension of hostilities even for a short time.

"Grover, have you ever played with these clubs before? They look like something you bought off an infomercial advertised by Suzanne Sommers," she chided him.

"Just because I'm not a golfer, Dr. Aymes, doesn't mean I'm an idiot. Who would buy golf clubs from Suzanne Sommers? With her chest, there's no way I could get the same angle on the ball."

Mitch was twittering, trying not to show it, and I was amused, too. Maybe they did deserve each other.

We were being signaled up to the tee. Mitch hit his first drive of the day about 250 yards, long for him. I went next, then Marilee and finally Grover. We were required to take everyone's tee shot once each nine holes. I was praying Grover would be able to hit it more than fifty yards at least once. He went up to the tee, stood looking over the ball and the fairway and finally, finally, hit the damn thing—about three feet. It was going to be a long day.

Mitch and I got back into our cart and started off to where his drive had landed, stopping on the way to pick up my ball. As we headed down the cart path, we heard Marilee saying, "That's just great, Grover. Maybe we should get you some breast implants if you think it would help."

"I didn't think it was bad for the first ball I've ever hit," he said with mock innocence.

"You mean you've never played golf before in your life?" Marilee, a scratch golfer, was appalled. She'd sooner dine with gators.

"Nope. And I wanted to play with the best, so I paid extra to get teamed up with you," he grinned again.

I think I heard growling from Marilee, but maybe it was the cart engine.

A few times in the first six holes, I shared a cart with Marilee Aymes just to avoid the open hostility between her and Grover. On the fourth fairway, the talk turned to General Andrews and the nomination. All of Tampa had been discussing nothing else for weeks. Both of us expressed our sorrow at the crazy world that allowed someone to shoot John Hamilton, whom neither of us knew well.

"These anti-abortion nuts are getting to be a real problem, Willa. I've cut down my volunteer work at the free abortion clinic in the projects to one day a month just because I think it's so unsafe now," Marilee said.

"You're a cardiologist. Why are you volunteering at the abortion clinic?"

"Somebody's got to do it. I just mostly do counseling and help out with the medical stuff if there's no one else. Some of these patients are so poor they can't feed themselves and the kids they've already got. I sympathize with them."

"It's a tough issue, Marilee. I don't think I'd ever be able to get an abortion and I thank God I've never needed one," I told her.

"Amen," she said, in the first vaguely religious comment I've ever heard her make.

We reached the seventh hole with Grover never having hit another ball as well as his first three foot drive. The drink cart came around and we took a break for cold water and sodas. It was about nine o'clock. Grover ordered two beers and Marilee ordered scotch. Mitch and I tried not to laugh.

The pretty, young drink cart driver who doubles as a barmaid, told us that General Andrews had never arrived. They'd tried calling him for the past two hours, but got the answering machine. Someone had been sent out to his home to find him.

"No one can figure it out. Why, General Andrews hasn't missed a Blue Coat in ten years. What do you think happened to him?" she said in her whispery little Marilyn Monroe voice. She bent over to give the guys a good view of her rump while she dug down in the ice chest looking for Grover's beer.

Whether just to tweak Marilee or because he really is grossly rude, Grover punched Mitch conspiratorially in the side and said, "Don't you want to order one, too, Mitch? Sure improves the scenery."

Before anyone else could react, Marilee hauled off and punched Grover right in the jaw, knocking him onto the grass. Howling, he grabbed his face and shouted that he'd sue her for battery.

"Kiss my grits," she said. She got into their cart and drove off, leaving us to deal with Grover, a job the barmaid didn't seem to mind. So we left Grover with the drink cart. We got all the way to the eighth tee before we couldn't hold back any longer and laughed so hard we were holding our sides and trying not to wet our pants.

Marilee was back in a few minutes with my brother, Jason, in her cart. When they drove up, she said she'd gotten a new partner. She walked right up to the tee and hit the ball over 280 yards. Jason said, sotto voice to Mitch and me, "She just swooped into the club house and grabbed me. Is now a good time to tell her I've never played golf before?"

Mitch's turn was next and he gathered enough composure to hit the ball in the right direction and then join Marilee in her cart. I managed about 150 yards and Jason, who I think was kidding about never having played golf before, at least made contact with the ball. Marilee snorted when Jason's ball landed about fifty yards out and took off with Mitch toward her ball, which was clearly the farthest drive.

That left me with Jason and Jason with Mitch's clubs. What a day. And we had eleven holes to go. My head started to throb as I took the wheel and headed off down the cart path.

"Did General Andrews ever show up?" I asked Jason.

"No, and we're all pretty worried about it. He doesn't answer his telephone and no one has seen or heard from him. The chairman finally sent someone out to his house, but Andrews lives all the way out at Tampa Green, so it will take a while to get there."

"Does the Senator know of any reason Andrews wouldn't show up? It's not like him to skip an event he's been sponsoring for years."

Jason looked away from me and denied having any inside information, which I took to mean that he knew something he wasn't at liberty to divulge. I respected Jason's confidential capacity as counsel to the Senate Judiciary Committee, but Andrews' private sponsorship of a golf tournament shouldn't be an issue in his confirmation. There was no reason for secrecy.

"Are they worried about a repeat of yesterday's shooting?" I pressed him.

"I don't think so. The local cops wanted to give him police protection, but the General refused. He continues to maintain that the shooter wanted to kill the man he shot. He's refused all extraordinary security measures, even though we've told him it's standard procedure for any nominee. Andrews says a U.S. Army Four Star General can take care of himself. It would be nice if he'd start doing it."

"What do you mean?"

"We've all counseled him on how to get his nomination approved. But he just won't cooperate. He makes it damned difficult for the party to support him as the President's choice." Jason sounded disgusted, whether for the nominee, the President or the process, I wasn't sure.

"Despite what you told Frank Bendler last night, does the party want to support the President on this one?" I asked him. During the hearings, it seemed to me there was little about the process that was supportive, of the President or anyone else, but particularly General Andrews.

Jason looked at me shrewdly. "What have you heard from George about that, Willa?"

I was startled. George was very highly placed in Republican circles but his influence with Democrats was non-existent. To George, the Democrats were all one brick short of a load. He thinks they're all ideologically incompetent to sit on the Supreme Court and he'd told me that more than once as we discussed the General's appointment during the past few weeks.

"What would George know about the Democrats' strategy? He'll barely talk to your boss on the street and he threw him out of our house last night." One of the many subjects George and I disagree on is politics. George is on top of all the issues, fully cognizant of the nuances of each. He's the only man I know, besides maybe Frank Bendler, who can identify all 100 senators and most congressmen by sight. I, on the other hand, used to be able to identify the Florida senators and Sonny Bono. Since Sonny died, I'm down to two.

Jason shrugged. "I'm sure you're right. It's just that there are so many rumors floating around Washington and George knows everything that happens. I thought maybe he'd told you."

"Told me what?" I was really getting exasperated. If this cloak and dagger is how all of Washington works, no wonder they never get anything done.

Jason was considering the question, stalling until we got to the ball and he could get out of the cart near the others so he wouldn't have to answer. When he tried to get into Marilee' cart, I made it impossible.

Unless he wanted to acknowledge that he was trying to ditch me, he had no choice but to get back in the cart with me.

"I'm not going to let this drop, Jason, so you might as well tell me now," I said with the courtroom sternness I reserve for lawyers who are about to spend the night in jail for contempt.

"You know, you've always been so supremely stubborn." He said it fondly. I think. "How much do you know about the history of Supreme Court appointments?"

"Very little. Why?"

"It's fascinating, really. For instance, did you know that when Taft was President, he was promised a Supreme Court appointment by Teddy Roosevelt in exchange for political support?" Jason asked. "Then, Roosevelt didn't live up to the bargain, so Taft asked President Harding to appoint him Chief Justice and Harding did it."

"You're right, Jason. That's just fascinatingly irrelevant. What does that bit of history have to do with Andrews?" He ignored the question.

"Do you know how the selection process works?"

"Not really."

"Most people don't. When a Supreme Court Justice resigns, retires or dies, the President asks his chief of staff for nominees. The chief works with the Attorney General and White House Counsel on a list of potential candidates. A tentative choice is made and then the Chief of Staff asks key party senators for their views. The President usually talks to the opposing party whip, to judge the opposition. It is a highly political process." He must have sensed I was chafing with impatience.

"The point here, Willa, is that none of that was done. None of us knew about Andrews' nomination until it happened. The senators are not happy about that. It discounts their power. And it means none of their favorites got a chance."

"So this is some sort of sand-lot squabble between the big boys over who's more important?" I asked, not bothering to hide my disgust. The only difference between men and boys is the price of their toys–and their battles.

Jason sighed. "Partly. But it's more than that. The rumor is that the President appointed Andrews because of some secret deal between them. President Benson's part of the deal was just to make the appointment. Which he did. The President doesn't want the nomination confirmed. Andrews has too much baggage and will be too uncontrollable if he gets on the bench."

"And what about Warwick? Where does he fit in all this?" I asked him.

"Exactly where you'd think. He's furious with the President. But he can't show that on national television."

"So Warwick's joined forces with George and the Republicans to defeat the nomination?" My incredulity was plain, even to Jason, who can be a little thick sometimes.

"Politics makes strange bedfellows, Willa. You know that." Jason was resigned and tired of talking about it. "Are you happy now that you know the whole story?"

"I don't know if I'm happy or not. It sounds like politics at its worst to me. What possible reason could there be for the President to ignore the best interests of the country and appoint Andrews in some sort of horse trade?"

"That would depend on what the trade was, wouldn't it?" Now Jason just sounded tired. I noticed deep circles under his eyes suggesting he'd had another sleepless night. It didn't occur to me to wonder what he'd been doing all night. He was resigned to see this thing through, but he didn't like it. Nor did I. I could only imagine how George would feel when he learned about this secret deal, and I just wanted to avoid the fall out.

At the next hole, Mitch ended up back in my cart and Jason took care to see that we didn't have a moment together for the rest of the game. We finished ten over par; not a stellar score for a scramble and we had no hope of winning, even after we applied Grover's big handicap. When we got back to the clubhouse, several other foursomes had finished ahead of us. The topic of conversation was General Andrews' whereabouts. He still had not arrived and no one seemed to have heard from him.

The rubber chicken lunch was to be served at noon on the patio, and Senator Warwick delivered the keynote speech after letting us all know that General Andrews "sends his regrets and apologies." The mayor's foursome won the tacky and cheap blue sport coats that were the first prize, along with bragging rights for the next year. My group finished in the middle of the pack.

It wasn't until I was showered, dressed and in my car heading for home that I heard the news. General Albert Randall Andrews had been found dead about eleven-thirty. The radio story was short and to the point:

Tampa's first Supreme Court nominee, General Albert Andrews, is dead. The General apparently committed suicide, despondent over the course his confirmation hearings had taken and the shooting of his long time secretary, John Hamilton, yesterday. Police Chief Ben Hathaway announced just a few minutes ago: "Early this morning, it appears that General Andrews placed his revolver to his right temple, holding the gun in his right hand and pulled the trigger. He was found still sitting in his fishing boat, facing away from the dock in the small lake in back of his Tampa Green home. His family believes the General had been upset over the Senate confirmation hearings."

I pulled over to turn down one of the side streets off the Bayshore and sat there with my hands shaking for several minutes. I couldn't believe it. I'd talked to Andy just last night. I still had a bruise on my forehead from Victoria Warwick's tantrum throwing. I'd discussed his appointment with Jason today. Of course, the General was upset over the turn the hearings had taken. But enough for a man who'd fought and survived three wars to kill himself? How could this be true? I sat there a long time trying to deal with the news and listening to the radio for more information. Finally, the driver of a city garbage truck behind me laid on his horn and shouted to me to get out of the way so he could pick up the trash cans lining the curb where I sat.

4

By the time I recovered enough to drive home, the same story had been repeated on three different stations. No one knew any more than what Chief Hathaway had said at the press conference. I wasn't practicing my mindfulness the rest of the way back and I don't have any idea what scenery I passed. I was numb.

At Minaret, I left Greta with the valet and went up the stairs two at a time, running on adrenaline. I burst into the living room calling for George. Harry and Bess came bounding toward me, but George was nowhere to be found in any of the ten rooms of our flat. Granted, I looked quickly. But I'm sure I would have found him if he was there: there just aren't that many places he could be.

I went back downstairs and into the Sunset Bar, where neither the bartender nor the waitress had seen George all day. I checked the kitchen, the dining rooms and the outdoor dining areas. There were a few late lunchers, but no George. Finally, I found Peter in the office tallying up the sales for the morning.

"Peter, have you seen George?"

"Not today. I thought he was with you." I must have looked skeptical because he followed up, "Not to play golf, of course. I just thought he had gone out to the club early this morning when you did. When I got here, his Bentley was gone and so was your car."

I walked slowly back to the veranda of the Sunset Bar and sat at my favorite table overlooking the water—the table where George and Jason and I sat at last night. Being able to sit outside and watch both the sunrise and sunset over the water is one of the best things about living on Plant Key. Today, I barely noticed the view. Where could George have gone? It was unusual for him to be gone anywhere early in the morning. He sleeps late every day because he's up so late at night. To be gone on a Saturday for the lunch business was something he'd never done since he opened the restaurant. George thinks the owner needs to be visible, even though, or maybe because, everyone loves Peter.

I ordered a Sapphire and tonic with lemon on the rocks, and sat there thinking about where George could be, how Andy could possibly have committed suicide and why. An hour later, I still had no answers. I decided to let my subconscious do some work by taking a nap. I walked slowly through the restaurant, still looking around, then back upstairs. When I got into our bedroom, the heavily lined, floral damask drapes were drawn and there was George, snoring as if he hadn't slept in weeks. I was so relieved to find him, I just lay down on top of the sheets and, worn out by the emotional strain, the early morning, the fresh air and exercise, fell fast asleep, too.

A few hours later, I awoke disoriented and foggy. I turned over to reach for George and he wasn't there. Again. My eyes opened quickly. I was immediately awake. I hopped out of bed and walked into the hallway, slipping into my pink silk robe as I went toward the kitchen. George was sitting at the table, having coffee. "Hello, sweetheart," he said. "How'd you sleep?" Just like he hadn't been gone all day, without a word as to where he'd spent the morning. Instead of focusing on how relieved I was to see his sleep-rumpled self in his green summer cotton bathrobe and white silk pajamas, I lost it.

"Where the hell have you been?" I was almost vibrating with tension and anger.

"What do you mean? I left you a note."

"Oh, really? Where'd you leave it, in the refrigerator?" Sarcasm now, too. It didn't seem to bother him, though.

"No," he said with exaggerated patience, like he was dealing with a mentally deficient person. He put his coffee cup down softly. "I left it on the table beside your pillow."

I whirled around and marched back into our bedroom, over to my side of our king-sized bed and looked down at the pedestal table holding my reading glasses, an alarm clock, a small crystal lamp and, damn damn damn, a handwritten note on one of George's personal monogrammed cards propped up against the telephone. In his strong, almost indecipherable scrawl, it said:

"Darling, Gone jogging and then to breakfast. See you after the Blue Coat. Good luck. I love you." I read it, then I picked it up and looked at it like it was some sort of nasty laboratory specimen. It was his paper, his writing and it was a note that had been about eight inches from my face when I woke up both this morning and just now. I'd missed it. I'd gotten all upset for no reason. I hate to eat crow. I just hate it.

I carried the note with me back into the kitchen where George was still calmly having his coffee and reading today's *New York Times*. "Find it?" he asked, just a little too sweetly. I could almost see the canary feathers on his lips.

"I found it. I'd like to say I didn't find it, but it was there. Next time, how about leaving it on the kitchen table where you know I'll be sure to look?" If I have to eat crow, I'm certainly not going to be gracious about it. "Let me share the paper." Like Mark Twain, I, too, have been through some terrible things in my life, some of which actually happened.

We drank coffee and read the paper. For about half an hour, I was pouting and feeling very put upon, which is why it took so long for me to remember to ask George if he'd heard about Andrews' death. I asked him just as he was sipping and he almost choked.

"What? How? When?" He was shouting. What did I look like? Maria Shriver?

"I don't know exactly when. I heard it on the news on my way back from the club. Why don't you go turn on MSNBC. There's bound to be more information by now." I was talking to his back because he was already on his way to the television in the den. I got up and went in behind him, just as the headline news story started.

The reporter said General Andrews had been found at home, an apparent suicide. The details given by Chief Hathaway on the radio earlier were repeated. There was nothing new except the very last sound bite: "A source close to the investigation claims the General left a suicide note, but the police have not confirmed the story."

The reporter then went on to rehash yesterday's shooting of John Hamilton outside the capitol building. Since yesterday, they'd learned that the shooter had indeed been trying to kill General Andrews. The shooter's late night interview was replayed and his face came on the screen. "I expected him to come out of the car first. I'm sorry I hurt Mr. Hamilton. It was the General I was after. He has no right to kill unborn babies. No murderer will sit on the Supreme Court. We won't allow it."

George was flipping channels and shaking his head. "What is this country coming to? Why is it that people think they can just kill someone they don't agree with? Why don't people trust the process?"

"Jason says that's the problem," I told him.

"What?" He sounded startled.

I told him what Jason had said to me about Andrews' appointment. "That's true, Willa, but it's not unprecedented. And most people have no idea how behind-the-scenes politics in judicial appointments work anyway. I meant why can't people trust the confirmation process."

"Well," I said, "that didn't seem to be going so well, either. Just yesterday, citizens were worried enough about the process to protest, picket and shoot at Andrews. More than two thousand names of law school faculty members who spoke against him were listed in the Congressional Record, even more than spoke against Bork when he was defeated. I've seen countless advertisements in the papers addressed to senators by citizens against Andrews. The process wasn't working. How much patience do you expect the lunatic fringe to have?"

George hung his head, his arms resting on his thighs. "Supreme Court Justices aren't confirmed by sound bites. There's a long history of nominees who weren't confirmed. More than twenty percent aren't. Not being confirmed is no reason to kill yourself."

"Maybe Andy didn't like those odds," I replied.

No further information about Andy's death was to be had on any station. When the stories degenerated to the brawl in George's restaurant last night, with witnesses describing the verbal volleys between Warwick and Andrews and George's more physical approach, George finally turned off the set and we sat together on the upholstered love seat in the quiet room, Harry and Bess laying near the door. After a while, George said, "You know he didn't kill himself, don't you? There's no way Andy would have done that. Someone murdered him."

"George, you don't know that. If they say it was suicide, they believe it."

"No. If they say it was suicide, they want the public to believe it. That doesn't mean it's true."

"Why would you think he didn't kill himself? You've barely talked to Andy in years."

"Because I know Andy and I know he would never, never kill himself. Goddamn it!" George threw the remote control across the room and stalked out. It's amazing how tough those things are. It didn't even crack. I heard him slamming drawers in his dressing room and then leave by the front door. And I was totally bewildered. Who was this man in George's body? My George never lost his control, but I had seen this stranger lose it twice in the last twenty four hours. George had put so much of himself into this fight, felt so strongly about it, spent so much energy and time on it. I had hardly seen him in the past few weeks and when he was home, he was so preoccupied that he either spoke of nothing else, or didn't speak at all.

But I know George didn't plan to win the battle by losing the General. For once, my Mighty Mouse routine didn't seem to be called for. There wasn't anything I could do to fix this, and I had no choice but to wait it out. For the third time in two days I was reminded that we never really know another person, no matter how comfortable we've become with them. The dogs didn't like it either. Both of them came over and put their heads in my lap for me to rub their ears as I tried to calm all of us down.

After a while, when it became obvious that George wasn't coming right back, I turned, as I often do, to my work. A celebratory dinner always followed the Blue Coat, but under the circumstances, even if they had it, I didn't feel like getting dressed up and going. So I put on a pair of black jeans and a cream tee shirt and went into my study to wrestle with *Newton v. The Whitman Esquire Review.*

The file hadn't gotten any smaller since I'd left it on Aunt Minnie's chair yesterday. The only way to get started was to start. I picked up the last of six pleadings files looking for the final pre-trial order I entered on the case outlining the parties' expectations for proofs at trial. Generally, it was a defamation case; count one alleged libel and slander, and count two alleged breach of the "private facts tort," claiming obliquely that private matter had been published without consent. I had the case in my court because the parties were citizens of different states. Newton was a Florida citizen and *The Review* was incorporated and had its principal place of business in San Francisco.

The Review, it was alleged, had reprinted some anonymous local gossip labeled "About Town" without sufficiently checking facts or disguising Mr. Newton. Mr. Newton alleged that everyone in his business circle knew the story was about him, causing him great personal harm. What he didn't say was that it would likely cost him votes if he ran for mayor, which, rumor was, he planned to do in the next election. Mr. Newton claimed that *The Review* printed the gossip with malice, that is, with reckless disregard for its truth or falsity, and that the story had harmed him to the tune of $25 million.

The Review, for their part, denied any wrongdoing and stood by the story, which had appeared in the popular but gossipy "Mr. Tampa Knows Best" column. Truth, they said, was Mr. Tampa's absolute defense. Alternatively, *The Review* argued that it printed the story without malice and was not liable because Mr. Newton is and has been a public figure.

Well, I wasn't so sure about that, but I had ruled earlier in the case that whether Newton was a public figure or not was for the jury to decide. Since trial court judges are not required to be without opinions, I had mine about the case. Aside from the titillation factor, what possible difference could it make? In the first place, who cared whether Nelson Newton is gay? The world wouldn't stop. It's not a crime. It's not even a problem with his marriage since he isn't married. Not now anyway. Wife number four left him just before the story appeared. Indeed, that was one of the facts cited in support of the truth of the story by the paper. I mean, it wasn't like Tom Cruise suing the *Enquirer* for the same type of rumor. Cruise had won his suit, but whether Nelson Newton would win or not remained to be seen.

It looked to be a long trial, though, and I hate long trials. The witness lists took up three single spaced pages and Mr. Newton was representing himself. He might, as the old adage goes, have a fool for a client but what it meant to me was a longer than normal trial with many more opportunities for reversible error and a serious strain on my limited judicial resources. I've had cases with Nelson Newton before. He can't say his name in less than twenty minutes. Just the thought was making me tired.

I pulled out the offending news story that was going to become indelibly imprinted on my brain in the next few weeks and read it again.

What prominent Tampa lawyer lost wife number four and won't get married for a fifth time because he likes men better? Those in the know have seen him in the locker room with his hands where they shouldn't be. Shame on you, Mr. N., for staying in the closet. You should have the courage to be who you are.

The item contained few facts. I wasn't sure how *The Review* planned to prove the story was true and I wasn't really interested. Did I become a Federal Court judge for this?

The Review, a very radical, controversial gay paper, had been publishing a series of articles "outing" gays all over the country, and particularly on October 11, "national coming out day." They employed stringers in each major market to add some "local color" to the stories. "Mr. N" was only one of several items *The Review* had published along similar lines, but Newton was the only one who had sued in my courtroom. If avoiding unfavorable publicity was Newton's true goal, making the case a media event in Tampa wasn't the way to do it. If Newton was a different sort of guy, I'd believe he had pure motives. To educate the public, say, or to promote privacy. But this was Newton–a publicity hound of long duration. I knew there was a hidden agenda here. And I didn't like being used to foster it, whatever it was. Unfortunately, I had no choice. I'm a public servant and Newton is a member of the public. Open access to the courts gives him the right to be in my courtroom for the $120 filing fee. Open access to the courts is something I normally support, but cases like this make me reexamine my opinions.

I spent some time going over the exhibit lists, reviewing the trial briefs and the proposed jury instructions submitted by both parties. Before I knew it, it was after ten o'clock. I'd worked right through dinner and George had never come home.

I called down to the kitchen and ordered a late night snack to be sent upstairs. If I went downstairs I'd run into someone I know and I just wasn't in the mood. I did go into the den and turn on the news. I watched for over half an hour as I ate, but there was nothing new reported on General Andrews' death or anything else of interest. I soaked in my tub for a while, read my most recent Carolyn Cain mystery and then called it a night.

When I turned out my bedside lamp at about one o'clock, I tried not to think about George not being home and instead focused on Kate. I hadn't seen her in over a week, and I don't like being out of touch with her. Kate has been like a mother to me since my own mother died. I try to see her and talk to her every couple of days.

I closed my eyes and thought about George's recent behavior. Why was he acting so strangely? I was worried about him. He'd always been a political player, but he'd gotten so much invested in this battle. It was completely different from his usually detached manner of dealing with life. Long nights with the party chairman, working with Jason whenever possible. Even working closely with Senator Warwick, a man whose ideology and personality George detests. I had heard him on the phone into the late hours talking to all of the senators he knew personally, urging them to vote against Andy. I suspected he'd attempted to meet with the President. Which sounds farfetched except that George does know President Benson. Politics is like any other world. If you stay in it long enough, eventually everyone you knew in your younger days rises to positions of power and influence—by processes of aging and attrition.

What I didn't understand was why defeating Andy's confirmation mattered so much to George. I knew he believed Andy was not suited to the job, and we'd talked for hours about why. But a lot of people aren't suited to their work–like my boss the Chief Judge ("CJ") for instance–and it never seemed to bother George. The strain was turning him into someone I didn't recognize. And maybe he felt a little guilty. If Andy did kill himself, George would feel at least partly to blame. I counted on my subconscious to answer my questions since it was pretty obvious George wouldn't. Eventually it did, albeit not soon enough and certainly not as I expected.

5

There is a scientific explanation for why time seems to pass more rapidly as we age. According to this theory, we humans measure time against our experience. The older we get, the more experiences we have and thus the shorter it seems a year will last. Or ten years.

This is a great theory and it's probably even true, but it doesn't explain why time passes so slowly when you want terrible things to be over. That Sunday was one of the worst ones I'd ever spent. The days would get a lot worse, but I didn't know that then.

I woke up early, groggy and heavy-eyed from lack of restful sleep. George had come home some time during the night and he was snoring soundly. I eased out of bed, thinking that if he got enough sleep, he might be back to his old self today. I didn't know the man that had been inhabiting George's body for the past two days, but I didn't like that man and I was hoping he'd gone back where he came from.

My George is tall, dark and handsome. At least, to me. He's patient, kind, loving and full of that old concept: honor. This guy looked like George. He wore George's silk boxers just now, the ones I gave him for Valentine's day with the red hearts on them. But he was obviously someone else. My George sleeps in pajamas.

I crept out into the kitchen and put on the coffee, whispering to Harry and Bess to be quiet as I let them out the back door and picked up the newspapers off the back porch. We get three newspapers every day, the two local ones and *The Washington Post*. By the time Harry and Bess got back, my coffee was done. Cuban, strong and sweet, my caffeine of choice. I took my papers and coffee mug, the one George had given me that said "I Hate Mornings," out to the veranda and sat at the table overlooking the bay, the dogs at my feet. The sun was just starting to peek through the horizon again. Sunrises are truly glorious miracles even though I prefer to sleep through them. This morning, I tried to appreciate the pinks, oranges and blues in the sky. That's hard to do when your eyes are closed.

I opened the *Post* and saw the headline, much as I expected. Barring some terrorist airline hijacking, the death of General Albert Randall Andrews would be front page news everywhere today. ANDREWS COMMITS SUICIDE, it said. That was certainly creative. Everything above the fold dealt with Andy's death and, for the first time, printed the note he left in his study before he went out to the boat to kill himself. Tears sprang to my eyes as I read it. I had no idea he was so sensitive. It certainly wasn't a side of himself that he allowed to show very often. The note was reprinted in full:

Good bye my darling Madeline. Please take care of our children. Make sure they understand how much I've loved them all. I just can't go on under such attacks, especially by my friends and colleagues. I wanted to serve my country once again as a Supreme Court Justice. Now, this Old Soldier's career is over.

All three papers carried the same story on the front page, which was from one of the wire services. It reported that General Andrews was found dead after suffering a gunshot wound to the head early yesterday morning. He was found in his fishing boat, still tied to the dock behind his Lake Thonotosassa home. It was his habit to go out every night to fish, the report said, and his home was so remote from others that no one heard the shot. He was survived by a wife, two sons, one daughter and no grandchildren.

The papers rehashed the low points of the recent confirmation hearings and speculated that the contentiousness and the potential vote against him were the reasons for the General's suicide. Senator Warwick was quoted, "It is a tragedy that the Republic should repay him for his decades of service by publicly humiliating him to the point where he felt he had no choice but to take his own life." There was more in this vein for about six pages, which I dismissed as the worst sort of public grandstanding, particularly when I knew Warwick's real views on Andy's appointment. Honest politician. Now there's an oxymoron.

The local papers carried a number of stories and columns about Andy's contribution to the community, his charitable activities and his commitment to education. There was even a story on the sports page about yesterday's Blue Coat golf tournament. I was mildly amused to see that one of the teams had been disqualified, my group had come in fourth and our designated literacy program would get $250 prize money.

I'd refilled my coffee mug several times and the sun was moving quickly toward the yardarm, as the pirates who once sailed these waters are believed to have said, when George came out in his bathrobe. He brought his own coffee—he detests mine—and rubbed his stubbled face across my cheek before he sat down across from me at the table. While he was sleeping, I had decided to act like nothing untoward had happened between us, so I just said "Good morning, sweetheart. Did you sleep well?" I said it sincerely, too. Really I did.

"No, not really." Was all he said in reply. He looked out on the water and appeared to be concentrating on some inner conflict, but he didn't say what it was and he didn't talk any more. I went back into the house to make more coffee before I finished my papers.

When I came out with two carafes on a tray, one for him and one for me, George said, "Do we have anything planned for today? I'd really like to go out to see Madeline, if that's alright with you. I'd like you to come with me, please."

I looked at him over my reading glasses. "Why do you think we'll be welcome there? You haven't talked to Madeline Andrews in years, unless you count the words you said while throwing them out of the restaurant the other night."

He might have winced, but it could have been my imagination. "I know. And I'm sorry about that now. Andy and I were close once. I really respected the man years ago and I've always liked Madeline. I just feel like I should go out there. You don't have to come along, but I'd like it if you would." He was talking quietly, almost as if he was speaking to himself.

"Of course I'll go with you. It's the right thing to do, anyway. It's just that I'm not sure we'll be welcome. But I suppose we can turn around and come back if we're not wanted."

I continued to read the papers in silence for a while longer and then went for my morning jog. When I got back, we dressed and drove out to Thonotosassa.

Lake Thonotosassa is an old lake community about fifteen miles east of downtown Tampa, out in the country. The Andrews house was built on land leased to him by the University of South Florida in a sweetheart deal several years ago. It was a good public relations gesture to practically give the ten-acre estate to Andy when they were trying to get him to agree to become president of the university after he retired. He declined the presidency, but he kept the land. Rumor was that he paid a fair price for it when his memoirs were published last year, but I'd never seen any evidence to support that. Where Andy was concerned, the locals had so much pride they'd never consent to any real or imagined blemish on his honor. Andy's accepting the land with strings attached was something Tampa wouldn't acknowledge, even if it had happened.

We had to park George's silver Bentley about half a mile down from the driveway and walk up to the house. The media vans were on the public road, but as close to the drive way as they could get without actually trespassing: no chance they were going to miss anything.

As we approached the driveway, we were spotted first by NewsChannel 8. Frank Bendler, who seemed to be everywhere these days, came up to us with his photographer and his microphone, looking for that "film at eleven." Before he let the camera roll on an "interview," he had the good manners to ask us if we'd mind.

"I don't think this is the time, do you, Frank?" George asked him. "Besides, we don't know anything. We're here to pay our respects, that's all."

Frank looked at me beseechingly, but I backed George up on this one. I wasn't feeling too friendly toward Frank after Friday night, anyway, and if there's anything I hate about the media, it's their ability to make a circus out of a tragic event. I'm not sure just how much the public does have a right to know if it means depriving loved ones of privacy they need when they've suffered the ultimate loss in death. And that is true even if the deceased was a Four Star General and a Supreme Court nominee.

But Frank wouldn't give up. His camera was rolling, so he said, "Tell me this, Judge Carson. Do you believe General Andrews committed suicide?" Just as I was ready to tell him that was a police matter, the gremlin inhabiting George's body resurfaced.

"No, Frank, she does not think that. It's unthinkable. General Andrews was a war hero and one of the bravest men alive. He would not kill himself. Now turn that damn thing off and have a little respect, will you?"

George took my elbow and escorted me through the gaggle to the driveway. Fortunately, I'd worn my low-heeled Tods, because the gravel driveway was uneven and difficult to walk on. On either side of the driveway were orange and live oak trees. Spanish moss hung down from the branches and a dense blanket of kudzu covered the ground. Someone had cut the kudzu vine back on either side of the driveway to keep it from taking over the entire area, but any surface was fertile for the vine that strangles everything it touches. I shuddered, thinking of all the snakes that must be living under there.

We walked past cars lining both sides of the driveway all the way up to the house. There were limousines, army vehicles and every imaginable type of car and truck. That current status symbol of the middle aged white American male, Harley Davidson, was also well represented. Who would ride a Hog to a condolence call?

We eventually reached the front door of the Andrews' Georgian-style home. It was about thirty seconds before someone I'd never seen before in my life opened the oversized oak door and let us in. The house was teeming with people standing so close together we could hardly get through them. Whether we'd even be able to find Madeline, let alone talk to her, was doubtful.

The room—and the whole house for that matter—was filled with both familiar and unfamiliar faces. Some were in various types of military uniforms, and others were in the usual Sunday- -go-to-meeting clothes worn to comfort the bereaved. We stood a little uncomfortably in the foyer for a few minutes until George spotted Police Chief Ben Hathaway across the room. Ben was heading in our direction, a little too purposefully for my comfort.

Ben is a big man and I always have the impression that he won't be able to stop his forward momentum in time to avoid walking right over whoever is in his way. He's not only tall, but heavy. Yet, he maneuvers like a ballerina. He's clever. And secretive. He's probably been a cop too long to betray his true intentions.

"Hello, George," he said, extending his hand. "Willa," as he bent to kiss my cheek. "This certainly is a mad house, isn't it?" I remembered exactly when Ben Hathaway became the kind of friend who could kiss me hello and it was clear that he thought he had that privilege. I tried not to feel too prickly about it. I don't like people to touch me. Kate says it drains my energy. Maybe she's right, but I just know it makes me uncomfortable. I always feel like I'm being manipulated. I hate that.

"I didn't expect to find so many people here, Ben. What's going on?" George asked him as they shook hands.

"I don't know really. Most everyone likes Madeline. I think people are just shocked and want to affirm that what they believe about life still exists. No one can accept that the General killed himself." Ben was trying to speak softly. The trouble was that everyone in the room was speaking quietly, which had the effect of a low rumble over which truly quiet voices could not be heard.

"I'm certain he didn't." George said, with the same vehemence he'd been using to Frank Bendler outside. Ben looked at him curiously.

"Why?"

"I've known Andy for twenty years. Served under him in the army, did you know that?"

"No, I guess I didn't." Ben said, a little cautiously. His army career isn't something George usually talks about. I was surprised he'd bring it up here.

"Well, the Andy I knew would never have killed himself. He thrived on adversity. He thought suicide was the coward's way out. There's no way he did this to himself. No way. At least, not on purpose."

None of us had seen Frank Bendler come in the house, but he was standing nearby, listening intently. He'd probably been invited. Frank was a local celebrity, just like Andy had been, and we all knew him. He was entitled to pay his respects just like the rest of us. But Frank wouldn't leave anything he overheard out of his professional life, either.

Ben's attention was focused on George and a small crowd was gathering. Some had their backs turned, pretending they weren't eavesdropping on our conversation. But they were.

"Did you ever talk to him about it?" Ben asked.

"Yes, we did talk about it, years ago. One of our mutual friends committed suicide and Andy wrote him off as cowardly. Then again when Admiral Boorda killed himself over the alleged disgrace of wearing the wrong medals, Andy was incensed."

"About what?"

"He thought the Admiral should have shown more courage in the face of adversity, that the issue was a small one and the Admiral should have been above it."

The crowd around us had grown and they were very quiet, listening intently. Bendler was still standing there, along with everyone else. "Anything else?" Ben asked George. I didn't like the sound of it. Not at all.

"Andy never believed Vince Foster killed himself, either. He said he knew the man and Foster'd been murdered, plain and simple." There was a shocked murmur rippling through the surrounding crowd now. I spied Madeline Andrews a few feet inside the house. I turned to George and took his arm.

"Will you excuse us, Ben? We need to pay our respects to Madeline." I started walking away, pulling George with me and the crowd of polite, but frankly curious, onlookers parted for us to walk through. Madeline's back was turned to us and I leaned over to whisper to George. "You need to curb your views while we're here. It's not the time or the place."

"You're right, of course. I'll do better." He squeezed my arm gently to emphasize his agreement while people we didn't know continued to look at us, pretending not to stare.

Madeline Andrews had been petite and polite since birth. I noticed, as I hadn't on Friday night, that her brown hair was streaked with grey and her brown eyes were old. She'd added a few pounds over the years and she looked every nano-second of her age, which I guessed to be about sixty. Today, she was dressed in a black silk dress with short sleeves and a jewel neck. She wore the obligatory pearl choker with small pearl earrings clipped on her lobes. Her only other jewelry was her wedding ring, the plain gold band Andy had put on her finger over thirty years before. The way arthritis had swollen her knuckles, she wouldn't have been able to get the ring off if she'd wanted to. Which, we all knew, she didn't.

Standing next to her in the darkened living room of the large, unkempt, rambling house, was her daughter, Robbie. Nothing about Robbie resembled her mother. Robbie was taller and about a hundred pounds heavier. Her hair was mousy brown. She wore round glasses which made her round face appear fuller than it was, if that was possible. She had three chins. Robbie was holding onto Madeline's arm as if Madeline would fall without the support. In the years I'd known Madeline, I couldn't imagine her needing support from Robbie. If anything, it had been the other way around. Robbie was the flighty one.

Today, Robbie had cried off all her makeup, if she'd had any on to begin with. Robbie had the kind of face that needed every bit of a makeup artist's skill. She stood there, looking lost and without any clue as to what had happened to her father.

Madeline, gracious as always, held out a hand to George, who took it and at the same time, bent over to kiss her cheek. This cheek kissing seemed to be the male response to sorrow, at least today. I bent over to give Madeline a small hug, myself. She seemed to need the contact. Or maybe I did. The house smelled strongly like cats, but I didn't see one. Not that cats would have been visible in this crowd.

"Hello, George, Willa. It's so good of you to come. I wasn't sure you would." Madeline said quietly.

"I didn't think you'd have the nerve, after the way you behaved," Robbie said with more honesty and hostility. "If it wasn't for you, my father would still be alive."

Madeline turned to her smoothly. "Robbie, dear, George was justified in protecting Willa. Your father would have done the same for me."

"That's not what I meant, and he knows it. He was the one who led the opposition to Daddy's nomination. Without him, Daddy would be on the Court by now and still living." The spite was palpable, oozing off her like oil off a hot turkey.

"He did what he thought was right, Dear. We can't hold it against him now." Madeline was always generous of spirit and kind to others.

She was a woman who loved too much. Or maybe it was just what George's Aunt Minnie would have called breeding.

Robbie glared at us both, but kept further opinions to herself. She didn't leave and let us talk with Madeline alone, though.

"We're very sorry about Andy, Madeline. Neither one of us can believe it." I said, in a serious bit of understatement. Madeline's eyes glassed up and tears welled.

"I can't believe it either, Willa. I've known Andy all my life. We lived next door to one another from the time I was born. I don't know what my life will be without him." Her voice was shaky and I was afraid she'd break down completely, but she didn't. Robbie, to her credit, took over, thanked us for coming and said her mother should go lie down for a while. They headed off to one of the other areas of the house, presumably toward the bedrooms.

I needed a little time to myself, too, and I left George in search of the bathroom. I was unfamiliar with the layout but after a few false starts, I found what must have been the General's den. It was filled with army paraphernalia. Flags, guns, plaques, framed certificates and photographs. Lots of photographs. I looked around the room, which was dominated by a large wood desk with a brown leather armchair behind it. I wondered if Andy had used this room to write his memoirs.

Andy's memoirs had caused quite a stir when he published them a year or so ago. He had extensive notes of all his army experiences and he used those notes to write his autobiography. He was sharply criticized for taking official army documents and using army personnel for the project. The suggestion was that, for years, Andy had been using the U.S. Army as if it was his personal corporation and he was the CEO. Andy denied any wrongdoing, offered to return the documents and pay for the personnel. But the damage to his reputation was already done. The scandal didn't drive him to suicide, lending further support to George's disbelief.

A fireplace, a couch and two chairs fronted the massive desk. It would get quite cool out here on winter nights. A fireplace would make the evenings cozy. There was a soft antique Iranian rug in front of the hearth and several other souvenirs from Andy's trips overseas in the room.

To the left side, a door led to the outside of the house. The General would want a way to admit visitors for meetings without disturbing his family. Again, the cat smell was close to overwhelming, but I didn't see a cat.

The powder room was just opposite the outside entrance. I ducked in and took care of things. It wasn't the cleanest bathroom I've ever been in, clearly the province of a man.

As I was leaving the bathroom, careful to return the seat to its original up position, I heard two guests talking in the den. "Madeline said Andy was sitting up reading in here Friday night around eleven. They have separate bedrooms so she didn't know what time he went to bed." The other guest said, "They'd been arguing and she went to bed angry. How would you like to have to live with that?" I've never been a comfortable eavesdropper. I let myself out the door to the hallway that I'd entered through.

I wandered around the house for a while, eventually stumbling into the large country style kitchen, overlooking the lake. Here, too, the house could have used a good cleaning and some maintenance. The cat smell was stronger. I saw a litter box in the corner. The lake and the dock in back of the house were visible out the french doors.

The fishing boat where Andy died was still tied to the dock. Yellow crime-scene tape and a uniformed officer I didn't recognize at the entrance kept anyone from walking out onto it. I went out the back door and across the yard. I stopped in front of the officer, who had watched me make the journey from the house.

"This certainly is a beautiful lake, isn't it?" I asked him. I didn't recognize him at all, and he apparently didn't know me.

"Yes, ma'am," he said. "You gotta admire a man who can afford to build a place like this."

"Is that the boat where he died?"

"Yes, ma'am, it is."

"It sure is a mess, isn't it?" I was trying to look out into the boat about eighty feet from where we were standing. It was full of blood and other things not identifiable from this distance but which I didn't think was left over from Andy's fishing experiences.

"Yes, ma'am, it is." I was beginning to get the picture that I wasn't going to get any information from this officer, whether he knew me or not. Nothing ventured, nothing gained. So I asked him, "Do you think the General committed suicide?"

"I'm sure I don't know, Ma'am."

"Is there anything at all you can tell me?" I asked him.

"Not if I want to keep my job, Ma'am."

I was trying to find out if there was any possibility that Andy didn't kill himself, as George seemed to believe. But if there were clues I could see from the shoreline, they weren't obvious to me. I gave it up, went back inside, found George and insisted that we leave. He was more than ready, so we ran the gauntlet back through the television cameras and ignored Frank Bendler's questions about whether George would like to comment on Robbie Andrews' accusations against him.

We finally reached George's Bentley and drove home. By the time we got there, I was bone weary and ready for a quiet evening, which is just what we had. Our last one for some time, as it turned out. If I'd foreseen the next few weeks, I'd have spent the evening discussing everything thoroughly with George, because for the first time in a long time, he seemed willing to talk about it. But I thought we'd had enough for one day, there would be many long, leisurely hours to hash it all out, and our relationship would get back to normal. Once again, I was wrong, wrong, wrong.

6

Monday morning, I had to get up and get moving to get into court by eight-thirty. I ran the dogs, showered, dressed, picked up the *Newton* file, made plans with George for dinner and scurried off down the back stairs to the garage. Greta's top was still down from Saturday, and I didn't bother to put it up. It can't hurt my very short hair, and the morning was already turning into a fine Florida day.

Some federal district court judges use their law clerks as chauffeurs, but I really enjoy my time with Greta. My boss, the CJ, has told me Greta's too flashy to drive now that I'm on the bench. But if you're from Detroit like I am, cars are the essence of life itself. How could I give up Greta just for a job?

I drove down our version of Palm Beach's avenue of palms, over the bridge off Plant Key, away from Minaret and turned east onto Bayshore Boulevard toward downtown Tampa. The view was, as always, spectacular. Hillsborough Bay, particularly along the Bayshore, is truly beautiful. Not many years ago, the Hillsborough River, the Bay and Tampa Bay were completely dead. After a massive clean up campaign, fish, dolphins, rays and manatee are regularly spotted here. In fact, you can eat the fish. If you're brave enough.

Practicing my mindfulness, I really looked at the old mansions along the north side of the Bayshore, interspersed with the newer condominiums and a few commercial establishments, like the Colonnade

Restaurant. It was closed this morning, but by lunch time, it would be filled to capacity with the Old Tampa crowd, as well as the current crop of blue haired snow birds who filled the place to capacity every day. The food was pretty good and the view spectacular. It would never be competition for George's restaurant, but they had good grouper at good prices.

The drive down Bayshore, over the Platt Street bridge, toward the Convention Center is one of my daily pleasures. I could feel my mood lightening and I actually felt better physically. As I approached Davis Island, then Harbour Island, and turned north on Florida, I passed what used to be called Landmark Tower and is now the Sun Trust building. It reminded me again of my late friend, Hainsworth Waterman. I don't know why I thought of Hainsworth today. He'd been out of my mind for several months. Maybe it was Andy's death that did it. The recent deaths of my friends had been appearing in my mind at every opportunity since Saturday. I passed a series of storefronts and Sacred Heart Church along the four-block stretch to the courthouse.

My office is in the old Federal Building, Circa 1920. It is a beautiful old building with wood details way too expensive to duplicate today. In 1920, the Middle District of Florida was a much smaller place than it is now. The building is old, decrepit and much too small. So now we have a new court house just down the street. Maybe, when the CJ (who I'm sure hates me) is promoted or retires, I'll get to move to the new building with all the other judges. For a while yet, I have to make do with my small courtroom.

As the most junior judge on the bench, in terms of seniority, age and the CJ's affection, I have the least desirable location. It's the RHIP rule; I have no rank and no privilege. My courtroom and chambers are on the third floor, in the back. Getting there from the parking garage helps me keep my schoolgirl figure.

I pulled into my reserved spot and parked Greta as I always do, illegally across two parking places. Building security got the meter maid to write me a ticket the first time they found my car parked like this. I vacated it. I may have no rank with the CJ, but I certainly rank higher than a meter maid. This parking garage was built with the very minimum allowable tolerances. Greta's sensitive to being banged by other car doors. I won't subject her to that.

Fortunately, the trip from Plant Key to the garage at the old courthouse is a short one. I was able to park Greta, jog up three flights of stairs, walk into my office, grab my robe and get onto the bench only two minutes late. Not bad.

The parties were at their respective tables, the Defendant represented by counsel and seated next to an army of lawyers, looking very subdued. Boxes of defense files, exhibits and other papers were stowed behind the rail that separates the gallery of visitors from the rest of us so as not to be seen by the jury. *The Whitman Esquire Review* attorneys numbered six, with two additional paralegals in the gallery. The President of the paper was the client representative. The woman sitting next to him was "Mr. Tampa," the author of the offending piece of trash they were all here to defend. I'm told Ann Landers was once a man, too. Go figure.

In what every trial lawyer would recognize as deliberate contrast, the plaintiff, Nelson Newton, sat by himself at the counsel table closest to the jury box. He had only one wrinkled, dirty, letter-sized manilla folder on the desk in front of him. He was holding an ink pen that looked like he'd picked it up at a car rental desk. His somber navy blue suit, shiny from too many trips to the cleaners, could have come from J.C. Penney ten years ago or the Salvation Army this morning. He wore a yellowed, dingy and frayed white oxford cloth shirt with a button down collar. His red, white and blue striped tie had soaked up its share of spilled lunches.

Dressing for court is a little like selecting the right costumes for a play. The idea is to have credibility with the jury, to look like a person they can root for, one they'll want to win. A trial is a contest and there *are* winners and losers here, as much as we try to pretend otherwise. The game is not decided on points. It's one roll of the dice when the case goes back to the jury room; you never know who's going to get lucky and who'll go home broke. The last time he tried a case in front of me, Newton had worn this same outfit every day for three weeks. The jury gave his client two million dollars that time. Maybe it's his lucky suit.

"Counselors, any last minute issues before I bring in the jury venire?" I looked around the room. Media types, if they were in attendance, were of the print variety. No cameras were allowed. Both lawyers said, simultaneously, "Ready, your honor," and the Court Security Officer went to bring in the jury pool, the sixty men and women who had been waiting out in the hall for this moment.

They filed in, one at a time, and sat in the gallery. The clerk called out the numbers and names of each potential juror and the tension in the room rose to a level that resembled a high hum. As each name was called, the clerk directed the jurors to take one of the twelve seats in the jury box and then filled the six extra chairs the Court Security Officer had set up in front of the box.

You could take a bite out of the tension in the courtroom. After a few days, a trial takes on a more relaxed feel. But in the beginning, the participants are uncomfortable and the jurors are mostly bewildered; the parties are trying like hell to select a jury that will be biased in their favor; everyone is tired and sleep deprived, worried about that one last thing they hadn't done in preparation. That tension is like nothing else in the world: The trial lawyer's equivalent of an Olympic event. Ready, set, go. Sometimes, I really miss the entire experience. And then I come to my senses.

This jury venire looked like all the rest. Mostly women, casually dressed. A few men, college-aged students or retirees. Everyone here either because they couldn't get out of jury service one more time or they didn't have anything else to do.

I ask the preliminary questions from a prepared list I use in every trial: Does anyone know the litigants or the lawyers; do they have personal knowledge of the facts; is there any reason they can't be fair?

Stuff like that. Yes answers get them released from service. Then, unlike a lot of federal judges, I turn the questioning over to the lawyers. After some earlier mistakes when I first took the bench, I've learned not to let the lawyers get out of control, though. I limit their voir dire to one hour each. How they use that hour is up to them, but they get one hour, no more, no less. On television, they try two or three cases in an hour. In real life, a trial is slow and tedious. Even the short ones.

As the plaintiff, Newton went first. He stood up and slowly buttoned the middle button of his single breasted jacket, fumbling a little on purpose. He walked over to about the middle of the rail in front of the jury box and stood there, letting them get a good look at him. He was short and overweight. What hair he had left was grey and cut in a fringe around his spherical head. His eyebrows were grey, too, making his violet eyes more startling somehow. He put on his best good ole boy accent, even though he was educated at Harvard just like I was, and said, "How many of you all believe you're entitled to personal privacy regarding your own life, assuming you're not doing anythin' illegal and ain't hurtin' nobody?" The jurors identified with him instantly. It was the one thing he had that couldn't be contrived. Every hand went up. He looked at them all, one at a time, and nodded slowly.

"Are any of you all public figures?" No one admitted it, if they were. "Does anyone know what a public figure is?" He said it like it rhymed with "jigger."

One juror, a young man in the back row dressed in a Pewter Pride golf shirt, raised his hand. "A public figger like Warren Sapp?" he asked, naming one of the Tampa Bay Buccaneers football players. Everybody nodded, apparently in agreement that Sapp was a public figure.

"Yes, that's right," Newton nodded, too. "Does anyone here recognize me to be a celebrity or a politician?" All heads shook negatively. That must have been a blow to his ego at the same time it supported his case. Newton had never been modest. In fact, over the years his name has probably been in the paper at least as many times as Warren Sapp. The walls of Newton's office are lined with the newspaper and magazine accounts of his trial successes. He's been on television enough that some of the jurors might have seen him.

"Well, lemme ask y'all this," he started, and I knew I was going to have trouble from the defense table just from the posture of lead defense counsel.

Newton continued talking to the Bucs fan in the third row who had answered his last question. "Suppose your wife had an affair, Mr. Roberts. Now, I'm not sayin' she did, because I don't know nothin' of the kind. But let's just s'pose she did, for the moment, alright?" Mr. Roberts looked unsure, but he agreed by nodding slightly.

"Would you like it if *The Tampa Tribune* printed that information in the paper?"

"No!" Mr. Roberts looked quite indignant about it, too.

"If *The Tribune* printed that your wife had an affair and it wasn't true, do you think they should get away with that?" Newton put his hands in the pockets of his suit coat, which made his elbows look like chicken wings while he and rocked forward on the balls of his feet.

"Certainly not!" Mr. Roberts was really getting into the issue now.

"And if *The Tribune* did print such a thing, such a scandalous untrue thing, do you think it would hurt you or your wife or your children in any way?"

"Your honor!" Defense counsel was on his feet, almost shouting his objection. "He is trying to prejudice this jury by asking questions that he knows do not represent the true facts in this case. He knows he is a public figure under the law and what was printed about him was absolutely true. He's trying to mislead this jury and taint the whole panel. I move for a mistrial." Newton was guilty of all this, just as the defense attorney was posturing to undo the damage as early as he could.

"Judge, I think it's for the jury to decide what the true facts are in this case. That's why we're here. And I'm entitled to explore their opinions. That's what voir dire is for, as counsel well knows. I oppose any motions for mistrial and I promise to be polite and not interrupt defense counsel if he will stop interrupting me." The jury snickered. Newton was smooth and sure. He knew the game and he knew how to counter all the other side's moves. I overruled the objection, but instructed the jury that defense counsel was well within his rights to make it. I denied the motion for mistrial and instructed both counsel to make any such motions at the bench, out of the hearing of the jury, because I did not intend to have my trial interrupted by grandstanding.

It was familiar territory to all but the jurors. Like a play in its tenth year, each of the actors recited the well-worn lines and like the untutored audience they were, the prospective jurors remained ignorant of the truth of the performance.

Newton continued his voir dire in the same vein, raising the issues with the jurors and making *The Review* out to be a scandal sheet of the worst order. Which, of course, it is. A couple of times I reminded him that this was not argument, but jury selection. Otherwise, I allowed him enough rope to hang himself. The jury would remember Newton's voir dire and that "the facts" he portrayed didn't resemble what they heard in the trial. Whether they'd hold that against Newton during their deliberations or not was the multi-million dollar question.

Newton finally ran out of time and yielded the floor to the blue chip, silk stocking law firm partner from New York who had been admitted to practice in my court specially to handle this case. He stood up to adjust himself before he began his voir dire. He was about 6'2", with a full head of expertly coiffed and colored blonde hair, manicured nails and a medium-grey plaid Armani suit. He wore brown cap toe shoes and the hose (for they were not mere socks) picked up the pale brown threads in the suit. His brilliant white shirt had French cuffs with Tiffany gold knot cuff links just peeking out of the bottom of the sleeves of his suit, as he pulled down on first one cuff and then the other, straightening them just right; clear nail polish reflected the glare of the flourescent lights. The tie was a yellow print, knotted in a half Windsor and hanging straight on his flat stomach to just above the shiny gold monogrammed buckle of his brown Louis Vuitton belt. He looked the picture of what he was: an $850 an hour hired gun. His name was A. (for Archibald) Alexander Tremain, VI. No kidding.

Tremain stood in the same spot Newton had used to hold the prospective jurors enthralled for the last hour and then he turned to look at the remainder of the jury pool in the gallery behind where Newton was now seated. To each group, Tremain nodded his head slightly, but he didn't smile.

"I want each of you to know that today, if you are selected for this jury, you will have the responsibility of deciding whether the United States Constitution is something we all live by, or whether it's not." He stopped and looked in turn at each of the eighteen prospective jurors in front of him. At this rate, his hour for questions would be up before he got any information at all.

"At the end of this trial, the jury that is selected here will be asked whether the First Amendment still means anything in this country, or whether true speech can be punished. Mr. Roberts," he picked out the juror who had seemed so sympathetic to Newton earlier, "do you believe in the United States Constitution?"

"Yes, sir, I do." Mr. Roberts gave the expected answer. Our voters are a pretty patriotic and conservative lot. Florida has had a strong, conservative Republican electorate for years. Remember Anita Bryant?

"Do you believe that you have the right to say just about whatever you want in this country? Not the privilege, but the *right*?" He raised his voice when he said "right" and pounded a closed fist into his flat palm.

"I guess so, yeah. But I don't think you should hurt anybody by saying things that aren't true. That's not constitutional." Mr. Roberts remembered Newton's hypothetical about his wife's adultery.

"You're right, Mr. Roberts, you're absolutely right. If you knowingly say something that's not true, that shouldn't be protected by the Constitution most of the time. But what if it is true? Shouldn't you be able to say anything that's true and not be afraid of being sued?" Tremain pushed his advantage and his theory.

"Sure." Mr. Roberts gave in. He was a true lawyer's nightmare. He wanted to be on the jury so badly that he'd agree with anything you asked him. The lawyers had no way of knowing which way he'd vote, so leaving him on the jury would be a wild card. The trial lawyer's equivalent of white knuckle time.

Tremain nodded approvingly, giving Mr. Roberts a figurative gold star. Then he moved on. "I certainly hope none of you are gay or lesbian?" There was an uncomfortable silence in the room. The jurors were shaking their heads and looking from side to side, almost involuntarily, trying to figure out where this was going. The statement of the case that was read to the jury at the beginning of the voir dire never mentioned what it was that *The Review* had printed about Newton. It was out there now.

"If any of you eighteen potential jurors are gay or lesbian, please tell us now, because you must be excused from this jury," Tremain said.

"Objection!" Newton shouted, jumping to his feet and shouted as I banged down my gavel and sternly admonished the defense attorney. The jurors chuckled self-consciously, looking around for raised hands. I asked to see both counsel in chambers and we left the courtroom for my smaller hearing room, each of the members of the defense team following behind Tremain the way goslings follow their mother.

I turned to defense counsel as we entered the room, "Just what exactly are you trying to do here? Is this standard voir dire in your part of the woods, because I can tell you that's not the kind of question we routinely ask here in Tampa."

"Your honor, the issue of Mr. Newton's homosexuality will be at the heart of this trial. He denies it, but he has put the truth of the matter squarely before the court. I think my client is entitled to know whether any homosexuals are on that panel. They should not be sitting in judgment on the decision to publish this material. I want them all dismissed for cause." The rest of the defense team nodded on cue.

"Judge," Newton responded, all pretense of the country bumpkin magically erased. "Assuming some potential jurors are homosexuals, the defendant would not be entitled to excuse them on that basis alone. If he tried, it would be objectionable and possibly even illegal. That last question should be stricken and no others like it should be allowed in the rest of the voir dire." Newton was hot and I didn't really blame him. But he had to know it was coming. Like a lot of things, though, knowing and experiencing are vastly different.

"Do either of you have any law on this for me?" I looked at them both, sternly. They didn't, which made me suspect that the defense knew what the law was and it wasn't good for their side. If they'd had any support for the idea they'd have been waving it in my face. In triplicate. "I don't know what the legal answer to the question is, but I found your question personally offensive, Mr. Tremain. On that basis, I will not allow any further questioning into the personal sexual habits of jurors. And if any more questions like that are asked in violation of my order, I will direct a verdict for the plaintiff. Understood?"

To his credit, Tremain didn't argue. His point had been made with the panel and we all knew it. Newton requested a curative instruction to the jury, which I agreed to give, but it wouldn't help. The cat was out of the bag. I asked both lawyers whether they wanted a mistrial, to start over. Newton refused. So we went back to the courtroom and finished up the jury selection without further incident. Not surprisingly, Tremain used one of his pre-emptory challenges to dismiss Mr. Roberts. By three o'clock, we had our jury sworn and I adjourned until the next morning for opening statements.

I was planning to finish up a few orders I'd started last week and all of the law clerks wanted to talk to me about their research projects. But I just couldn't concentrate and had a strong desire to see and talk to Kate.

Kate lives in a bungalow, four houses from the Bayshore on Oregon. It's charming, but the house is on a corner lot and the kitchen looks out over the side street. Both George and I were worried about just anyone being able to drive up and see her standing in the kitchen, but she said we watch too much television. She wouldn't even put blinds on the windows. She said she moved to Florida for sunlight.

I pulled into the driveway and walked up to the back screen door, calling her name as I approached. I didn't want to startle her, since I hadn't called to tell her to expect me. In the back yard from the dining room window, I saw her working on her newest project, an English garden. I watched her for a few minutes, still supple enough to get down on her knees in her garden easily. Kate had been doing yoga for flexibility for thirty years and she was still as flexible as any twenty-five year old.

Almost as if she knew I was there, she turned around and waved to me. She put away her tools and offered me a glass of iced tea—the quintessential southern hospitality offering. We chatted about nothing in particular for a few minutes in the kitchen as she washed up, poured the tea into tall glasses, added a sprig of mint and a slice of lime to each one. Then she carried the glasses and some shortbread cookies she'd made from an old family recipe on a small tray out to her patio. We sat, enjoying the companionable silence overlooking her wonderfully overgrown flowers.

Kate's garden is so wild and uncontrolled, like nothing else in my life. All the flowers are mixed together erratically, the colors both brilliant and subdued. Our gardens at Minaret are beautiful, too, but they're perfectly ordered, weeded, matched and wouldn't dare encroach on the brick paths or the grass. Kate's garden was creative and free, a reflection of Kate herself.

After a while, Kate said, "Dear, why don't you just ask me what you came to ask? The suspense is more than my heart can take on such a beautiful afternoon."

My connection to Kate is intense, almost as if she were my real mother. She can sense my moods and can usually tell when I'm troubled.

She says it's because she's a channel for the universe and she trusts her intuition. That may be true. Or it may be that I rarely come by just to chat anymore, so that every time I come over it's because something is bothering me. That's George's theory, anyway. Whatever it is, whenever I'm in trouble, to Kate is where I come. She knows it and I think she likes it. Everyone wants to be needed.

"It's George."

"George? Mr. Wonderful? Your knight in shining armor? That George?" She teased. Actually, Kate thinks more of George than I do, if that's possible. They have some kind of mutual admiration society that makes it not fun to complain about one to the other.

"It's not funny, Kate. George has been acting very strangely the past few days and I just don't understand it. It's got me worried." So I told her about his outburst at the restaurant and how he threw the Warwicks and Andrews out for good.

"Good for him." She sounded almost as indignant as George had been. "It's about time Tory started acting her age instead of like a thwarted toddler. Throwing crystal glasses, indeed. Are you alright now?" She reached over and moved my hair away from the right side of my forehead so she could look at the lump, which was going down, but the bruise was still slightly visible.

"I'm fine. It's George I'm worried about. That night, I don't know what time he finally came upstairs. The next day, he was out and gone before I got up. He made up some story about jogging, but you know George never jogs," I said, continuing my litany of grievances.

"Maybe the man wants a little privacy, Willa. He stays right where you can find him ninety-nine percent of the time. Isn't he entitled to a little mystery? Once in a while?" Kate's never been one to accept criticism of George. When we first married, she told me I should never tell her about arguments with my husband. She said that he and I loved each other, so we'd make up, but she would not be able to forgive him if he hurt my feelings. So, I rarely complained to her about George. But in truth, there was seldom much to complain about at all in the seventeen years we'd been married. George was near perfect as far as I was concerned. Until lately.

"Sure he is. But he could just say that. Why does he have to make something up that we both know is untrue? I'm not used to George lying to me." As we discussed this, I was becoming more upset, not less.

"Ok. George is protective of you and occasionally wants a little privacy. What's so terrible?" She ate a cookie and offered the plate to me. I shook my head.

Then I told her about his temper tantrum at Andy's house with the reporters, his insisting Andy didn't commit suicide and how interested Chief Hathaway was in George's murder theory. She looked a little concerned, but she was trying to reassure me.

"Tell me what it is, exactly, that you're worrying about," she said. Solemnly. Seriously.

"I think George is in some kind of trouble, but I can't imagine what it would be." Unlike turning on the light to look for the bogey man in the closet erasing the fear, voicing my concern seemed to make it more real.

Kate reached over and patted my hand. "I think you're worrying unnecessarily. Let me think about it and we can talk some more. But now that you've told me, don't you think about it any more or that will just confuse the energy." She poured another glass of tea and changed the subject. Unfortunately, I couldn't just decide not to think about it and make my concerns go away. When I was younger, Kate would have me symbolically put my worries in a box and she would lock them in with a small gold key that she wore around her neck. I'd forget about my troubles and she would tell me that she let them out in the woods for the Universe to handle. What worked when I was twelve didn't work as well at thirty-nine. But I was still willing to try it. As it turned out, my intuition was right.

7

The evening news had Frank Bendler reporting an "exclusive" story on the latest events about General Andrews' death. When I came back from Kate's, George was in the den watching his image on the screen repeating what Frank was calling George's "murder theory." After the clip with George, Chief Hathaway was cornered. Frank asked the Chief whether there was any evidence to support a cause of death other than suicide. Ben said he couldn't comment about an ongoing investigation beyond the official statement he'd already given. Frank's commentary correctly pointed out that the Chief didn't deny the possibility that General Andrews had been murdered.

I was shocked that Frank would air such a thing, and said so. George was more calm about it. "Frank has a responsibility to air the truth, Willa. Andy didn't commit suicide and we all know it. If Frank puts it on the air, the truth will come out. Otherwise, it will just be another Marilyn Monroe speculative story for years." He turned off the television and asked me if I wanted a drink. I wanted a dozen. He poured me a full glass of Sapphire and tonic.

"Frank asked you if he could run the story before he did it, didn't he? That's the reason it wasn't on last night." I accused.

George was unperturbed. "Of course, he asked me. But I'm sure he would have aired it even if I'd objected. Frank is our friend, but not at the expense of his journalistic ethics."

"You've always thought 'journalistic ethics' was an oxymoron. When did you get to be so supportive of the media?" My tone was just a touch sarcastic, but George just turned and walked out into the night air. Whether he heard me or not, I don't know.

I followed him out to the veranda and the dogs followed us both. We sat in our usual white wicker rockers and I took a big gulp of my Sapphire and tonic. "George, don't you see how this makes you look? It looks like you know something. Like you have some inside information or something." I took another swig, looking for the instant tranquilizer. It wasn't working.

"I do have inside information," George said quietly.

Not only was the gin not tranquilizing, every nerve ending was buzzing throughout my body. Maybe this was the intuition or spirit guide Kate was always telling me I had. And maybe it was just years of experience as a lawyer and judge, but I knew this was not good news.

"What inside information is that?" I squeaked out, really afraid to ask.

"You'd better get another drink. This will take a while," he said, eyeing my now-empty glass. I didn't argue. I traded my highball glass for a tumbler and refilled the ice, Sapphire and tonic. We were out of lemons, so I substituted a lime. I wasn't about to go out into the kitchen to slice fruit right now.

George sat in deep reverie for a while. I didn't rush him. I just had another sip or two of my drink, looked at the water and concentrated on my breathing until I finally started to relax. Really, what could be so alarming? This was George, after all. The man I'd been married to for seventeen years. I knew him better than he knew himself. What could he possibly tell me that would be so bad?

Finally, he began, in a quiet, slow "telling a story" kind of way. "You know that before we met, I was in the army and I served under Andy overseas." He seemed to need me to acknowledge this, so I said, "Hmmm." George's army career was exactly the kind of thing that made me love him as I did. He'd enlisted in the army right after college, even though he didn't have to, because "it was the right thing to do." George was always doing "the right thing" and he never had any trouble figuring out what that was. Maybe it was his Lutheran upbringing, or that WASP noblesse oblige. Dependable George wasn't likely to throw too many curve balls at his wife and that was just what I wanted. I understood Barbara Bush on that score very well.

"Andy was the best kind of officer the army could turn out. He was an honorable man who looked at his career as a calling. He insisted his men abide by the best code of honor he and the army could exact. There were so many examples of this during the time I served under him that I can't name them all and I'm sure I've shared some of them with you before." Again, an affirmative response seemed to be called for.

"Hmmm."

"Andy and I came to be friends. I didn't make the army my career, but he didn't hold it against me. We had a connection regardless of how infrequently we saw each other. Whenever we could, we'd have dinner or drinks, but the years put distance between us." He paused again, sipped his drink this time, and added, "Until Andy was promoted to Colonel and stationed in Tampa not long after you and I moved here."

I remembered the time well. We were new in Tampa and the Andrews family was one of the few we knew. We saw Andy and Madeline and their children as frequently as Andy's busy travel schedule would allow. I'd come to like Madeline immensely. Andy was a bit too much of a man's man for my taste and his views on women were misogynistic. Mostly, he just acted as if women didn't exist. I remembered several social occasions where Andy stood tall and straight, quiet and polite while women in our circle talked. He wasn't listening and he rarely responded unless we asked him a direct question. It was more like waiting for the noise to stop. Then he'd turn to one of the men and start a totally new conversation about something none of the women would be the least interested in. He wasn't disrespectful, but he treated women as if they were flies buzzing around a picnic: Something that couldn't be helped and were best ignored. Both Andy and I had made allowances for each other because of our affection for George, our common friend.

George continued, in that same far away, remembering kind of voice. "Derek Dickson was another officer I'd served with under Andy in Korea, the third member of our triumvirate. Derek made his career with the army, but he served in a different unit from Andy and his career stalled out after he made Colonel.

"One day, we heard that Derek's boy, a young First Lieutenant, had committed suicide. Derek was crushed. The boy had gone to West Point and was Derek's heart." George sounded emotional about the issue, even now. He got up to refill his glass, and he took his time about it, gathering his composure.

When he sat back down, he was more remote. "I wanted to send a gift of some kind to Derek or go to the funeral and I wanted Andy to go with me. He flatly refused. He said the boy was a coward who couldn't face his responsibilities and the army didn't need him. He said the army didn't need Derek either because he obviously sired the boy with bad seed. Andy saw to it that the boy received a posthumous dishonorable discharge for cowardice. Derek killed himself the next day."

"That's despicable! I had no idea. Why would Andy do such a thing?" I was incredulous. To deliberately hurt a man and his family when he'd suffered the death of his child was cruel and unnecessary. I'd known Andy as a single-minded military man, not a harsh, heartless monster.

"I don't know. But it was obvious to me that the Andy I had known years before was not the man who literally ruined Derek's life. Andy and I fought about it and some pretty harsh words were said. Words I never regretted, even once. After that, I distanced myself from Andy and I guess he distanced himself from me, too. Over the years, you know, you hear things. I heard a lot of similar stories of Andy's lack of compassion. Even the way he treated his kids was overly rigid and controlling. He acted like they were his to command, too." George stopped and sipped his drink for a while, but there was more and if I would but wait, he'd tell me what it was.

"I finally came to believe that Andy was mentally unbalanced. As he rose further and further up the ladder, and eventually became Chairman of the Joint Chiefs of Staff, I was truly alarmed. That's why I worked so hard to defeat his nomination. Why I couldn't let such a man sit on the highest policy-making court for the next generation. He was unfit to serve. I knew it. President Benson and Sheldon Warwick knew it. I think even Andy knew it."

George turned and looked at me intently. It was important to him that I understand now, although he hadn't shared any of this with me before. I was working at not feeling too wounded about that. "But don't you see? Andy would *never* have given up on any fight. Fighting was how he solved all his problems. He would have seen this battle for the Supreme Court seat to the bitter end and he was damn close to winning. It might have killed him by a heart attack or maybe some other lunatic with a better aim would have gotten him, but he would never, never have taken himself out of the game early and definitely not by suicide. Someone killed him. This, I know."

When he finished, I wasn't sure if I was more upset by the story itself or by the fact that I'd never heard it before. I thought I knew everything there was to know about my husband. I'd believed we were soul mates in the way few couples are. I knew what his favorite meals were, where he preferred to vacation, what types of reading material he liked, even the type of underwear he preferred. To realize I knew all these trivial details of George's life, but had no clue about something as important as the demise of a serious personal friendship in a rather spectacular and awful way was more than a little unsettling to me. Maybe, I allowed myself to think, our connection had just never been tested before. My most significant personal tragedy, the death of my mother, happened long before I met George. Since we'd married, our lives had been pretty uneventful, upwardly mobile, middle class, white bread normal. Like the lives of our friends. Well, most of them.

George was my lifeline to the world. He provided my anchor, my sounding board, my protection and companionship. We lived in a special, protected world. He cared for me and I took care of him. We shared everything. He was my soul. Or so I'd thought.

If he'd kept something like this from me, even in the face of Andy's death, what else was there that I didn't know? And if I found out, what would it do to my life as I knew it? Could I live with it? I really wasn't sure. And it was that very lack of certainty that unnerved me. I needed to be sure of George, I wanted to be sure of him. Dammit, I had been sure. Until lately, I was dead certain I knew who and what my husband was.

Because I didn't know what to say or how to say it, I said nothing. I was so lost in my bewilderment, so focused on my personal feelings, that I didn't hear George get up and leave the flat a while later. On Peter's night off, George acts as his own Matre d'. He must have gone downstairs to work. By the time I came back from my self-imposed introspection, it was dark out and getting cold. There were no lights on in the flat and the dogs were outside, howling to get in. In fact, that was the noise that roused me.

I went over to the back door to let Harry and Bess run headlong into the room. After petting them for a while and giving them a few treats, I changed clothes and got to work on the *Newton* file in preparation for the opening statements. When I don't know what else to do, I work. I know I use work as an escape from life, a substitute for life. It's where I go to get away from everything that I can't cope with. I know it's not healthy, but it's better than other self destructive methods of escaping the world. And it works.

In the den, I sat at the desk where Aunt Minnie had done her household accounts as a young bride. It was a partner's desk; one person could sit at either side and both could work in the middle.

At some point, hours later, noticing I was hungry, I called downstairs, asked George to send up whatever tonight's special was and join me for dinner. When he said he had already eaten, I realized it was ten o'clock. I'd been working for over three hours and didn't remember a thing I'd read. I'd have to start over and try to concentrate this time. It was going to be a long night.

Making room on the desk for my dinner tray a while later, I noticed the black leather book Kate had given me last year for Christmas sitting on the small table beside my favorite reading chair. It was embossed in the center with Andy Mellon's words "When your heart speaks, take good notes." The pages of the book were blank. Kate intended that I keep a journal. She insisted that it would provide guidance and connection to my intuition. Every time I saw her, she asked me if I'd started to use it. She'd asked me today, in fact, but I had ignored the question. Maybe now was a good time. If I wrote down some of these thoughts I was having about George, maybe I could at least leave them there on the page and pay attention to my work.

I wrote for over an hour, putting down all the things that had happened in the past three days and how I felt about them. I wrote long paragraphs describing how shaken I was over George's lack of forthrightness about such a significant event in his life. And I wrote one short sentence about how stupid it was for him to tell Frank Bendler about it. Finally, I got to a big issue that wasn't all about me and my hurt feelings. If Andy didn't commit suicide, who killed him? And was it possible that George knew the answer to that question?

My hand was shaking so badly that I wouldn't be able to read what I wrote next: If George knew something about Andy's death that he wasn't telling, what would the State Attorney do to George?

I slammed the journal closed and threw it on the floor. It landed face down in the corner under one of Aunt Minnie's twenty wing chairs that seemed to sprout full blown in their ball and claw feet every time I wasn't looking. It would be a damn long time before I touched that thing again. Not only did it not make me feel better, I'd come to a conclusion that everybody else must have reached yesterday. I left George a note, got my car keys and stomped off down the stairs, out into the night.

Greta and I drove over to St. Pete beach. I had a long, long walk and just as the sun was coming up over the horizon, decided to drive home, get dressed and go to the courthouse. Nothing was resolved and I didn't feel any better and if either of these lawyers messed with me today, they'd be damn sorry they had.

I stopped at Cold Storage, my favorite Cuban coffee place, on the way to the office. Cold Storage lost its lease on Florida Avenue when the City sold the land to new development after the Ice Palace increased business over there. Now, it was located at the corner of Whiting and Tampa street in a much bigger building. Sometimes when restaurants move, they lose their ambiance. Cold Storage managed to reproduce its graffiti on the walls, pictures of patrons and welcoming atmosphere in new, larger surroundings.

When I arrived at the Courthouse, I saw the news vans in front and my only thought was that if the lawyers in my case were giving press conferences I'd throw them all in jail. I don't want my cases tried in the media. The courtroom is where all evidence is presented. If I had to put a gag order on the participants to get the point across, that's what I would do. I'd done it before and if that big city lawyer didn't know it now, he'd know it in the next ten minutes.

By the time I got up to my office, I'd worked myself into a fine snit and I was ready for bear. All of which I blamed on the caffeine in the Cuban coffee. I pushed open the outer door to Margaret's office and stormed through without even so much as my customary good morning. She knew better than to say anything when I was in one of my rare moods, so she kept her head down and looked busy. I snatched my robe from the hook on the back of the door, put my arms through it and marched out into the courtroom, ready to vent my rage.

Absolutely no one was there. I asked the Court Security Officer where the parties were and he said he didn't know. The clock said eight thirty-five, five minutes after we were to start. The ruckus from the hall was the media circus I'd witnessed out front just a few minutes before. I turned to the Court Security Officer. "Please go out in the hall and tell both Mr. Newton and Mr. Tremain that if they are not in here in five minutes, this case will be the first in history to have judgment entered against both parties. Tell the media they are, from this point forward, barred from the courtroom and do not let them in." I couldn't keep them out indefinitely, but I could do it for the next thirty minutes at least. Until one of them got an order from the CJ to get back in–which I knew he'd give them the second they asked for it, just to tweak me. And because he'd be right.

"Yes, ma'am!" the officer said, on his way out as he said it. The court reporter gave me one of those, "What's with you?" looks, but I didn't care. This was an issue I'd always felt strongly about, but on no sleep and less patience, I would definitely have made good on my threat to give Mr. Newton the fifty million dollars he requested and to dismiss his case with prejudice at the same time. Let them figure *that* out in the Eleventh Circuit Court of Appeals.

Apparently, the officer got the point across, because both lawyers hurried into the courtroom and remained standing at their respective counsel tables while the officer kept everyone else out. I was still standing as well and we all looked a little silly. I gestured to the court reporter to begin taking down the proceedings.

"Counselors, listen closely because I am only going to say this once and I expect no misunderstandings. This case is pending before the United States District Court for the Middle District of Florida. We spent the entire day yesterday selecting a jury. The case is not being tried to the media and the jury is not the public. From this point forward neither of you are to discuss this case with any member of the media, on or off the record, until the verdict is returned and the jurors are released. This order includes any conversations of any kind. If I so much as hear a *rumor* that you are talking to a friend over coffee who happens to be employed by one of the newspapers, I will enter judgment against you so fast you won't know what hit you. And I will award fees and costs to the winner in an amount I deem appropriate. Is that perfectly clear?"

"But, Your Honor—" Newton sputtered.

"Judge, you can't—" Tremain spit out simultaneously.

I cut them both off with a slam of my gavel. "There will be no argument and no further discussion on this subject. I can't bar the media from the courtroom forever, but I can stop you from talking to them. It is completely within my discretion to do all that I've told you I will do. Don't test me, gentlemen." I turned to the officer and told him to bring in the jury in ten minutes.

One of the most exciting days of any trial is when the lawyers make their opening statements. It's like reading a table of contents on a book, giving you an overview of what's to come. It's the first time the jury, the judge and the other side all hear the whole story. No matter how much a lawyer prepares for this moment, you're never quite sure what the other side is really going to say. Sometimes, it's something you never even considered. The closer a lawyer gets to trial, the more he begins to believe his own bullshit. This is a dangerous road to travel because it makes you believe you can see what's around the blind corners. *Newton v. The Whitman Esquire Review* was one of those cases for both lawyers and I knew, if they didn't, that there were surprises in store for both.

Back in my chambers, I attended to the thousand and three details that somehow just multiplied on my desk like rats in a laboratory. I've never had, nor do I want to have, any actual experience with rats. Pink telephone slips must be related to rats in some molecular way, though. What else could explain the proliferation? There were two messages from my boss, the CJ. I gleefully put them at the bottom of the pile. As usual, I was so caught up in other things, I was unaware of the time. The courtroom was full when I went in again. I vowed to work on this problem. I hated judges to be late when I practiced law. I'd been convinced it was a personal snub, that they just couldn't be bothered to be on time for the litigants who were, after all, their reason for being. Or that they thought their precious time was more important than ours. Life is just one long, educational experience, isn't it?

When we started again, I nodded to Nelson Newton who rose to his full five feet four inches, smoothed down his stained red tie over his protruding stomach, and sucked it in a little so he could button the rumpled blue suit jacket. I've seen Nelson at social functions and at George's restaurant. I know he owns more than one outfit.

Continuing his personal mime game of "me David, they Goliath," Nelson picked up his one manilla folder and pulled out two or three sheets of five by seven note paper that probably came from the same car rental desk as his pen. He looked the sheets over, front and back, put them back in the folder, and stepped up to the podium. Of course, he knew very well he couldn't see over it, but he wanted the jury to know. He turned and asked permission not to use the podium. I granted the request. He knew I would. He asks every trial. More elaborate play acting. But this time, Tremain hadn't seen it coming. Before he ever said a word in his opening, Newton had the jury on his side. Christians one, lions nothing. I hid my smile behind my hand as I pretended to cough.

"All of us were told growin' up that sticks 'n stones would break our bones, but names would never hurt us. Our mamas didn't want us fightin' in the school yard, so they told us to just ignore kids who called us names." He had the jury nodding in agreement.

"But we knew then, just as we know now, that names do hurt us. Calling someone names can not only hurt their feelings, but hurt their business and their relationships with their family and friends. That's what this case is about. *The Whitman Esquire Review*, a newspaper printed out in San Francisco, called me a name. They don't know me and they don't know our town. But they called me a name anyway, and they printed it in the paper, and it's hurt me. They shouldn't have done that. I know you won't let'em get away with it. I don't know about San Francisco, but here in Tampa, we're decent folks and we've got standards. It's up to you all to let *The Whitman Esquire Review* know that. Thank ye." He actually ducked his head when he finished and sat back down at his table. The jury looked over at Tremain with interest. How could he hope to compete with Mom? The jury was still interested in the answer at this point, but it was a critical juncture for Tremain. For my part, I was wondering whether that $850 an hour *The Review* was paying him would turn out to be worth it.

Tremain had a large, black three-ring binder in front of him on the table containing his trial notebook. It was filled to three quarters' capacity, tabbed and organized with white, pink, blue and yellow paper in the different sections. It definitely conveyed the impression of preparedness. And maybe more than a little overkill. He closed the binder and rose to give his opening without it. No crutches. Except for his slow, deliberate adjusting routine which he performed only when the jury was in the room. What was the subliminal message? To me, it was just annoying because it took him so long before he ever got started on anything.

Tremain had no trouble standing behind the podium; He towered over it. He gripped the sides with both hands, the better to give the jury a look at his plain gold wedding band. He leaned into the podium, toward the jurors, but leaving both the podium and the rail between them so as not to invade their space.

"First, I want to thank you for your service as jurors in this case. I know you are not the country bumpkins Mr. Newton makes you out to be, just as he isn't the bumpkin he pretends to be. I know you have busy lives and taking time out to help us is a hardship for you. I want *you* to know that we appreciate it. But more than that, aside from going to the polls to cast your vote, serving as a juror is the most patriotic thing many of you will ever do. This is your chance to uphold the laws of the United States." Not a bad contrast, actually. Mom versus patriotism. The sides were chosen. Let the game begin.

Tremain went on about the constitutionality of free speech, the right to print what's true, newsworthiness and the legitimate concerns of the public for about thirty minutes. By the time he finished, the jury would have had a hard time remembering anything Newton said. They were all puffed up with the importance of their job to the continued viability of the nation. It promised to be more than a fair contest. It was a little hard to tell the Christians from the lions at this point, but I was on Newton's side. I know first hand what it's like to have your life the subject of everyone's morning coffee conversation and I don't like it, either.

Newton's first witness was "Mr. Tampa" herself. She was a youngish woman, about twenty-five, with purple-black hair and a pierced nose. She was dressed like a member of the cast of "The Rocky Horror Picture Show," or a Frederick's of Hollywood catalogue. She took the stand, raised her hand and swore to tell the truth, "Of course."

"Are you a man or a woman?" was Newton's first question.

"A woman."

"Were you born that way?"

"Of course."

"Then calling yourself 'Mr. Tampa' is misleading to the public, isn't it?" The jury snickered. The questioning went on in this vein for a while, Newton trying to show that "Mr. Tampa" was a fraud and her column full of lies. We took a break after the direct, but Tremain would have some rehabilitating to do when we reconvened.

By the time we got to the lunch hour, I'd had as much grandstanding by both of these lawyers as I was willing to put up with. I told the jurors they could go home for the day and I told the lawyers that I would hear argument on their various evidentiary motions at two o'clock, before Newton put on his next witness tomorrow. Then I left the bench, seeking sanctuary, and maybe a nap, in my office.

When I got to my desk, Margaret had ordered a Chicken Walnut Salad from Carlino's new place for my lunch and had it set on my conference table with spring water and flatware. She'd put out my messages from the morning and a list of matters I had on my schedule for the afternoon. Right on top, she'd written a note that George had called three times and said it was urgent. Oh fine, I thought. For days he's been acting like I don't exist and now he wants to talk so it's urgent. Well, I was busy, too, and whatever he had to say could wait until I got home. Maybe if he had to wait a little while he'd find out how it feels.

I was wrong. At three o'clock, in the middle of Newton's argument that Tremain should not be able to put on witnesses who allegedly had homosexual affairs with Newton in the late seventies because such affairs were irrelevant to the truth of the assertion that Newton is gay, Margaret came out with a note and handed it up to me on the bench. It said, "George has been arrested for the murder of General Andrews." I told the lawyers I'd hear the remainder of the argument tomorrow and adjourned. If I hadn't been so emotionally wired, if I hadn't stayed up all night, I could have handled it. As it was, I didn't start to shake uncontrollably until I was safely locked in my office.

8

For the second time today, a gaggle of media were swarmed at the front door of a building I wanted to enter and I had to sneak around to the back entrance of my own house. I'd called home and was surprised to find George there. He made his own bail and was released with the standard admonition not to leave the jurisdiction, even though homicide suspects aren't usually allowed bail in Florida. His release was unusually quick. I gathered some small comfort from that, although I had no idea why it had been allowed. As he had the day before, he'd turned on the afternoon news and was watching the story of his arrest played out on national television.

"Are you so pleased with your celebrity that it wasn't enough for you to live it, you have to watch it all over again?" I sniped at him.

"I want to know how they're justifying arresting me. The police won't tell me anything, so I have to get my information the way the rest of America does. Come and watch with me and we'll talk when it's over." He patted the place on the sofa next to him and I vacillated between sitting down to watch and continuing with my outrage.

Again, Frank Bendler had the local report and it had been picked up by the networks. This must be Frank's moment in the sun and I was resentful that someone I had counted among my friends would capitalize on the complete disruption of my life.

I wasn't prepared for the strength of the evidence supporting George's arrest. Just hearing about it made me weak in the knees and glad I was sitting down.

"George Carson, local restauranteur, surrendered himself to authorities today. He was picked up for questioning at his home here on Plant Key in South Tampa. After questioning, Mr. Carson was charged with the murder of General A. Randall Andrews who died early Saturday morning from a gunshot wound to the head. Although initially reported as a suicide, the police quickly discovered that General Andrews was a murder victim. In the face of increasing pressure on the State's Attorney from outraged citizens and prominent politicians, Mr. Carson was charged with first degree murder. NewsChannel 8 has discovered the gun that killed General Andrews was registered to Mr. Carson. We've been given little information about the grounds for Mr. Carson's arrest, except that Police Chief Ben Hathaway told us Mr. Carson had means, motive and opportunity. Mr. Carson is now free on bond."

What followed were the inevitable interviews with Andy's family, his friends and anyone who would talk about George to the press. I was dismayed, and I know George was, too, at the number of people who didn't really know us but were willing to talk about us just for their fifteen minutes of fame. I made a mental note to cross every one of them off our Christmas Card list. Trying to hold on to my humor kept me sane. I've never cared what people think of me, and I still don't. But they should have been more charitable.

George had turned off the phones, so the answering machine was blinking like mad. I got up and turned it off, too, and went into my room to lay down. Later, I asked myself why I didn't talk to George. Or why he didn't explain things to me. But at the time, it was all just too much. I'd had no sleep last night. Sleep deprivation is a form of torture and I wanted to believe that some of my emotionalism was attributable to sheer exhaustion.

The rest was fear. I'd had enough experience with the feeling to recognize it for what it was. Losing my mother when I was sixteen and my Dad, who just couldn't cope, leaving me to live with Kate and her family, left me with an all too healthy fear of abandonment. If I couldn't deal with the world right now, at least I could escape it. In less than five minutes, I'd fallen into a deep slumber. I slept through until the next morning, not waking even when George came to bed.

I decided to run to clear my head, so the dogs and I sneaked down the back stairs. We ran our usual path around the island, but when we came back to the house, the news vans were still parked out front. Don't these people ever give up?

Upstairs, George had put on the coffee and brought in the papers. Front page news in all of them was his arrest yesterday. Looking like he hadn't slept in three days, George was sitting at the kitchen table drinking coffee and eating a bagel. I needed to shower and get fortified for the day, so I took my coffee in to begin the beautification process. I tried not to think about the whole sorry mess until I was dressed in the professional suit of armor that gave me the judicial detachment I desperately needed.

In my den, I called Margaret at home and told her to advise the lawyers that we would begin with Plaintiff's first witness, as planned, tomorrow. She wanted me to take the week off, but I couldn't fill all those empty hours. She said I should call the CJ and explain what was happening, that I was needed at home and he'd understand. Of course, I knew damn well my putative boss, Chief Judge Ozgood Livingston Richardson, Senior—"Oz," to his friends, which don't include me—wouldn't understand anything where I'm concerned. He has no real control over my life and his petty games were more than I needed right now. I am a United States District Court Judge, appointed for life by the President. I take my responsibilities seriously and I don't care whether the CJ thinks so or not.

I'd mistakenly taken his parking place my first day on the job, the revered first spot next to the door reserved for the Big Guy, the CJ, Oz himself, had been on my case ever since. I thought his reaction was more than a little bit strange for such a minor infraction. I got the worst case assignments, the smallest chambers, the most meager courtroom redecorating budget. The rest of the judges had moved to the new courthouse but I was the last one on the list to be moved when the CJ conveniently ran out of money in this year's budget. Or so the he said with what I swear was a twinkle in his eye. At meetings, he ignored my suggestions and just generally made it known, without saying so, that I was far from his favorite. I know he has aspirations to higher office. He might be holding a grudge against me for some trouble my sister was in recently, or maybe it's a black mark against him if he can't keep his junior justices in line, and he won't be considered for the Eleventh Circuit Court of Appeals. If so, that would be most unfortunate. The only chance I have of getting rid of him is the Peter Principle: get him kicked upstairs. I prayed for it every night.

I told Margaret not to reschedule anything on the calendar and I'd see her as planned. I gave her strict orders not to allow anyone to contact me unless it was a life and death emergency. Like the one I was living in.

Then I squared my shoulders, took several balancing deep breaths and went into the kitchen to have a serious talk with my husband. The man I once believed I knew better than I know myself. The one who had been charged with murder.

George was still at the table, still reading the papers, still mainlining coffee. He looked wired. His eyes were bloodshot; you could see red veins not only in the whites but in the hazel irises as well. His pupils were dilated. Deep wrinkles that weren't there last week had appeared between his nose and the corners of his mouth. I've heard stories of hair turning white overnight and never believed them. I looked anxiously for grey hair and didn't find any on George's beloved head, but that was the only thing missing from making him look twenty years older than when I'd seen him yesterday.

All my defensiveness melted away. This was George. The man I loved, whom I'd loved for years, who had taken care of me and supported me since we'd first met. George, my pillar, my strength. He wasn't a murderer and that was that. I had no idea what was going on here, but I intended to get to the bottom of it and I intended to see George cleared. God help anyone who stood in my way.

"George," I said, as I poured yet another cup of coffee and sat down across from him at the table. He looked up at me and then through me. He didn't appear to be listening at all. I reached over and touched his hand. "George. I need to talk to you. Okay?"

He said "Sure. What do you want to talk about?"

I didn't scream at him. And people say I have no self restraint. "I want to talk about how it is that I'm sitting across the table from a man charged with murder. I want to talk about how your gun got to be a murder weapon. I want to talk about what the hell is going on here." My voice had gone up of its own volition with every sentence until I was almost shouting the last question. I was losing control. My precious control. I wasn't used to it and I didn't like it. I tried again. I lowered my voice and slowed it down.

"George, please. I need to know what we plan to do."

"Do? What is there to do? I'll wait until Ben Hathaway finds out who killed Andy. The charges against me will be dismissed and forgotten. In the meantime, I'll continue with my life the same as I always have. What else would I do?" He sounded calm, collected, as if we were discussing one of the dogs being sick on a rug he didn't particularly like.

"What else is there? You've been married to a lawyer in a family of lawyers for seventeen years and you can ask me that? How about hiring the best defense attorney we can find, for one thing?"

He looked surprised. "What for? Willa, I don't expect these charges to go beyond the stage they already have. Chief Hathaway has assured me that they are continuing their investigation. I feel certain that he is being truthful with me. And the man who killed Andy will be found and brought to justice. Don't worry."

I was losing what little sanity and patience I had left. People think I'm not patient. But I am. It's just that no one recognizes my patience when I'm exercising it. "Has it ever occurred to you that what the police are looking for is more evidence that they have already arrested Andy's killer?"

For the first time, he looked shocked. Alive. Attentive. Thank God. "Willa, are you saying that you think I killed Andy? Because if you're saying that, then we have a much more serious problem here than my arrest."

That wasn't quite the response I was going for. I didn't know what to say, because I didn't know what to think. "Of course I don't think you killed Andy," I said. "But how did your gun get to the scene of the murder? And where were you at the time Andy was killed? You were so sure that Andy would never be confirmed as a Supreme Court Justice. Unless you knew Andy was going to die, how could you have been so certain?"

Now, George was truly angry. At me. He got up from the table and turned over his chair in the process. "You let me know when you figure it out, Willa. In the meantime, I'm getting dressed, packing my things and moving to the club. I'm sure you don't want to be sleeping with an accused killer. And I don't want to sleep with a woman who's supposed to have complete faith in me. But doesn't." He stalked out and I didn't go after him. Maybe some time apart was a good idea. Maybe we both needed time to reflect. I submitted to my exhaustion and George left while I was sleeping.

I woke up with my dreams so fresh in my mind that I could see them like a movie. I was sixteen again, spending the last year of my mother's life as her constant companion. She was telling me that she'd never leave me, as her life was slowly ending. I saw her after-death experience, saw her spirit leave her body and move toward the light. And I was laying over her, sobbing. Just as she left me completely, she said "Be brave. Take care of Daddy for me." Then she was gone, and I was startled awake by the dogs jumping on the bed. They were afraid of thunderstorms and had jumped up when the lightening and thunder started.

The dream left me badly shaken. I don't often dream of my mother and when I do, it always upsets me. My almost forty-year-old brain understands why mom died, and I try to believe that her spirit lives on with me. But the young girl I was then still feels the loss deeply. In an emotional crisis, I always dream of Mom.

But since she died, I've learned a thing or two about fear. Fear is always with us, lurking around the corner, waiting to jump out and scare you when you're most vulnerable. If you let it, fear moves into your head and takes over your life. The only thing to do with fear is to face it, deal with it, and dispose of it. What I knew was that I could choose to be afraid and just wait for the worst to happen. Or I could take charge of my life. I've done it before. I knew I could do it again. It's what Aunt Minnie would have called "pluck." You've got to have some, or fear will overwhelm you.

Just then, the doorbell rang. The dogs ran barking to the door. I wanted to ignore it, but I didn't. When I looked through the peep hole, I saw Kate was standing there in the hallway. Seeing her standing there, my resolved wavered. I invited her in, tempted to fall into her arms as she held me and let me cry. It was what I would have done as a child, the solution that was so much easier. Just let someone else deal with it, retreat and wait for the worst to pass over. What had I done? Why was everyone in my life leaving me? Where did George go? Would he come back? My heart was truly broken and it was up to Kate to mend it, as she'd done so many times before. I did none of that, of course. Judges don't cry. Except at sad movies, and funerals, and weddings, and when someone sings the National Anthem beautifully. And when their hearts are broken.

When we were seated in the den with hot tea, Kate's cure for all that ails you, she calmly asked me what the problem was. Intuition again? Probably she'd seen the same news reports we had. If I hadn't been so emotionally and physically exhausted, I'd have treated her the same way I had George when he asked me that question.

"Am I the only person on the planet who believes being accused of murder is not the best way to live your life?"

"He's *accused* of murder, Willa, not convicted. There is a difference." Kate's tone, as always, was gentle with me.

"Of course there's a difference. But neither one is all that desirable, in my view." Defensiveness caused me to be impatient. Weapons launched, like Patriot missiles, unerringly hitting their target.

Kate set her cup down on the butler's table between her chair and the couch. She looked at me closely for a long time. "Have you started writing in the journal I gave you at Christmas?"

"Kate, for God's sake. My husband is accused of murder. Writing in a journal about my feelings on the subject is not going to change it," I snapped at her.

"I was thinking you might try using it to figure out how to get yourself out of this mess you've made," she said quietly.

"I've made? You think I've made this mess? Is it my gun that killed an army general? Am I the one that now has mug shots down at the police station? Was it my face on the evening news describing how it wasn't possible that Andy committed suicide? Are my whereabouts at the time of the murder unaccounted for? Am I the one who's been making it plain to the entire world how I would *never* allow Andrews to sit on the court?"

And the clincher, "Am I the one who told General Andrews that I'd kill him if he ever hurt my wife again the very night before he died? You floor me, Kate. You really do."

When I'd vented my spleen, I didn't feel better and Kate didn't look the least perturbed. She sat quietly, picked up her cup again and said nothing for a long while, waiting for me to stop staring at her like a pit bull thrown into the ring with a scared rabbit. She was no rabbit, even if I thought I was a pit bull.

"Actually," she finally said, "I was thinking more of the mess you've made of your relationship with George and whether you are going to be able to repair the damage before the rift between you becomes the Grand Canyon."

As ever, Kate put her finger right on the pulse of my anxiety. I could love George in prison, but I didn't want to live without him and I wasn't interested in finding out if I could.

"Use your intuition here, Willa, not your fear. You know George didn't kill General Andrews. Why don't you prove that first, if that's what it takes to get your life back in order? I suggest, though, that you might use your journal to work on your priorities." She gathered up her things and gave me a hug before letting herself out of the flat.

I knew she was leaving because she thought I had some serious soul searching to do. I was too stubborn to do it, though. Her comments had just made me madder than ever at George. How could he put us in this situation? If he ever came back, I might throw him out for this. Now there's the Old Willa, I thought. That scared, trembling female was someone else. Someone I didn't have any intention of spending any more time with. I began exorcizing her by drinking hot milk and going back to sleep.

9

The next morning, I had to make my own coffee. Usually, George has downed half a pot by the time I get up. Mornings not being my forte, I heated milk in the microwave and put a tablespoon of instant Bustelo espresso in it, a trick a Cuban friend once taught me. It wasn't quite the same, but it was enough of a jolt to get my eyes open.

I took Harry and Bess out for a run. The day was a little cool, but the sun was coming up nicely. It would be another beautiful day in paradise. Some people claim to get tired of the sunshine every day. They are the same people who think suffering is good for the soul. Surely those Calvinists who deprived themselves in the time of our forefathers are not reaping their rewards now. If they are, I have no hope.

The second cup of instant Cuban coffee was really not bad. Strange how quickly your taste buds adapt. I'd have to get some solid food soon though. I've never been a good one for fasting. If I'm not as thin as Twiggy, it's too late now to worry about it. Besides, George likes me just the way I am, a pretty solid size twelve.

I was in the shower when the telephone rang. Thinking it might be George, I nearly killed myself sliding from the shower to the handset in the bathroom. By the time I picked it up, the machine had already kicked on. "George? Is that you?" I said, over the tape.

"No, Willa. It's Frank Bendler. Isn't George there with you?"

Shit! Now what should I do? Swearing at myself for not screening the call, knowing it would make a bigger impression on Frank if I hung up than if I tried to give him some explanation that he would, hopefully, accept. I said, "No, Frank. He went out for some bagels and he's not back yet. I thought he might have forgotten something. What can I do for you?"

Frank took my explanation without comment, but he'd be watchful of what was going on from this point forward. George had to come home today, or it would look like we'd split up over his arrest. Which, of course, was what we'd done. But it wouldn't help in the court of public opinion, which I didn't give one whit about except that it would matter to the State's Attorney. I crossed my fingers, hoping discretion would rule Frank on this issue until I could get George to see my point and come home. We have three guest rooms, for God's sake, if he wants to keep pouting.

"Do you want to comment on the latest information we've gotten on the Andrews killing? It concerns George." Business as usual with Frank.

"What information have you got?" I asked him, simultaneously wanting to know and dreading the answer.

"Robbie Andrews is giving interviews. She claims George met with Senator Warwick and the President the night before her father was killed and that they hatched a plan to defeat his confirmation. She says George was so intent on defeating her father's confirmation that he had allowed himself to be used as the front man by her father's political enemies. She said that's why George killed Andy. Would you or George care to respond to that?"

I slammed down the phone. Frank would report that as a "no comment," and it was just as well. If I'd offered my comments, they would have done both me and George more harm than good. I stepped back into the shower to rinse off the shampoo and soap. I was getting more and more pissed off, first at Robbie Andrews and then at George. What business did Robbie have trying to put another nail in George's coffin? And what the hell had George been doing the night before Andy was killed? A secret meeting with the President of the United States, no matter how far-fetched that seemed, was as plausible as George's own claim to have been jogging.

Of course, I had only myself to blame for the fact that everyone in Tampa knew George hadn't been home with me. Why did I say that he'd gone jogging to all those people at the Blue Coat? Because I'd thought there was no harm in it. What you don't know can hurt you.

My anger was covering up fear. George didn't commit murder, but one of the other people he'd been spending time with since Andy's nomination could have done it. Presidential aides have done worse and lived to tell about it. I could name a few who are still in prison. After that, there is always talk radio.

Trying not to get distracted, I dried my hair, put on minimal makeup and dressed in jeans and a long-sleeved cotton shirt. I slipped on my Tods, picked up my minuscule handbag, drove Greta over to the club and went into the dining room for breakfast. Just as I expected, George was seated, fully dressed, having coffee with the *Wall Street Journal.*

Mindful that the wait staff was no doubt watching and unsure of his reaction, I didn't go over and kiss him. But I certainly wanted to. The relief I felt to find him there, right where he should be, in the first place I looked, was palpable. He looked so perfect this morning. He'd rested well. He was shaved, dressed as he always is and eating his usual breakfast. George's steady behavior has always been my rock. I feel better when I know how he'll behave. Predictability isn't always a bad thing.

"Good morning, George," I said, loud enough to get his attention away from the financial pages. He lowered the paper and smiled at me. My heart melted.

"Good morning, sweetheart. Care for some breakfast? Please sit down." He folded the paper, stood up, gave me a kiss, and held the chair so I could join him across the table for two. "I tried to call you last night for dinner, but apparently you weren't home." He said this without an ounce of accusation in his voice and once again I accepted how much bigger a person he is than I am.

"Actually, I was home, but I'd taken the dogs out. I saw the machine blinking, but I thought it was just reporters, so I didn't pick up the messages until much later. I did try to call you around seven for the same reason," I said, inviting him to explain his whereabouts. He didn't.

"I'm sorry I missed you," he said with genuine regret. The waiter came by to take my order. I asked for a three-egg ham and cheese omelet with toast, orange juice and coffee. George raised his eyebrows. Usually, my breakfast consists of coffee with cream. George is the big breakfast man.

"I didn't get to have dinner last night, so I'm famished," I explained to him. I wanted to keep this conversation on the right track, not get off into any kind of bickering. I came here to convince him to come home and I was trying to focus on that goal. So I asked him about the stock market. That's always good for a half hour of friendly conversation. Ever since George left the bank, he's been an investor. He says it's the perfect occupation—very lucrative, you're your own boss, and you can do it in your pajamas. I've tried to follow his stock tips, but I don't devote enough attention to it. He's always twenty-five to thirty percent up at the end of the year and I lag around ten percent. Not that we're competitive about it.

We discussed his recent stock moves through breakfast and when the waiter had removed the dishes and freshened our coffee, I broached the subject of my visit. George waited for me to come to the point in my own good time. Surprisingly, I found it hard to begin. I'd never been in this position before and I wasn't used to apologizing.

I decided just to get to the point, to use that directness everyone always says I have. "George, I'm sorry we fought yesterday. I'd like you to come home."

"I'd like to come home, Willa, but I just don't think I should," he said calmly.

My heart sank. I had hoped he'd reviewed the situation and come to the same conclusions I had. I'd wanted him to miss me and to want to come back.

"Don't look so crestfallen," he said. "It's not that I don't want to come home. It's just not good for you to have me there at the moment. The spillover publicity can't be good for your career and you're edgy and nervous about my arrest. Think about how the CJ will use this against you, if he can. I think it'll be better for you if we live apart until this is over." He sounded so calm, so reasonable. I could tell he'd thought this through and as with so many other discussions we've had in the past seventeen years, he wouldn't be persuaded to change his mind. No matter how wrong he was. He'd made up his mind to do this for me, whether I wanted him to or not. It made me think of that old story about the young couple who wanted to give each other a meaningful present. Each of them gave up the one thing the other loved best to get something neither of them cared about.

"I'm sure you believe you're doing the right thing. And I won't tell you it's easy for me to see you on the news and in the papers and have everyone we know willing to believe you're a murderer. When I know you won't even kill bugs."

"Thanks for your concern, Darling," he said dryly. I felt chagrined and I might have even blushed.

"You know what I mean," I faltered and lowered my voice. "But have you considered how bad it looks for you to have moved out of our house? People will think that I believe you killed him and that's why you left. They'll think I have no faith in your innocence. They'll think that if your wife won't support you and stand by you through this crisis, I must know that you've done something wrong. Don't you see? It will prejudice everyone if you don't come home." I was distraught and almost pleading by this point. But he was unmoved.

The course of public opinion has never mattered to George, and usually I agree with him. He feels his true friends will stand by him, will know he would never have killed Andy. As for the rest of the world, George just doesn't care what they think. For himself, anyway. On my behalf, he was ready to choose pistols at twenty paces over the smallest perceived slight. In this instance, though, public opinion mattered. I don't want to believe it, but maybe it always does.

We talked about the situation for a while longer, but he wouldn't change his mind and in the end, I left the Club without him. We planned to have dinner together and he said he'd be at his restaurant all day, as usual. But he wouldn't move back to our flat. Not until this whole issue was resolved. He said he just wouldn't put me in that position.

If I hadn't planned to solve this murder already, now I had an even greater reason to do so. For I understood that if George was convicted, he would likely divorce me. He would never agree to let me have a husband in prison. I knew he did not expect to be convicted. George has a lot more faith in the judicial system than I do. George wasn't even considering all of the ramifications and he would not turn from this course. He believed he was protecting me by leaving me until justice prevailed and he would not change his mind, no matter how it hurt both of us. Germans can be so stubborn.

So I turned the conversation back to what we knew about the evidence against George. Since no human can be in two places at once, I started with the biggest question. "George, I have absolute faith in you. You know that. But State Attorney Jasper obviously doesn't. Let's just tell him where you were when Andy was killed, he can check it out, and this will all be over." I took his hand across the table.

"It's not that easy, sweetheart."

"Why not?"

"Because I gave my word not to disclose that information."

"Even to me?"

George looked right into my eyes and gave my hand a little squeeze. "All these years, you've never wanted to get involved in politics. Now that you're on the bench, you're supposed to be politically independent.

I won't compromise that and I won't let you compromise it. You've kept many professional secrets from me and I've respected that. You have to respect my decision on this one."

"So it was something to do with the confirmation," I accused. He said nothing. "Alright, then. How about this one. How did your gun get to be a murder weapon? Maybe if we know that, Jasper will still let you go. It's the only real evidence they have against you."

"I truly don't know the answer to that one. I'd tell you if I did." I must have looked skeptical because he said, "Really. I would. I haven't seen that gun in a while."

"Well, where was it the last time you saw it?"

He let my hand go, sat back in his chair, and said, "On that, I'm still checking."

"You don't remember?"

"I'm not prepared to discuss that just yet," he said.

I didn't want to start another fight, and this was getting me nowhere, so I gave it up for now and turned our conversation to other things.

If possible, I was more troubled when I left the Club than I had been when I arrived. I was glad I had to go back to work. Before I took the bench, I got out my Florida Bar Journal directory issue and looked up Florida's best criminal defense attorney, Olivia Holmes. No kidding. She could be the poster child for the idea that names determine our destiny. I called her and made an appointment to meet with her at Minaret this afternoon.

When the *Newton* trial resumed, I was barely aware of it. Newton began his case in chief by calling his expert witness to the stand. No surprises here for the Defense, since the expert was previously deposed and fully explained his opinions. He testified that Mr. Newton's sexual preference, whatever it was, was a private fact that had been publicly disclosed. He said disclosing Mr. Newton's sex life was offensive and objectionable to all reasonable people of ordinary sensibilities and could not be of any legitimate concern to the public. Further, unless Mr.

Newton admitted he was a homosexual, which he most certainly had not, labeling a person "homosexual" without his consent denies a basic human right: the right to self-identity.

Most of it was above the jury's head, steeped in history and philosophy. The short of it was, though, that personal relationships are private matters and ought to stay that way. Most of us in the room agreed with that, except, presumably, Mr. Tampa herself. And her employer.

When Tremain rose for his cross, he covered truth, justice and the American Way. He questioned the expert about hypocrisy, lying and misleading others. He covered the social necessity to eradicate AIDS, which kills indiscriminately, and the courageous "coming out" of characters like Rock Hudson, Chastity Bono and Ellen DeGeneres. Finally, in rapid succession, he asked,"Sir, are you married?"

"Yes, I am."

"How long have you been married?"

"Twenty-five years."

"Do you have children?"

"Yes. I've got three adult children, two girls and a boy."

"Are you heterosexual?"

"Absolutely."

"Did you mind telling us these things about yourself, sir?"

"Of course not."

Tremain turned around and looked at the jury pointedly. "You don't consider these facts about your life private?" We couldn't hear the answer over the laughter in the galley and the jury box, but the court reporter got it down.

I had arranged to meet Olivia Holmes at two o'clock at Minaret. When I got there, she was waiting. Thankfully, the media circus hadn't yet arrived and was it unreasonable of me to think she'd be driving something a little less conspicuous than the bright red Ferrari parked in our driveway?

Olivia Holmes lived in Miami, but she had offices in Tampa, Orlando, Gainesville, Jacksonville and Tallahassee. Today, I had been fortunate to reach her in her Tampa office. I hadn't asked George for his permission to hire a lawyer, but I hoped I'd be able to talk him into it if Olivia would take the case. Since defense attorneys were calling the house almost non-stop since George's arrest, offering to work for no fee just so they could get the free publicity of the trial and a subsequent book and movie deal, I was pretty sure Olivia would want the job. After all, a Supreme Court nominee had never been murdered before. This was the case of a lifetime. George's lawyer didn't have to win his case, just to get her name in the paper was all that mattered. Look what the O.J. Simpson trial had done for Marcia Clark and Christopher Dearden, not to mention the defense team.

But, Olivia is particular and she has to be not only asked, but persuaded. Olivia Holmes made her reputation defending high profile defendants in political crime cases. When the senator's mistress is killed, when the congressman's son is arrested for dealing drugs, when the mayor's wife is charged with vehicular manslaughter for driving under the influence, Olivia gets them off. Sometimes with a plea bargain, sometimes with a little back room dealing, sometimes with a spectacular trial, but Olivia's clients never go to jail. In the early days of her career, she represented anyone who would hire her. Now, her clients had to be innocent. At least that was the rumor. George could add to her reputation and not spoil her record.

Olivia has never tried a case in my courtroom, which isn't surprising since there just aren't that many women trial lawyers in Florida, let alone that many who do criminal trial work. Besides that, it takes an iron will and a strong level of self confidence to hold a man's freedom in your hands and know his life depends on your skill and judgment. Not many women lawyers have the stomach for it. I don't.

Olivia and I have had a professional association over the years. We haven't been friends, partly because neither George nor I can agree with

Olivia's politics. A criminal defense attorney usually justifies the work of putting criminals back on the street by believing she's serving "the system" and it's "an honor" to do so. They believe the prosecution must always prove its case, or lose. They believe they are guarding basic constitutional rights that must, at all costs, be guarded. They believe that drivel about how it's better to let a thousand guilty men go free than to jail one man who is innocent.

All of that stuff sounds good in theory. The problem is that theory and reality are so far apart. These days, an innocent man is rarely, if ever, brought to trial. It's hard enough to get the guilty ones arrested, tried and convicted. If they are arrested, if they don't plea bargain, if they go to trial, they're usually guilty. And when the defense attorney puts them back on the street, they commit another crime and we do the dance again. The recidivism rate is astronomical and the justice system is losing ground every day.

A criminal defense attorney is, to my way of thinking, a necessary evil. But they aren't crusaders or heros or protectors of the American way. Not to me. At least, not until now. Like so many people before me, as soon as I needed a good criminal lawyer for a bogus charge, I bent my principles. It's the age old problem of being an American lawyer: we know the difference between right and wrong and good and evil but we also see the similarities. Maybe there's something to the criminal defense lawyer's role in the system after all.

Olivia is as unusually short as I am unusually tall. Standing together, we must have looked like the female version of Mutt and Jeff. Her impeccably tailored suit reminded me of Tremain, but hers must have been custom made. Nowhere could she buy such beautiful suits in size two. Finding shoes must have been even more impossible. Her feet were smaller than my hands. Standing next to her made me feel freakishly large and gawky. I moved away a few paces, hoping for perspective.

After we exchanged the obligatory social graces, I offered Olivia a drink. When we were settled upstairs in the living room, she came right to the point. I was grateful, having had a hard time trying to find a place to start. "First, Willa, let me say right off the bat that if you've called me here to ask me to defend George, I accept. If you hadn't called me, I'd have called you."

I couldn't have been more surprised. The tales of Olivia's refusals to represent the accused were legendary. I couldn't believe I hadn't even had to ask her, and I said as much.

She laughed. "I love those stories. They make it possible for me to charge my exorbitant fees. After the client begs long enough, if I say yes, he's willing to offer me his first born child. If I'd wanted children, it would have been an easy way to get some."

"You're joking, surely."

"Actually, no, I'm not. You'd be surprised how many unwanted children there are in the world. But some of what you've heard is true. I do have plenty of work. More than I want, really. And I'm sad to say that there are always more criminals than good lawyers to defend them. So I do turn a lot of work down. I'm swamped right now, actually, and it will be hard for me to handle this case. But I'm hoping there won't be much to do for very long. I'm sure George didn't kill General Andrews. We have someone else to thank for that. As soon as I find out who, I'll probably volunteer to defend him, too."

I don't think this last was meant facetiously. I set my tea down on Aunt Minnie's highly polished mahogany coffee table, unconcerned about water stains. "Olivia, I'm not sure whether you're teasing me or not, but I want you to understand that this is very serious business to us. Neither one of us has ever been in a situation like this and we want it over with as quickly as possible. In fact, I'm so angry with Ben Hathaway that I could personally strangle him without any hesitation. I can't believe he'd arrest George!"

"Of course it's not a joke, Willa, and I'm not joking. I am more than willing to defend George. First, because I feel sure he's innocent. Unlike a lot of criminal defense attorneys, I've gotten to the stage in life that I don't have to defend the guilty ones anymore. And second, I do believe that General Andrews was the worst possible candidate for the Supreme Court. So, yes, I'll take the job if you and George want me. And I'm proud to do it." Maybe she'd been sincere all along.

"Well, you should know that I certainly believe there's no one that will do a better job than you. But there are a couple of problems." I hesitated a moment and she noticed. "George doesn't even think he needs a lawyer, let alone the best we can get. Obviously, I disagree."

"George has always struck me, at least by reputation, as someone who had more sense," she said and she reached for her glass and sat back in her chair. She reached into her pocket and pulled out a cookie. "But I'm not accustomed to forcing my services on someone who doesn't want them," she said as she ate the ears off her Mickey Mouse shortbread.

"I know. I think I can persuade George that he needs not just a lawyer, but you in particular. I just wasn't going to try to talk him into it until I found out whether you were interested. Please leave that part to me."

"Alright, I can live with that. What other problems do we have?" she asked, brushing the crumbs off her fingers.

"According to the news reports, there's a lot of evidence against George, and he refuses to explain any of it. He seems to think that the truth will set him free and someone else will find out what the truth is. I was hoping you would be able to convince him it's in his best interest to help himself." If it sounds like I was pleading, that's because I was. Husbands have a tendency to ignore their wives' advice. Sometimes an independent expert can present the same arguments and be more persuasive. George had plainly rejected my opinion this morning. Maybe Olivia would have better luck.

Olivia considered the implications. It's almost impossible to defend an uncooperative client. If she knew the case would never go to trial, it wouldn't matter. But if she actually had to make an opening statement, cross examine witnesses and mount a successful defense, not having George's cooperation would make the task a daunting one.

Finally, she said, "Well, you're experienced. You know what the risks are. Why don't we wait and see if we can persuade him. If we can't, I'll have a talk with the State's Attorney and see where they're going with this. If it looks like it's going to be the whole shebang, then George will have to decide whether he wants to trade his gourmet cuisine for prison slop. I'm a great lawyer, but I'm not a miracle worker." Modesty didn't seem to be one of her faults. Nor could she be accused of being coy. Success does strange things to a tiny woman.

"What else?" she asked me, seeming to know that while I'd already delivered some seriously bad news, there was more to come. I just told her, without dissembling. She was the type to take it better straight.

"I am personally investigating the murder. And I will control the defense. No arguments." I looked her right in the eye. I didn't waiver, look down, blink, smile or anything else to diminish the declaration. For her part, she didn't back down either. She didn't say anything for several minutes.

This last condition might be enough to cause her to turn down the case. It was outrageous. And, for her, unethical. Most lawyers wouldn't stand for it, wouldn't even believe I'd said it. Interference in the progress of the investigation, making the spouse a potential witness when her testimony could otherwise be protected by a privilege, second guessing by the client. Each was enough to make a good lawyer run, not walk, in the opposite direction. I wouldn't have allowed it if I had been in her shoes. But I wasn't. I was in my shoes and I was not comfortable with leaving anything to chance. Kate believes the Universe handles all the details. I've been a lawyer long enough to know that it doesn't. George wouldn't hire her if I didn't talk him into it, and I wouldn't even try unless she agreed to my conditions. Some lawyer would.

Finally, Olivia drained the last of her tea and asked if we could take a walk down on the beach. To my mind, we hadn't gotten all the issues resolved yet. "I think we need to get to know each other a little bit before I make a commitment, don't you? Let's have a talk," she said.

Like everything else she'd done, it was unconventional. But then, my demands were unconventional, too. I didn't have anything more pressing to do, so I led her down the back stairs and let Harry and Bess out ahead of us. We walked around the island, away from the house and, hopefully, any reporters who might be out there.

She took off her four-inch heels and left them on the beach, walking just out of the water line where her feet only got wet when a larger wave came up, which was rare. There's no such thing as surf in Tampa, most of the time. She walked quite a while in silence. I was occupied by my own thoughts, so I ignored the quiet.

Eventually, still looking straight ahead as she put one foot in front of the other, she said, "My parents were so happy when my brother, Thomas, was born. They'd waited over ten years for a boy and they feared they wouldn't ever have him. Not that they weren't happy with me, but my dad was the last of his line and he wanted a boy to carry on the family name. We lived on a plantation in Louisiana at the time. The old farm place. It had been in the family for generations, but the taxes and maintenance were making it impossible to keep. Dad was about to sell it when Mom got pregnant. He was so sure there'd be a boy to inherit, he kept it. The struggle to keep the old home place going nearly killed him, but he knew his son would want to live there."

I said nothing, wondering what the point of this story was. She seemed to need to talk about it, and she continued after a time.

"Thomas was a wonderful child. I loved him as if he'd been my very own present from God. To my parents, he was a miracle. Unlike some kids who get that kind of adulation early in life, Thomas wasn't wild or spoiled really. He loved everyone and everything. He was a gentle soul who really could have been the model for Margaret Mitchell's Ashley Wilkes, you know?"

"Ashley Wilkes has captured the hearts of generations of women. I can't imagine why, though. I always liked Rhett Butler better."

She laughed at that. "Well, Rhett was a take charge, get it done sort of fellow. I probably liked him the best, too. The point is that Thomas never should have been in the army. But he joined because generations of Holmeses had served in the army and he was steeped in tradition, the family heritage and so on.

"So, he joined up. Actually, he got into West Point and he came out an officer. A second lieutenant." She bent down and picked up a pretty good size conch shell that had washed up since this morning. It looked to be in good shape. I like to keep all of the shells that come up onto our beach, but letting her have one would show some good will. Besides, she just held on to it and didn't ask me if I minded. It would be petty of me to ask her to give it back.

"Anyway, Thomas was just starting his career. He served under General A. Randall Andrews." I was beginning to see where this was going. Some personal reason made her willing to defend George. I wasn't too happy with that, but maybe it would make her accede to my demands.

"Thomas died. You know there aren't that many American casualties in peacetime, but Thomas was one of them."

"I'm sorry. How did it happen?"

"General Andrews killed him, that's how it happened." She threw the conch shell with so much force it hit a live oak tree and shattered. If you've ever tried to break a conch shell, you know how much force it takes. She had a lot of strength for a little girl. Something to keep in mind.

"In the military, these things happen, Olivia. Tough decisions have to be made. You can't just blame General Andrews because he was the commander of the Army." I tried to reason with her.

She turned then, and looked at me steadily. "You misunderstand me. General Andrews literally shot Thomas. He killed him. There was never any inquiry into the incident, and the official version is much different. But I did my own inquiry and that's what happened." Her tone was quiet and firm; her look challenging me to disagree with her. Discretion was the better part of valor here, so I just nodded.

Satisfied that I believed her, she turned to continue her walk. We were about half way around the island by now. I could no longer see downtown from where we were standing; we'd reached the northernmost point of Plant Key and started around the other side.

"Not long after Thomas died, Dad sold the plantation. Then he and Mom just seemed to give up. They're in a nursing home, their room a shrine to Thomas. Both of them live completely in the past. There's nothing that can be done. They're in kind of a living death brought on by grief.

"So you see, I owe the man who killed General Andrews quite a lot. I want him to get the best defense possible. If it was George, I want him to go free, just like General Andrews never answered for killing Thomas. If it wasn't George, I don't want him convicted just because the public wants to paint this as the murder of an *American war hero*." She almost spat out the last few words.

We walked on toward Minaret. She was still silent, giving me a chance to digest what she'd told me. I was thinking about the strengths and weaknesses of having someone with such an emotional stake in George's future at the helm of his defense. Her personal vendetta would make her more malleable to my demands and I intended to be sure George never went to trial. I needed the best possible defense attorney. I was still convinced Olivia Holmes was that lawyer. I felt confident then that I could control her, at least long enough to accomplish my goals.

"I see why you want the job. What you've told me doesn't change my opinion that you're the lawyer I want. But we need an understanding right now that I will be doing whatever I think is necessary to prove George did not kill Andy. If you can't live with that, you'll have to wait and volunteer to represent the real killer, when he's charged."

"This is against my best professional judgement. But okay. I'll agree to your terms. I won't take a fee for my work, though. I'll give you a graduated fee which you can donate to the Thomas A. Holmes Foundation. Until then, I'll be a volunteer. You can't fire a volunteer."

We both laughed at that, even though I caught the veiled threat that she would be on the case whether I wanted her there or not.

We returned to the point where she'd left her shoes. She bent down to pick them up and shake the sand out of them. She slipped the pumps on her bare toes. Then I walked her back to her car.

"One more thing, Willa."

"Yes?" I was cautious now.

"I won't let you surrender Andrews' killer to Chief Hathaway. Make no mistake about that. Andrews got what was coming to him. I don't intend to see anyone punished for it."

She got into her Ferrari and sped off over the bridge, leaving me to wonder if she wasn't the one who had killed Andy. She was certainly capable of it. Revenge is an excellent motive for murder, especially if you believe a heinous wrong has been dealt you by one truly evil man. I might not have cared whether she'd done it, and that bothered me more than knowing there was a real possibility that she had.

I got Harry and Bess out of the parking lot and around to their outside kennel. Of course, they had to be showered again. Then I went upstairs, climbed under the wing chair and retrieved my journal. I needed to keep track of what was happening. From long experience I knew there were few people I could rely on in the world. George and Kate. And myself. I am always more confident when I control my own life. You get what you expect to get. I intended to get my life back. Soon. George felt he was protecting me by moving to the club and I intended to help him clear his name as quickly as possible. I was playing beat the clock. I had a narrow window of opportunity to convince State Attorney Jasper not to indict George. And it was time to get started.

10

What Kate calls a centering ritual was in order, so I put on the tea kettle using bottled water. While the water steeped, I pulled down my mother's Royal Albert tea pot and a matching cup and saucer. I took out the infuser that sat down inside the pot and put two tablespoons of loose raspberry herb tea in it. I dug out the tea biscuits left from a small box George had brought me from London a few months ago and arranged all of this on a silver tray.

When the kettle started to whistle, I finished the tea, and covered the pot with Mother's rose-colored cozy. I took the entire tray out to the veranda where I could watch the water, think, and write in my journal.

This journal was rapidly becoming a habit. I seemed to have it on my mind constantly. Without George to talk to, I was carrying on a conversation with myself in writing. But some gremlin, or maybe what Kate would call my spirit, was talking back. It was energizing, in a strange way. Is this what it feels like to be schizophrenic? Is the only difference between me and them that my voices don't talk in my head, but rather write in my penmanship, in my journal pages, in response to my questions?

I sat down with the tea and my journal and began to write the events that had transpired since I'd gone to see George this morning. My thoughts were slowly developing and I could see them on blue and white, unlined, recycled paper. I listed what I knew so far about General Andrews, Olivia Holmes and George.

After a while, I began to wonder whether the Malathion spray for medflies they'd been putting in the air might have infused all of us, just as the raspberry tea in the pot. None of us was acting the way I was accustomed to us behaving. Maybe Thomas Holmes' family weren't the only personal enemies General Andrews had made in the past 65 years. The list had to be a long one, even if you discounted all of the faceless, nameless multitudes that had been attending the confirmation hearings. They were the best and most obvious choices because I didn't know any of them. But what if there were countless others, too? Some of whom I did know?

One way to get George out of this mess was to find other likely suspects, creating reasonable doubt of George's guilt and assuring he'd never be convicted. Olivia had said "no certain conviction, no indictment." That was my goal. I needed to look at the police investigators' file, to know what they had, where they'd been. Then I'd know what to do next.

I looked at the investigation plan I'd so carefully thought out and written down in the past few hours. Some revisions were in order and I made them. Then I left for Ben Hathaway's office.

Ben, who had been sort of a friend of mine until he'd arrested my husband, was at his desk when his secretary ushered me into his minuscule office. You'd think the Tampa Chief of Police would have better quarters. His office was in the Sun Trust building where the Tampa Police Department had moved a couple of years ago.

He stood up as I entered. He started to come around the desk and give me a hug and a kiss, just as I allowed him to do as recently as last Sunday. I tried not to physically recoil and sat down before he got to me, making it awkward for both of us. He took it gracefully and merely leaned up against his desk.

"What can I do for you, Willa?" He asked me gently, sounding like the friend I once believed he was.

"I'll come right to the point, Chief." His eyebrows went up a little at that. Recognizing this was to be a business meeting, he crossed his arms over his chest. He was much more foreboding when you realized the power he had over your life. I began to feel sorry, just a little, for some of Tampa's more sensitive criminals, if that's not an oxymoron.

I continued, "I want to see your file on the Andrews murder investigation. Now."

He stood up a little straighter and walked back around to his chair, putting a little official distance between us. "We've been through a lot together, Willa, and I'd like to help you. You know George is one of my favorite people. But I can't break the rules, even for George. Or for you."

"I'm not asking you to break the rules, Ben. I'm only asking you to bend them. You know the defense will get the file eventually anyway. Once George is indicted, the prosecutor is required to turn over anything in it that's exculpatory. In George's case, I already got the evidence against him from the six o'clock news. So where's the harm?" This last was a little more sarcastic than I'd intended. It still pissed me off that Ben Hathaway had come to our home to get George instead of allowing him to come downtown for questioning. It was one of the many things I'd never forgive him for, when this was all over.

"That may be. But it's not my call. That one will be made by the prosecutor, when and if the case ever comes to trial. This office doesn't open its investigative files to the families of accused murderers. And the Florida Supreme Court will back me up on that."

I returned his steely look. Ben Hathaway and I had played the power game before. Usually, he only asserted the power he had. He played by the rules, knowing the rules and the resources were stacked in his favor. I had been known to bend the rules, especially if I wanted something we both knew I could get in the long run. For every task there's the easy way and the hard way. The easy way is, well, easier, but the hard way works just as well. I'd expected his initial response and come prepared.

"Ben, how much of your department's resources are directed at finding General Andrews' killer? Not yesterday, or two days ago, but right now?" I asked him. Still being reasonable.

"As much as we need to devote to it." He sounded a little defensive.

"In other words, nothing. Am I right? You think you have a suspect in custody, arraigned and turned over to the State Attorney's office. You have other crimes to solve and you don't have that much manpower. You're not even looking for the real killer, are you?" I was getting a little belligerent, now. He was looking down at his hands clasped on his government issue imitation walnut desk. His ears were getting more than a little crimson at their tips.

He answered me slowly, as if he was talking to someone with poor hearing or less than full mental acuity. "We don't need to look for the General's killer. We found him. We arrested him. He's awaiting trial. If you want to see the file, go ask the prosecutor."

I stood up to my full five feet eleven inches, making me two inches taller than Hathaway when he's standing and about two feet taller while he was still sitting down. "Chief, I want you to know that George Carson did not kill General Andrews. If you want to take him to trial for this, you certainly can. But if you do, you'll lose. And then you'll be the laughing stock not only of Tampa, but the entire country. Everyone is watching this. Everyone."

He sighed. "What do you want me to do, Willa? My hands are tied. They wanted an arrest. They got one. Our State Attorney is a political animal and George is on the wrong side of that ambition. They've done battle before and now it's Jasper's turn to have the winning cards. It's out of my hands." He held his hands out, palms up, to demonstrate his point.

"I want you to let me look at the file. I'll make you an offer, just once, right now. Here it is: You let me look at the file, help me unofficially and I'll tell you when I've figured out who killed Andy. If you turn me down, I'll be sure you never hold any job in this city for the rest of your life. You know what a small town Tampa is. You'll have to move. How well do you and your family like it here, Chief?" I could see him thinking it through. Eventually, he would realize he had nothing to lose and everything to gain. I was promising not to embarrass him, not to let the situation get out of control. He knew I could make good on my promises, the positive ones and the negative ones.

And, to give him a little credit, Ben Hathaway does like George. He likes me, too, for that matter. He wanted the killer to be someone else, but he was not his own boss. Someone higher up called the shots and that someone wanted a quick solution to this incredibly thorny issue. Bringing down a powerful member of the opposite party was a bonus.

"I can't do it, Willa. I'm sorry. If President Benson himself asked me, I'd have to say no. I want to help you. But you can't just march in here, let God and everybody see you, and demand special treatment. I've got no discretion in this. The answer is no." To give him credit, he did look sorry. He looked like a sorry S.O.B.

I gave him my best steely stare. No impact. "Ben, you disappoint me. I thought you had some integrity. I didn't know you'd be part of a plan to ruin my husband just for politics. If you change your mind and develop some backbone, you know where to find me," I told him sorrowfully, just before I walked out.

Like I said, there is the easy way and the hard way. I'd tried the easy way. It didn't work. At least, I thought it hadn't. I'd been home twenty minutes when the door bell rang. I was surprised to see Ben Hathaway at the door. With a briefcase. I let him in.

"Okay," he said, holding up his thumb and forefinger on his right hand. "But I have two conditions of my own. One, you keep me up to date as you go along." He folded the fore finger down.

"No problem." I lied and he knew it.

"Two," he held up his thumb. "You tell me who you think killed Andrews and I'll arrest him. None of your elaborate confession schemes. I don't want you or George getting killed over this. This guy killed a decorated army General, for God's sake. He won't stop at a judge and her husband."

I nodded my agreement. He wasn't impressed. "I'm serious here, Willa. We may be on opposite sides at the moment, but if you think arresting the wrong guy will get me run out of town on a rail, think what would happen if I let you and George get killed by the same perp. Do it for me. Please."

Only because I was beginning to worry that he'd change his mind again, I agreed. Realistically, it was the sleeves out of my vest anyway. What was I going to do with someone who would shoot Andy in the head and coolly walk off? I had no interest in being a hero. All I wanted was my husband back. And my life.

He handed me the briefcase. "I'm going downstairs for dinner. I'll be back in two hours. Can I leave this here? I'll pick it up after."

I smiled at him. Now it was my turn to kiss his cheek. Mom always said people would do the right thing if you gave them a chance. "I'll keep it right here until you're finished." Before he left, he gave me two more rules: No copies; and never tell a living soul he'd done this. I thanked him and he left me alone.

When he'd gone, I took the briefcase to my study and opened it. Inside, I found the file labeled "State v. George Carson," which was nothing more than a five-inch redwell jammed full of papers. It was scheduled to go the prosecutor's office shortly. Timing is everything.

I reached into Aunt Minnie's desk drawer and pulled out my dictaphone. It would be faster if I dictated what I found and transcribed it later. My mother had told me when I was in high school, "learn how to type and you'll never be without a job." It was some of the best advice she ever gave me. I could type about 80 words a minute on a computer keyboard and the skill was invaluable for doing confidential work. I planned to set up my own shadow file as soon as possible. Organization is the key to a lawyer's life. Legal documents multiply like rabbits in the dark. They're worse than rats and telephone pink slips.

First, I went through the file and dictated a list of its contents. Things have a way of disappearing from police files once they're turned over to the prosecutor. I'd had a number of experiences like that as a lawyer and since I'd been on the bench, it happened in my cases more often than I'd like to admit. I'm not big on conspiracy theories. I don't believe that Kennedy's political enemies conspired to kill him, that AIDS was deliberately transmitted to the gay population by the CIA as a test of biological warfare, that the Government introduced drugs to the black community, or that the defense department is concealing aliens in Roswell, New Mexico. But I know that things legitimately get lost and over zealous prosecutors sometimes pull out all the stops to win the case. Competitiveness in America is alive and well in more than just professional sports.

When I went through the first time, nothing particularly incriminating to George jumped off the page. I also didn't notice anything missing, except the full autopsy report, which apparently wasn't done yet. It looked like the usual homicide investigation file. I saw the initial report of the first officers on the scene, crime scene photographs, autopsy photographs, toxicology report. There were a few interview notes with members of the family, George, friends, colleagues. An inventory of Andy's pockets, the boat. Pictures of the gun, ballistics report.

I returned to the beginning and went through more slowly. The homicide squad and the medical examiner's office had been called at the same time. Regardless of the cause, where a death is unattended or a death certificate cannot be issued by a competent physician, someone from the medical examiner's office had to examine the body, to estimate the time and probable cause of death.

The science crew in this case was just two technicians. Their job, I knew, was to locate, identify, preserve and remove for analysis all substances that might be clues to solving any crime that occurred.

These two criminalists had apparently worked together before. They had a routine they'd developed that looked pretty thorough. That doesn't mean they didn't overlook anything, just that they'd likely be good witnesses, able to describe in meticulous detail everything they found and how they found it. If they'd found anything to incriminate George, they'd be able to get it into evidence easily. Half the cases a criminal defendant wins are won because evidence against him is excluded. That wouldn't be happening in George's case.

The photographs of the scene weren't too gruesome. Mostly, it just looked like Andy had slumped over in the boat before the body was moved. The photos taken from every angle, though, revealed that he'd slumped due to the hole in the side of his head.

The fingerprint reports showed fingerprints everywhere. Most of them belonged to members of the family and Andy himself. A few were unaccounted for, so far. George had been finger printed when he was arrested, but none of the unidentified prints were his. That was a break.

They'd bagged the gun and taken samples of the blood stains. There didn't seem to be too much other physical evidence, but what there was had been gathered, photographed and sent to the various laboratories for analysis. Except for the body, of course, which had been sent for autopsy by the medical examiner.

Around the area, the investigators found nothing remarkable. No footprints or car tracks that the killer might have left. That's not surprising since they didn't find the body for several hours after Andy was killed. It was January and it's pretty dry here in January. Some years, I leave Greta's top down for the whole month, even though I have to turn the heat on. The ground would be hard and resist imprints of any kind.

The gun found on the bottom of the boat was a snub nosed .38-caliber Colt revolver, serial number Y327141, which had five shells in the cylinder, one having been fired. No question about it. The gun belonged to George. The police officer at the scene, apparently having better training than I would have given him credit for, picked up the gun by sliding a pen through the trigger guard. This meant, of course, that no one obliterated valuable information by sticking something down the barrel.

The officer's report claimed he had smelled the fresh odor of burned gunpowder when he smelled the barrel, suggesting that the gun was recently fired. Fingerprints on the barrel, the cylinder and several of the shells belonged to George. Gunshot residue tests found no indication that Andy had recently fired a gun with either hand. Normally, a negative result might mean Andy had on rubber gloves, or held the gun in a plastic baggie, or maybe even that no residue escaped. But since he died instantly, it wasn't likely that any of those other choices were possible here. Elementary, my dear Watson: Someone else shot him.

One bullet had been removed from Andy's skull, a .38-caliber. Again, modern technology was working against George, because the ballistics tests confirmed the gun found at the scene was the murder weapon.

One interesting thing. The police had used a length of string to trace the angle at which the bullet had entered Andy's skull. While it's not exact, they did place the approximate spot the gun was held when it was fired outside the boat, on the dock.

The faint powder burns on Andy's head indicated that the shooter must have been about three feet away from him. The powder burns would have been stronger if he'd shot himself. No doubt about it. Andy was murdered.

I went through the file a third time, more carefully. I started with the interview notes. The interview with George was either the shortest suspect interview in history or there was another set of notes somewhere. These notes contained only George's assertion that he had no idea how his gun ended up at Andy's house and that he'd been jogging the morning of the murder. Thanks to me, everyone knew that George had not been jogging. George thought jogging was a sign of insanity. In his view, running was uncivilized. So, he'd lied to the police about where he was, too. What was George doing that was so important he'd keep the secret rather than exonerate himself by providing an alibi? If I'd known that, I could have ended the whole thing now. Damn George's honor. Whoever he was with certainly didn't feel honor bound to help George. It was like him to keep his word, even when others didn't.

As for George not knowing how his gun ended up at Andy's house, I took that to be true. And I made a note on the section of my journal where I'd been taking down notes, to follow that issue up with him. At least tracing where he'd last seen the gun should be easy. That the interview notes didn't say anything about his answer to those questions, if they'd been asked, was one of the reasons I didn't believe the notes were complete.

The interview with General Andrews' daughter, Robbie, was a little longer. Her alibi for the time of the murder was that she was working. Robbie worked at home and I wondered how her alibi had been verified. Further down in the notes I saw that Robbie had shown the investigator the column she'd been working on at the time. I made a note of that, and to follow up with a few questions of my own. That is, if Robbie Andrews would talk to me. She had also told the police that George had been plotting with Senator Warwick and President Benson to defeat her father's nomination. She said George would stop at nothing to keep Andy off the bench. This must be where they got the idea that George would have a motive for murder, but it seemed pretty weak to me. That motive would fit every protester at the Capital last week.

The other interviews were longer yet. The police had interviewed John Williamson, Robbie's husband, Madeline Andrews and both of the General's sons. They'd also interviewed Senator Warwick and my brother, Jason. And that was all the interview notes. The only consistent thing about the interviews was that all of the individuals they talked to had alibis that were more plausible than George's. Which is to say all the other alibis were confirmed.

As I dictated into my recorder, I noticed a few things but mostly I was just trying to get it all down for later. What was the most obvious was the coroner's conclusion on manner of death: homicide. The basis for the conclusion was that the "death is inconsistent with suicide." No kidding. The angle of entry of the bullet into the temple was inconsistent with a self-inflicted gunshot. There were also no powder burns on the general's temple, suggesting the gunshot was fired from some distance rather than with the gun placed on the side of his head as a suicide would do. They'd known it wasn't suicide from the start. No wonder people don't trust the government. They lie.

Two hours later, I was finished. I put the file back into Chief Hathaway's briefcase. He picked it up without a word shortly thereafter. From my review of the police file, I was beginning to sympathize with Chief Hathaway. Really, how could Ben not have arrested George? George had no alibi, his gun—complete with his fingerprints—was the murder weapon, he had made it plain to one and all that he would make sure Andy never sat on the Supreme Court. Add to that his fight with Andy at the restaurant the night of the murder. It was a set of facts that would definitely support an indictment. They'd need a lot more for a conviction, so the prosecutor's office probably was still investigating. But what they were looking for was more evidence against George, not the real killer.

11

George and I were having dinner together and I tabled the issues for later. George had some explaining to do and I was determined he'd do it tonight. I would call downstairs and have something romantic delivered.

I decided to order the specialty of the house, Rack of Lamb Julius Caesar, a cherry vinaigrette salad with Gorgonzola cheese, broiled tomatoes and french bread. For dessert, we'd have the Chef's specialty: creme brulee, which he served warm in a cereal bowl, with raspberries and blueberries on the bottom. I was getting hungry just thinking about it. When I looked at my watch, I saw that I had about an hour until dinner.

I took a long, scented bath, opened a bottle of Merlot and relaxed. I tried to stay in the present and not catastrophize. I was determined to discuss the issues with George, but I wanted to keep our relationship on the same plane it had been this morning. This, too, shall pass, I knew. When it did, I wanted my life right back the way it had been. I was trying to expect the results I wanted instead of assuming the worst. Catastrophizing solves nothing. I've tried it.

I dressed carefully. I put on my black lace Natori bra and matching black bikini panties. A cream silk shirt George liked with a knee-length dark green silk skirt that I left unbuttoned up the front to well above my knee. You could see the bra through the shirt, which was the effect I was going for. I'd had a pedicure a few days ago, so I put on open sandals. I slipped on my diamond stud earrings and the diamond pendant

George gave me for my last birthday along with my slim platinum wedding band. I did my makeup lightly, just enough to accentuate my eyes and a little bronzer on the cheek bones. A rosy copper lipstick completed the look. I was sure George would approve. For some reason, he thinks I look good without makeup. Which is one of the reasons I'm still married to him.

I went out to the curio on the wall in the living room that contains my Herrend zoo. The animals had been Aunt Minnie's. I think she'd had a Hungarian admirer at one time. He gave her a beautiful set of Queen Victoria china and the whimsical porcelain figurines painted in the technically difficult fishnet pattern. Judging from how many she had, the relationship must have lasted for a while. Aunt Minnie gave all the animals names that she left in the inventory we received when George inherited the house.

To the extent Aunt Minnie's ghost or spirit still lives with us, she must be pleased that I admire her zoo and George is adding to her collection. Whenever a particularly special opportunity arose, he ordered an unusual piece from Hungary to give me. The animals are now available here in the states, but all of Aunt Minnie's pieces, and mine, were specially made for us.

I picked up Otto, the raspberry unicorn, the most magical piece. Aunt Minnie used to hold him and make wishes. I wondered if her wishes came true. And if mine would. No harm in trying.

I iced a bucket of Champagne and got out our special champagne glasses, the ones we got at George V when we spent a month in Paris for our tenth anniversary. We'd had such fabulous sex there. George would remember and get the hint.

I finished all the preparations just before he knocked on the door promptly at eight-thirty. So old fashioned, George is. He was acting like an invited guest. And he was.

I opened the door to watch George smile slowly and with appreciation. "Please come in, George. You do live here, after all."

"Indeed, I do. Any chance I can get a warm greeting from the hostess?" He put his arms around me and we went from there to the bedroom. Yes, that was what I wanted, but I had been thinking we'd have dinner first.

Quite a while later, George opened the Champagne and we finished the bottle. I vaguely heard the waiter bring the food about an hour earlier, and I was, all of a sudden, famished. "George, darling," I said, snuggling a little closer to his chest and running my hands over the curly black hairs that grow there in abundance, "Aren't you hungry? I ordered a fabulous meal."

"I'm starving, actually. Why don't we go see what you've got." So we got up, put on our robes and he brought the heated food into the dining room where I had set the table with Aunt Minnie's linens, china, silver and crystal. I even had flowers sent up. George got the food out and we sat down to a fabulous feast.

During dinner we talked about the things we always talk about: our friends, our neighbors, what happened with him today, what I did. Of course, my report of my day was a significantly abridged version. Time enough for that later.

When we got to the coffee, we moved out into the cool night, still just in our robes. Finally, seeing no way to gracefully bridge the gap, I just asked him what was on my mind.

"George, I talked to Ben Hathaway today," I started tentatively.

"Did you now?" He didn't seem too upset so far, so I plunged on.

"Yes. He said his department has been ordered to stop investigating Andy's murder. Seems the State's Attorney feels they're better off with the provable case they have now than an unprovable one if they start fooling around with it." I prepared for the explosion, but, thankfully, it didn't come.

George was thoughtfully quiet for a while before he responded to me. "I know you're worried about me, Willa. Truly, I'm worried about me, too. I recognize that political expediency is often served at the expense of justice. I just have to believe in Ben and that the truth will be told, either at the trial or sometime before they actually execute me." He smiled wanly.

"Look, I hired you a lawyer today. Olivia Holmes." I told him.

"What makes you think you have the right to hire a lawyer for me?" This was said softly, but I could hear the edge in it. George is the one who takes care of us. He doesn't like anyone to forget that. Sometimes he takes this knight in shining armor thing a little too far.

"Obviously, it's subject to your approval. You have to have someone. With your assets, the court isn't going to appoint you a lawyer, you can't represent yourself and I sure can't do it. Besides, I thought you'd like her. She has the reputation for being the best there is," I told him.

"Why do you think she's the right choice?"

"Because she has a reputation for representing only innocent defendants, for one thing. I didn't think you'd want a lawyer who's known for getting the bad guys off."

"True," he smiled. "I prefer to look like what we are. It's a good message for the media, too, I suppose."

I was encouraged. He'd started to think strategically, which was a big step from his philosophical rage of innocence. Strategically, George is one of the best. I often ran my strategies by him when I practiced law. He was really good at the conservative, majority, middle America approach.

"Yes, it is. No one except Olivia seems to be picking up on the fact that you are not a killer. Maybe our friends will even start to get the idea," I said, bitterness creeping uninvited into my tone.

George sat his cup down, reached over and took my hand. "You mustn't judge them too harshly, Willa. Andy was well-loved around here. People are outraged. I haven't offered any excuses for myself. And you saw how incriminating the evidence is. What are they supposed to think?"

"You're being a lot more forgiving than I'm willing to be with them all." Normally, I don't give a fig for what people think about me. I want them to think the best of George, though. He deserves it.

"Let's just wait and see how it turns out. I have gotten quite a few supportive calls, actually."

He hadn't even mentioned that. "Really? From whom?"

"All of your family. Your Dad. Kate, Jason, Mark and even a wire from Carly in France, for starters. Everyone in the restaurant. Senator Warwick. President Benson, although it has to be kept quiet. The President can't be seen to support Andy's perceived murderer. How would it look?"

"Since when have you cared how President Benson looks? He's not exactly a personal friend or your favorite politician." I wasn't to be appeased. As far as I was concerned, this lack of faith in George from the rest of our friends was inexcusable. If it's in times of trouble when you find out who your true friends are, then it didn't seem like we had as many as I thought a few days ago. Eric Clapton has it right. Nobody knows you when you're down and out. Except we weren't out. Down maybe, but definitely not out.

The time had come to spring my idea. "George, between the two of us, we're definitely smarter than the average bear, wouldn't you say?"

"It's one of our conceits." Again, that dry smile.

"Yes, but true anyway. We can figure this out. We have to figure it out. We're the only ones who want to." I knew I was sounding a little desperate, but I saw the police file. He hadn't. There would be no investigation of other suspects if we didn't do it. I was not willing to sit around and wait for the real murderer to take credit. If it was some crazy group with an anti-Andrews agenda, they'd have claimed credit already. Given that they hadn't, the murderer was someone who wanted to remain anonymous. And the possibilities were seemingly endless.

"I wouldn't say *the only ones* who want to find the killer, although we're certainly the ones with the most serious interest." He sounded almost academic and I was beginning to lose my carefully cultivated calm. Another argument was not what I wanted, so I kept putting a lid on my impatience. But I needed to get into the particulars or we'd just end up where we were before.

"Seriously, then, I can think of several people who might want to murder Andy. There's all those special interest groups who were attending the hearings: the right-to-life crowd already tried once and failed, the gay-rights groups were very vocal and angry, all of the races except the Caucasians were represented, not to mention the feminists and the Republicans." I ticked them all off on my fingers, each with individual members who were capable, ready, willing and able.

"That's the trouble with free speech, Willa. When you exercise it, people automatically assume you're going to act violently to secure your points."

"Maybe. But a lot of people do use free speech to incite violence. You know that as well as I do and there was a good example in John Hamilton's shooting. That man was an easily led ideologue. As far as I'm concerned, he was an instrument of destruction."

"But then you get into the concept of free will. Do you really believe that others can be made to behave in ways that are repugnant to them?" He asked.

"Do you really believe they can't?"

"Yes, actually. I think everyone makes his own life and is in control of his own destiny. We all have the ability to choose whether to do an immoral or illegal act. The choices we make define us."

"You sound like you've been talking to Kate. But truly, George, I'm not interested in discussing philosophy. I want to consider the possible suspects. It seems to me we've got to include every member of Andy's family and," I said, remembering Olivia's story about her brother, "every soldier he ever came in contact with, as well as his close friends and acquaintances."

"Is that all? Should be a snap to wrap this up by morning." He smiled his indulgence of my plan.

"You have any better ideas?" I challenged.

"No. But I will have in the morning. Now is not the time to panic, Mighty Mouse. You don't always have to save the day. Let me sleep on it." He sat his glass down, kissed the top of my head, and went into the bedroom. I took the glasses in and put them in the kitchen. I'd do the dishes later, as a sort of meditation. I looked forward to an occupation for my hands while my mind worked on knotty problems.

When I came out of the kitchen, George was in the den, fully dressed. I was stunned. How could he think of going back to the Club to sleep after everything we'd gone through tonight?

"Where are you going?" I asked him. "I have a lot to talk to you about yet. We have to examine the evidence. Figure this out. You can't just leave."

He walked over and hugged me. "Everything I said this morning still goes. I need to stay away from here until this gets resolved. I'll see you every day. I'll be in the restaurant, like always. And we'll have dinner, just as we always do. But I intend to keep suspicion away from you."

When I started to protest, he put his index finger over my lips. "It's no use trying to argue me out of this. You got me to agree to Olivia and to investigating this thing ourselves. Count this as a successful use of your feminine wiles and get some sleep." He moved his finger, gave me a kiss and walked out.

12

By three o'clock I was still awake, so I gave it up and went to the kitchen for a cup of tea. I saw Aunt Minnie's dishes waiting to be meditated through, but I wasn't about to start that. So I took the tray with Mom's teapot, cozy and nighttime tea into the den, where I picked up my journal, sat down in the overstuffed chair, put my feet up on the ottoman and reviewed my last few entries. The journal reminded me about my police file dictation and now was as good a time as any to transcribe it.

I put the tape in the transcription machine and sat down at the computer. While waiting for the computer to come up, I skimmed through the last two entries in my journal. I made a few notes from my conversation with George tonight and flipped back to my plan of action. Despite my feeling that I was making no progress, I was surprised to find I was. Maybe there was something to this journal writing after all.

I put the earphones in and started to transcribe my notes. Unlike some of the secretaries I've had over the years, I haven't perfected the art of typing dictation without thinking about what is being said on the tape. So I reviewed the list of materials in the file as I went along. I pride myself on an excellent memory, but I was surprised by the number of things in the file that I had forgotten about, at least temporarily. I stopped as I went along and put in asterisks and notes to myself on items that seemed important or that tweaked my thinking in some way.

After I finished my dictation and saved the document, I printed out a copy, folded it and taped it into my journal. I looked at the desk clock and was surprised to see that the rising sun was right on time. It was five o'clock. The night time tea hadn't made me sleepy either, so I decided to run the dogs and start my day. Harry and Bess, who had slept through the night, were ready, willing and able to get started. So we did.

Sunrise is really beautiful on Plant Key. In all of Tampa, actually. It comes up behind the port, behind Harbor Island and Davis Island. The red slowly lights up the morning until the reflective gold and silver buildings downtown sparkle. On a clear morning, like this one, the water sparkles, too, a little like a mirror reflecting white twinkle lights. It's cool, rarely breezy, and always very quiet. As I rounded the northern tip of Plant Key I could see other early exercisers on the Bayshore. They were too far away for me to make out their faces, but I'd recognize quite a few of them if I could see them clearly.

Harry and Bess were way ahead of me. They circled back a few times, to be sure I wasn't lost. They'd run ahead, come back, run behind, splash in the water, then run ahead again. It could give you a complex if you weren't careful. Like you were pokey or something. Or maybe it was a guilty conscience. After no sleep last night, in truth, I wasn't moving very quickly.

We finally made it around. Twenty minutes later I was dressed in dockers and a Margaritaville T-shirt from last year's trip to Key West. On my feet were the dirty, ice-colored, tasseled topsiders I'd been wearing for five years because they've discontinued them and I can't get new ones. My favorite outfit. Under my robe and up on the bench no one knows what I'm wearing. The CJ doesn't approve, but that's not the only reason I dress like this. I also like to be comfortable.

I brought in *The Washington Post*, and both local papers to read any news that might be there about Andy and anything else that might be relevant. As I suspected, even in the local papers, Andy's murder was no longer on the front page. Since George's arrest, most of the news was speculation about President Benson's next Supreme Court nominee. I vacillated between relief and anger. Relief that we were no longer being hounded by news mongers and anger that something so upsetting to my life was tossed aside for the next nine-day wonder. Time to get to court. After that, I'd get back to business.

The trial day, which I had limited to mornings four days a week, promised to be substantially less mesmerizing than my private life, if I could stay focused on it. Newton had been married four times and there was no way he could keep that from the jury since it was right in *The Review* story he was suing over. He'd tried to take the sting out of it on voir dire by choosing jurors who had been married more than once, but Tampa is still a pretty conservative place. Divorce is common, but not desirable. Newton's five children, all boys, had been present throughout the trial and today he started by calling the most recent of his ex-wives to the stand.

"What's your name, ma'am?"

"Jennifer Newton," said the fourth former Mrs. Nelson Newton. She looked like a young Tampa matron on her way to church. She was clean and neat, but not overly showy. She was having a difficult time holding herself together and she looked like she could use a drink.

"Do you know me?" he asked her, with a wink to the jury. Several of them smiled.

"Yes. We were married for five years."

"Do we have any children?" he asked, turning around to look at his youngest son, sitting with the other four in the first row of the galley behind his chair.

"Yes. Nelson, Junior. He's seven."

"Now, Jennifer," he said gently, "I'm sorry to have to ask you this, honey, but please tell the jury why we divorced."

I remembered the divorce and it hadn't been friendly. He must have muscled her to get her here at all. I was just as curious as everyone else as to what she would say.

She looked down at her hands and then out toward her son. Her eyes were filling up. "You know the answer to that, Nelson. You fell in love with another woman." And then she did start to cry. Not quietly, either. We had to take a recess so she could pull herself together when Newton said he had no further questions.

After Tremain got up and got himself adjusted, he said he would have to ask Mrs. Newton some embarrassing questions that he didn't think children should hear. He asked me to have Mr. Newton's children removed from the courtroom and offered to have one of his paralegals stay with them out in the hall. When they were safely out of earshot, Tremain began his cross.

"Mrs. Newton, how many times was Mr. Newton married before he married you?"

"Three."

"Was Mr. Newton married when the two of you started your affair?"

"Yes."

"And, was Mr. Newton having an affair when the two of you were married?"

"Yes." She looked like she might start to bawl again, but Tremain waited until she had herself back under control.

"Mrs. Newton, how tall are you?"

"Five seven."

"And how much do you weigh?"

"About a hundred and ten."

"Have you always worn your hair short like that?"

"No. Nelson asked me to cut it short and I just did it for him."

"Now, Ma'am, I'm sorry to have to get personal with you and I certainly don't mean to be offensive. You understand that, don't you?"

Her chin began to quiver again, but she said "Yes," in a tiny, little voice.

"Ma'am, after you became pregnant with your son, did your husband ever make love to you again?"

This started her to bawling again in earnest. She never answered. Tremain just went back to counsel table and sat down. He said he didn't have any more questions and I let the fourth Mrs. Newton go. We could hear her caterwauling in the hall all the way to the elevator.

Newton tried again with his third wife. Belinda Newton Phillips was a physical copy of Jennifer Newton, but more flamboyantly so. She dressed to make a statement. She was about ten years older than Jennifer, and a hundred years more sophisticated. This woman probably hadn't cried since the doctor spanked her at birth.

"Tell us your name, please." Nelson, too, was less solicitous of her.

"Belinda Johnson Newton Phillips," she said, making sure the jury heard the full import of her impressive Tampa pedigree. Both the Johnsons and the Phillips' were long time, wealthy citrus families.

"Mrs. Phillips, tell the jury how you know me."

"Unfortunately, when I was young and rebellious, we were married for a short time."

"It's obvious you don't like me, Mrs. Phillips. Tell the jury why you've come here to testify today on my behalf."

"Because, to my everlasting regret, I allowed you to father one of my children." She smiled at another fair-haired, lanky boy who, even though he was very obese, bore an obvious familial relationship to Nelson and herself. "I don't want Johnson's life tarnished any more than it has to be by the fact that you're his father. There is no question in my mind that you are not gay. That's all I came here to say."

Newton quit while he had a chance of being ahead, and sat down. Tremain rose to face the fierce third Mrs. Newton.

"How do you do, Mrs. Phillips?"

"I'm fine," she said, leaving no doubt in anyone's mind that she'd like to give Tremain a sound thrashing, whether for making her appearance on behalf of Newton necessary, or for hurting her son, wasn't clear.

"Mrs. Phillips, I take it Mr. Newton wasn't much of a husband to you?"

"That's right."

"How long were you married?"

"Two years."

"And why did you divorce?"

She looked at Tremain, then at Newton and finally, at her son. "Because Nelson didn't love me. He never had. And I deserved someone who loved me. So, I left him."

"Nothing further." We all waited while Mrs. Phillips and Johnson left the room together, regally, as she had entered it.

Newton next called the second Mrs. Newton, and I was beginning to question his sanity if not his trial tactics. The last two witnesses proved he lived with women and fathered children, but they also shed grave doubt on his sexual preferences. He had to prove *The Review* had published a false statement about him, and it didn't seem to me that he was making any progress.

Mrs. Alice Newton was closer to Newton's age, but she, too, was a physical duplicate body type to the third and fourth Mrs. Newtons. She was tastefully attired, but not expensively so. She wore gloves and a hat. She was probably a sustaining member of the junior league, active in her church and a member of the Tampa Garden Club. She looked the part.

Just as he had with the other two, Newton began by asking her how they were acquainted. By now, we all knew what was coming. "I was once your wife," she said, with precision, and more than a little embarrassment.

"How many children did we have together, Alice?"

"Two boys, Tom and Samuel," and she smiled for the first time at her two sons. Both were short and had facial features more resembling Newton himself.

"How long were we married?"

"Seven years."

"And why did we divorce?"

She looked thoughtful, and this was the first time I appreciated the true motives Newton had for keeping his sons in the courtroom. She didn't want to hurt her children, any more than the third and fourth Mrs. Newtons had. But this woman seemed genuinely at peace with her past.

"Mrs. Newton, please tell the jury why we divorced?"

"I was young," she said. "I got lonely. I didn't understand why you had to work all the time. And I wanted you to spend more time with your sons. It was a foolish thing for me to have done and I've regretted it for years."

Newton wiped a tear from his eye and thanked the witness. Before he sat down, he went over to his sons and touched each of them on the shoulder. Alice Newton sat straight and tall in the witness box.

Tremain said "No questions, your Honor," from his seat, so we were spared the peacock routine this time. Newton declined to call the first Mrs., thank you God, and that concluded the day's trial events so I could get back to what really mattered: My life.

Today, I planned to meet with the General's daughter, Robbie Andrews. But before I did, I went back to the computer and signed on to the Internet. Robbie Andrews is a licensed psychologist. A few years ago, she started a revolutionary online therapy service. The same people who had been writing to newspaper columnists for free advice seemed willing to pay money to write to an online therapist. Anonymous psychotherapy seems like a concept that would have Freud turning in his grave, but I had heard Robbie lecture about how popular it was and how it really delivered a valuable service to those who would not seek therapy if they had to reveal their identities in public. I guess "public" in this context included an appointment with the therapist and payment by their employer-sponsored health insurance plan.

Anyway, I'd never looked for Robbie's Internet column because I'd never been interested. Now I was. She told Ben Hathaway that she was working at the time her father was killed and she used her online therapy business to prove it. The police file interview notes said Robbie had offered the Chief a look at her computer logs to prove she had been engaged in a therapy session on Saturday at five-thirty in the morning, the estimated time her father was killed, since exact times of death were impossible to establish without a witness. An electronic alibi. What next?

To be fair, the session she'd claimed to be involved in had lasted the conventional fifty minutes, twenty minutes before and after the murder. How convenient. And she wasn't the only one with an alibi for the exact time of the murder. I just wanted to investigate someone other than George and it was easy to start with my computer.

Robbie's online service was called "Ask Dr. Andrews." I'd heard her say it was a blatant attempt to be at the beginning of the advertising alphabet, but you can't blame her for savvy marketing skills. It took me several minutes to find her site. I marveled once again that anyone could find anything on the information superhighway, as everyone seemed to be calling it. There are over eight-hundred million web sites and the search engines are far from perfect. Nevertheless, I found Robbie's site and several other therapy services online, too, and I decided to browse them first.

Some of the services were exactly like "Ann Landers" or "Dear Abby." They were open to the public and consisted of a letter of general interest and an no nonsense piece of advice. Easy answers are often the best, but hardest to implement. Without continuous support, these services wouldn't be very helpful. Although sometimes, just a difference in perception created a shift in reality.

After reading a few of these columns, I moved on to the next type. These were fee for service arrangements where the "client" wrote a confidential, encrypted "problem" of two-hundred words or less and waited twenty-four to forty-eight hours for a two-hundred word response. The client paid a flat fee by credit card, in advance. These services were confidential, unless you could unencrypt them, which I couldn't do. So I couldn't really tell what the typical problems were other than through the type of service that was advertised. Management problems, workers compensation issues and substance abuse claims seemed to be the gamut of choices. And there was a specialist for every need. Truly, I'd had no idea there was such a panoply of Internet psychotherapy choices. Maybe Kate should go online. Her particular brand of "journal therapy" wouldn't be out of place and, judging from my own experience, might even be very lucrative. I wonder if insurance companies would pay for it?

Then I got to "Ask Dr. Andrews," which seemed to be a combination of the other types. There was a regular advice column that was new everyday. Then, there was the opportunity for personal advice. This, too, was an encrypted service. Like the other sites, "Ask Dr. Andrews" described the services offered for free, as well as the payment arrangements. "Ask Dr. Andrews" appeared to be unique among the other services because the confidential personal sessions were designed to be continuous therapy, much like the conventional type, just not face to face.

The web page actually had a clever design and I wondered if Robbie had done it herself or if she'd had a professional designer. Not that it mattered, but it suggested she was serious about the business. Robbie's credentials were prominently displayed, including her licensure in Colorado and Florida and her length of experience: fifteen years. She was the "pioneer" in the field and "devoted herself exclusively" to online therapy.

A few sample questions and responses from the therapist followed, with a list of the types of "common problems" for which Robbie provided therapy. Unlike the other services, she was willing to accept patients with depression, relationship problems, sexual orientation issues and antisocial behavior. It was a little scary really. How could she possibly evaluate antisocial behavior if she couldn't see the client? The liability issues must be tough to overcome. Maybe she's been sued over this, but if she has, I hadn't heard about it. Not that I necessarily would hear about it, but it's hard to keep a secret in Tampa.

I looked at Dr. Andrews' columns for the past few weeks. They contained the usual human hassles that could be found in the "agony" columns of most newspapers. The letters disguised the names of the problem people and had cute, anonymous names for signatures. There were more than a few letters about cheating spouses, wedding etiquette in the age of divorce and multiple families, and so on. The column had a search feature that would allow readers to search for common problems. Just for something to look for, I typed in "suicide."

Quite a few letters came up. Most were from anguished family and friends of suicides. Teenaged boys seemed to have killed themselves more than other groups. Near universally, the survivors of suicide were deeply troubled over the "why didn't I see it coming" issue. Dr. Andrews' advice was along the lines of forgiving themselves and recognizing that the suicide was determined to kill himself, so it couldn't really have been prevented.

One of the letters was a little more unusual. The writer was asking whether he should feel guilty about killing his boss and making it appear to be a suicide. He'd done it years before and hadn't gotten caught. Now that he had a fatal illness, he was thinking about confessing to "get right with God." Dr. Andrews advised him that long kept secrets should go with him to his grave and he should ask forgiveness when he arrived wherever he was going. Since the death was so many years ago, she said, it would serve no purpose to bring it back up to the family now. Could this letter have given Robbie a method for killing her father and getting away with it? At least I could prove she knew it was feasible.

I had to write a letter to Dr. Andrews' column because I couldn't do the regular online therapy anonymously. I'd have to pay with a credit card before I could even access the encryption software to submit to therapy. I made a note in my journal to figure out a way around this and also to ask Olivia whether we could subpoena the files Robbie had been working on the morning of the murder. The files would likely be protected by the psychotherapist/patient privilege, but we might be able to get them if we agreed to allow her to redact the names of the clients.

My letter was somewhat true and I kept it short. I told Dr. Andrews my husband had been accused of a crime he didn't commit and it was causing a problem in my marriage. What should I do? I signed it "Faithful Wife" and made a mental note to check for the answer tomorrow.

When there was nothing more I could learn from this approach, I decided the old tried and true face to face interview couldn't be improved upon, at least, from the murder investigator's standpoint. I picked up my journal, my keys and my tiny purse and left to visit Dr. Andrews.

Robbie Andrews and John Williamson lived in the section of South Tampa called New Suburb Beautiful. It was not as new or as tony as Beach Park, but the residents were mostly upper middle class professionals in John and Robbie's age group. The number of young children playing on the sidewalks made it look a little like another Pleasant Valley Sunday, if you're a Monkeys fan. Of course, this wasn't Pleasant Valley, and it wasn't Sunday, but you get my drift.

I consulted my notes from the police file for the Andrews/Williamson address and pulled up in front of an out of place, Midwestern looking, ranch-style house. It resembled a red brick shoe box turned long ways on the lot. It had white trim and black decorative shutters on either side of each window. A two-car garage at one end opened onto a driveway that went straight in from the street. The garage door was closed so I couldn't tell if anyone was home. The police file interview notes said Dr. Andrews worked at home every week day from five o'clock in the morning until at least six in the evening. So, if she wasn't here, it would almost be better than if she was. If she wasn't home when she was supposed to be today, maybe she wasn't here that Saturday, either.

Alas, when I rang the bell, a young Cuban woman with dark, curly hair dressed in jeans and an Outback Bowl jersey that hung below her knees, answered the door. "Hi. I'm Willa Carson. Is Dr. Andrews home?" I'd tried friendly. Actually, I wasn't prepared for an encounter with someone other than Robbie. I was counting on the element of surprise in getting Robbie to talk to me. Surprise is a nasty thing when it's me getting surprised.

The woman did let me inside the front door. So far so good. But only so far. "Dr. Andrews is working with a patient right now. She's booked until six o'clock. Would you like to make an appointment?"

"No. I'll just stop by some other time. It's a social call, really." I tried to look around and past this gargoyle at the gate, but I couldn't see much. The house was one of the older ones in the area and it lacked the vaulted ceilings and open feel of the newer Florida ranch-style homes built in and around Tampa. I couldn't hear or see any signs that anyone else was around. Online therapy must be quiet, if nothing else.

"Well, Dr. Andrews is booked every week day until six and Saturday mornings with standing appointments. I can tell her you called and have her give you a ring, if you like." It would probably be awkward for me to tell her I wanted to startle Robbie into talking to me. When all else fails, try the truth. Almost.

"Thanks. I'd prefer you didn't tell her. I'm in from out of town and I wanted to surprise her. I'll just come back later. Please don't spoil the surprise. I haven't seen her in quite a while." This was a small fib, but Robbie wouldn't see me if she knew I was coming. The woman got into the spirit of the supposed spontaneity.

"Oh. Okay. Sure. Just come back around six-thirty. I'm sure she'll be here then." I said my thank yous for her cooperation and left with smiles and waves. It's a wonder there aren't more home invasions than there are. People will tell you almost anything if you look friendly and harmless.

I walked out to Greta like a disappointed sorority sister unable to share the secret handshake with an old college chum after all these years. When I got off Robbie's street, I pulled into a convenience store and took out my journal looking for something to do that would advance the cause, but get me back here by six-thirty.

Then I remembered I had to meet George and Olivia at the house. I had invited Olivia to discuss the case and her representation with George and me together.

Back at Minaret, after introductions and hospitality, Olivia explained to us that George's private arrest and prompt release on $100,000 bond was primarily a favor done for me. Judicial comity, as it were. That George was a prominent citizen was also a factor. After all, they could be wrong and if they were going to have egg on their faces politically, they didn't want to look like uncivilized jackasses, too.

Olivia also told us that the next step would be for George to be formally indicted. Capital murder can only be charged by grand jury indictment in Florida. While it is theoretically possible that the Grand Jury won't return an indictment, that will only happen if that's the way the prosecutor wants it to come out. In George's case, we didn't know what the presumed probable cause was that had led to his arrest unless it was the evidence we'd read in the police file. Primarily, what they thought was his motive—to keep Andy off the bench—would be enough to support the indictment if the prosecutor wanted to get one.

George was appalled at the obvious perversion of the process. "Do you mean to say that he can railroad me?"

Olivia smiled at a question she must have answered a hundred times. "Sure. It's the American Way. Don't you watch television?"

George was not amused. In truth, neither was I. It's amazing how your sense of humor vanishes when your life is threatened by forces over which you have no control.

"As a practical matter, State Attorney Jasper isn't going to take a case to trial that he can't win. I've known Jasper for most of my life. He's tried over 250 capital murder cases and he's won every one of them. It's an impressive record, but all it means is that he pleads out the cases he can't prove. If he has an agenda, it's to keep his winning streak intact so he can someday run for Governor."

George relaxed a little. "Since we know I didn't kill Andy, then we shouldn't really worry about the indictment. Just as I thought." He looked at me pointedly, as if to say he was right all along and I was just being overly dramatic.

Olivia didn't let him off the hook so easily. "Not exactly. If Jasper thinks he can get a conviction on this case, he will go for it. This has been front page, lead story news on every available media. It's the case of a lifetime for a prosecutor. He doesn't want egg on his face, but he's not going to just go away, either. The case is a career-maker for him. All he wants to do is get a conviction. Believing he won't get it is the only reason he might not try.

"And don't forget," she continued, "the decision may not be solely his. He has people he reports to. He's up for re-election next year. A big win against a prominent member of the other party for murder of a Democratic leader would assure him another four-year term and maybe even set him up for the Governor's mansion. Make no mistake. This is the kind of case that comes along once in a career. They'll all be wanting to make the most of it."

"So, how long will all these shenanigans take? I have a restaurant to run, a life to live here," George's impatience with what he viewed as the silliness of all this was obvious, even to Olivia. She took the opportunity to display her leadership skills.

"Both of you need to understand something. This is a long process. It's unlikely that you'll even be indicted for another two weeks. After that, you'll be arraigned and then we can begin the formal discovery process. It will take at least nine months to get this case to trial, and we'll be working like crazy between now and then to be ready."

George exploded. "Nine months!!! I'm not going to be involved in this for nine months! This is outrageous!"

"Yes, George, it is outrageous. But there is nothing you can do about it. What we have to do is to try to end the process long before trial. We have to do our own investigation and try to persuade Jasper that they've got the wrong man. Our best shot is to do that before the indictment. If we can't, we'll just have to keep trying." Olivia explained things patiently, but firmly and without any particular optimism.

"I have no doubt that this will all be put behind you eventually and you'll be able to go on with your lives. But it won't happen quickly and it won't be painless. You two are just going to have to suck it up and show the world what you're made of. The last time I checked, you both had responsibilities. Keep going. Behave as normally as possible. Let me do my job and," this last was directed at me, "stay out of the way."

I showed Olivia out after promising to talk with her tomorrow. George and I talked briefly and I tried not to let him see how totally befuddled I was. How could this possibly have happened? I am a good person. A public servant. My husband is as honest, kind and traditional as any man anywhere. The idea that we were involved in this was a joke. A very bad joke.

George had to go down for the lunch service and I needed something do to keep me busy until I could interview Robbie Andrews at six-thirty. I decided to track down George's gun. This I could legitimately do, since he was my husband after all. And I tried not to get my anger up over the lack of such a trace in the police file. They just assumed George took his gun out to Andy's house and killed him with it. Knowing that didn't happen, the question I was asking myself was: how did George's gun get into the hands of the killer? I was sure George had no idea how that happened and, even if he wanted to, he wouldn't be able to tell me. George had told Ben Hathaway nothing about the last time he saw the gun, but George only uses his guns at the shooting range. So I headed out to the gun club.

I hated that George still shot handguns. He liked it as a carry over from his army days. He said it released tension and sharpened his skills. When we lived in Detroit, where the weak are killed and eaten, he used to keep guns in the house. No matter how much I insisted that I would never, ever use one to shoot an intruder or anyone else, George remained confident that I would if I had no choice. Fortunately, the issue was never tested.

When we first moved to Tampa, George did keep a couple of handguns around the restaurant, just because, he said, "you never know." Our home is open to the public and at least once a week or so, some diner wanders up toward the flat just out of curiosity and wanting to look at the house. We've never, knock on wood, had any kind of trouble. Until now. But that didn't count. This was not our problem.

The Tampa Gun Club and Shooting Range was out on Tampa's all purpose commercial highway, Dale Mabry, named after a popular local son. It was quite a distance from Plant Key and it took me over forty minutes to travel ten miles in the morning traffic.

As I drove out Dale Mabry, I took note once again at the homogeneity of America. All the fast food joints were there, more than once. If it's true that every American lives within three miles of a McDonald's, we're beating the national averages soundly. The standard franchise home improvement, furniture and discount stores were well represented. The franchise hotels and motels were gathered near the airport. The newcomers—book superstores—with coffee shops and live entertainment, had become the gathering places for Tampans after dark. They, too, were well represented: two of each.

These days, you could go to any city in America and see the same thing. You couldn't tell if you were in Los Angeles or Boston any more. Nervous travelers who used to feel uncomfortable leaving home for fear of bad food and worse sleeping conditions now worry needlessly. Whatever they have back on the farm, we have everywhere. But for me, all the individualism of the country's regions has been destroyed. You might as well stay home.

Eventually, I passed most of civilization and ended up on the very north end of Dale Mabry Highway. The gun club was on the right. Apparently, there wasn't a lot of money in running a gun club because the driveway wasn't paved and neither was the parking lot. It was dry and dusty now, but it must be a river of mud every summer afternoon when the skies open up and flood everything without man made drainage.

I was thankful for my casual clothes and that I hadn't put Greta's top down this morning. I got out of the car to a cloud of dust settling over us. I tried not to breathe in as a small breeze moved the dust imperceptibly. I walked the few yards to the door holding my breath.

There were about ten vehicles, mostly trucks, in the parking lot. I couldn't really visualize George's Bentley parked out here. It looked more like a gathering of rednecks, but wasn't.

The light was dim on the inside and the noise was deafening. The shooters were wearing ear muffs. I looked over at the counter and saw a middle-aged, over weight man also with earmuffs on. I walked over and introduced myself. He couldn't hear me. I touched his arm and he looked up, apparently used to being touched to get his attention.

He looked me over and must have decided I was harmless, because he gestured to a door at one side of the counter. I went through it into what must have been a soundproof room. He followed me in and closed out the noise with the door. The quiet was startling.

I was in a soundproof room with a gun nut I didn't know and no one knew where I was. I'm generally not given to paranoia, but this made me wildly uncomfortable. I decided to take care of my business and get out of here as quickly as I could.

"Can I help you?" He asked me.

I held out my hand and introduced myself as George Carson's wife, Willa. He took my hand in one big, hairy paw and covered it with his other paw. He looked so sorrowful, I was ashamed of my earlier paranoia.

"I am truly sorry about George, Mrs. Carson. He is one fine man. I just can't believe he killed General Andrews. If there's anything I can do for George, you just let me know, okay?" He was talking slowly and clearly, still holding onto my hand. As if I was hysterical and he needed to talk me down off a high building before I jumped. Maybe I'm not as good at hiding my feelings as I think. Or maybe he talked to all the "little ladies" this way. At least the ones who may be married to murderers.

"Actually, uh, what did you say your name was?"

"Curly, ma'am." I tried to pull my hand away, but he kept a tight hold on it.

"Um, Curly. Of course. George has mentioned you. It's nice to meet you." George had never said anything about this man to me in my life, but I wanted to get my hand back. I pulled gently. No luck.

"It's nice to meet you, too, ma'am." Yes. Well. Let's get to the point.

"Curly, I need to see George's locker and pick up some things. Is that okay with you?" I gave my hand another little tug, just to see if I could dislodge it. He tightened up. It was like playing with Chinese handcuffs. The more I tried to pull my hand away, the tighter his hold became.

"Sure it is, ma'am. But you need a key to get into George's locker. Did you bring one?"

"No. I guess I just thought you'd have a key. You do have one, don't you Curly?" I wasn't batting my eyelashes and blushing, honestly.

He hesitated a few seconds, looking at me with more curiosity than hostility. If George had guns in his locker, which I suspected he did, Curly had to be wondering what I wanted them for.

"I just need to look for the shooting log George keeps, Curly. I know he keeps track of when he shoots and how well he does. And he keeps an inventory of his guns. I want to look at that." And I wasn't pleading, either. If my tone was a little less confrontational than I use in the courtroom with recalcitrant litigants, it was purely expedience. Curly was thinking about it, at glacial speed. It wasn't smart to underestimate your opponent, but Curly was either dim witted or foxy and slow on purpose.

"You can come with me and watch what I look at, if you want." I suggested to him, as if he wouldn't have thought of that on his own. I wanted to look in George's locker by myself, of course, but if the only way I could get Curly the Giant here to let me do that was with supervision, it was better than no look at all.

About a month later, Curly finally nodded his head and let go of my hand. He told me to follow him and we went back out into the noise where conversation was thankfully impossible. He picked up his keys and walked through another door into the locker room. Apparently you don't have to shower and change clothes to use a shooting range, because there was only one room filled with lockers and nothing else.

The lockers were numbered and stacked in two, one on the top and one on the bottom, with a long bench separating them horizontally. They were next to each other in rows all around the room and there were two or three rows of back to back lockers in the middle. The noise was a little less loud in here, but you could still hear it.

Curly walked in front of me toward the back wall. There were men and, to my surprise, women standing in front of some of the lockers. I didn't recognize any of them and they didn't recognize me. It's an interesting human phenomenon that if you see someone outside the normal atmosphere for that acquaintance, you often don't recognize them. And to be honest, I wasn't looking too closely. The last thing I wanted was to see someone I knew.

When we got to George's locker, I almost laughed out loud. The locker number was "007." Did George see himself as some sort of James Bond? Reliable, sturdy, conservative George? Did he have a Walter Mitty life? Or was this just a joke?

Curly opened the locker for me, and stepped aside to let me look in it. There, on the bottom shelf, was George's shooting log. Under that was the list of his guns with their serial numbers and license numbers. The licenses themselves were in our safety deposit box. I looked at the log, flipping back through the last few entries.

George is a man of habits and rituals. Maybe all humans are. But I could see his habit of shooting each gun in the order it was listed on the inventory. He would shoot at random dates and times, maybe as he had the time. But he had come to the range every Wednesday morning for over two years. And on Wednesdays, he shot the snub nosed .38, the gun that killed General Andrews.

The log also showed that George sometimes lent his guns to other people. Most of the names I recognized, but some of them were strangers to me. I needed to take the log and the inventory with me. I just told Curly I was taking it, and he didn't try to stop me. I thanked him for his help and left, with the log and the inventory under my arm.

13

It was still too early to go back to Robbie Andrews house, so I stopped for a late lunch and reviewed George's gun logs. I thought about my favorite Thai place, Sukhotai, but everyone I know eats there. The Melting Pot is somewhere I like but don't go often. And it takes a long time to eat fondue, so I pulled into the shopping center parking lot. As if to mock my opinion that all the world's the same, on the corner of the strip center was a tattoo parlor. In the window was a sign: Tattoos while you wait.

I never ate at a restaurant in a strip mall in my life before I moved to Florida. Honest. Here, some of the best restaurants are tucked in between the Frank's Nurseries and Home Depots. Hard to believe. But it's the truth.

The Melting Pot was one such treasure. Fondue is sort of out of style, but here it's still alive, well and lucrative, if the crowds were any indication. It actually took me about ten minutes to get seated. I asked for a booth in the back. The restaurant itself was dark and the booths were the high backed variety. In the back of the restaurant, I could easily sit alone and not be bothered, or even seen, by other diners.

After I ordered the Swiss fondue and iced tea, I pulled the gun log and inventory out of my tote bag and began to look at them in earnest. I had brought my journal and my dictaphone but I was reluctant to dictate in the restaurant, even if it was secluded. So it was slow going making notes.

I had an unreadable pocket calendar going back two years and forward three more. To avoid having to wear bifocals to light up the tiny numbers on the calendar, I used the small, flat flashlight I'd been carrying in my purse the past few years. Even with the light, I could barely make out the calendar's numbers.

But my hunch had been right. The regular schedule of Wednesday morning shooting was recorded in George's log. Aside from that, his timing was irregular. Some days, he'd shoot in the morning, some days in the afternoon. Some weeks he'd go out two or three times, and some weeks, only on Wednesday. The really interesting thing was that on Wednesdays, he always shot the .38, the murder weapon. But he would sometimes shoot it on the other days as well, randomly.

If someone wanted to steal George's .38 without his knowledge, the best time to do it would be Wednesday afternoon. That way, they could keep it for about a week before he'd want to shoot it again. Maybe he wouldn't miss it during that time. The thief couldn't be sure, but it was as close to a reasonable bet as one could make.

George had listed seven guns on his inventory. He had bought the .38 about five years ago. Comparing the inventory to the gun log, George's meticulous rituals were evident again. He shot the guns in order, from the top of the inventory to the bottom. If you wanted to predict which gun would be next, it wouldn't be too hard.

The log and the inventory did not show whether each gun was in the locker at any particular time. That is, there wasn't the equivalent of a library card to show when the guns had been removed and returned. Knowing George, that made sense, too. He always keeps track of his possessions. If the guns were taken out of the locker, he would be the one to take them.

I ordered the chocolate fruit Fondue for desert and savored it as I reviewed my notes and pondered. I read Nero Wolfe books years ago.

His sidekick, Archie, reported that Nero was thinking when he closed his eyes and pushed his lips in and out. This, Archie said, was the sign that the genius was at work.

Nero the genius probably thought in complex mathematical equations, but I closed my eyes and tried to think in pictures while I ate chocolate. I could see George removing the .38 and using it. He would clean it thoroughly when he was done and return it to its purple velvet bag and then its black, clearly labeled box. I visualized the locker as I'd seen it this morning, and nearly spit out my chocolate covered mandarin orange slice. The box was still there! I remembered it clearly. I could see all the other boxes, too. They were all still there. All seven of them.

George, my ritualistic, compulsive husband, would never, ever, take the gun without the box. And without the box, the gun would be so much easier to conceal. So how did the gun and the box get separated?

I looked at my watch. If I wanted to get back to New Suburb Beautiful in time to catch Dr. Andrews, I couldn't go back to the Tampa Gun Club now. But I made furious notes in my journal and planned to go back out there tomorrow. I felt like shouting "Eureka!", but decided it would draw too much attention.

Looking up to signal the waiter for my check, two men walking toward me caught my attention. They were waking single file, both tall, good looking and involved in their conversation. I turned away as they sat one booth up on my left, John Williamson facing away from me talking earnestly with Archibald Alexander Tremain, VI. I recognized them both, even in the dim light, even outside their usual context. What could those two possibly have to talk about? How did they even know each other?

The waiter brought my check and then turned to acknowledge Tremain's gesture. When she did, Tremain saw me. I saw him whisper something to Williamson and Williamson turned around to greet me.

"Hello, Willa. How are you?" I called back that I was fine, signed my credit card receipt, followed the waiter to their booth and sat down.

"Tremain," I nodded in his direction and then turned to John. "I didn't realize you two knew each other."

"We don't," John said. "Mr. Tremain asked if he could interview me for a trial he's working on. What brings you here?"

This was more information than I wanted. I didn't want, and shouldn't be, involved in an interview of a witness in the Newton trial by the defense lawyer. I also didn't want John Williamson to be involved with Tremain and now I couldn't ask them why they were here. In fact, I was sorry I knew about it. So I said it was nice to see them, talked a little about our beautiful weather, told them I had to be going and left. Quickly. Before any more damage could be done to this wretched trial. I was sorrier than ever that I hadn't just granted Tremain's summary judgment motion weeks ago and let the Eleventh Circuit sort it out.

In the afternoon Dale Mabry traffic, even though most of it was going out of the city in the opposite direction, it took me twice as long to get back to South Tampa as it had taken me to leave. I finally made it to Robbie Andrews house, closer to six-thirty than I'd wanted to be. God watches over fools and children, because as I rounded the corner onto Jetton street, I saw Miss-Guard-the-Castle get into her Honda and pull out of the driveway. Mercifully, she went the other way and didn't seem to notice me.

I made a mental note to write down when she leaves. If I wanted to surprise Robbie again, I would make it a point to come by after her help had gone for the day. Which started me to thinking about when Miss Guard-the-Castle might arrive in the morning. Maybe ten? So how could she know when Robbie started working in the mornings?

I pulled into the driveway and parked Greta in the middle, blocking both sides. As I got halfway up to the front door, I heard the automatic door opener lifting the heavy double garage door. I returned to the driveway just in time to see Robbie getting into her car in the garage.

Miss GTC must have told her employer I'd be back, and she was trying to skip out on me.

"Hello, Robbie," I said as I approached her from the front sidewalk. She was holding her purse straps near her shoulder with the bag slung over her back. It was one of those fashionable Vuitton bags that everyone in Tampa seemed to have since Saks opened a store here. It looked like an open horse feeder, what the designers call a bucket bag. For a woman who worked at home on a computer where no one could see her, she certainly was well dressed. When I work at home, I favor cotton shorts and T-shirts. Robbie had on every imaginable designer label. Or at least the ones that come in extra jumbo size.

Robbie was a very large woman. But she was one of those women who always look well groomed. She had a fashionable haircut, great makeup and flowing caftan type clothes that made her look like a woman with a clothing budget exceeding her huge size. She wore spike heels, making her appear taller than the five-feet-three she really was. And she had beautifully manicured hands and feet. Except that she was the size of three runway models, she could have come straight from the fashion houses of Paris.

Looking at her, it occurred to me again why advertising works. The newspaper is full of bad news. Advertising sells hope, possibilities, potential. No wonder we want to believe. It's ironic that in a country where food is plentiful, where we can all have anything and everything we want to eat everyday of our lives, we prize thinness above all else. Robbie was a woman who tried to hide her size by covering it in expensive packaging, thinking people would focus on the wrapper and not the contents.

"Willa, I really have an appointment and I don't have time to deal with you right now." She was short tempered with me, even more than she had been at her mother's house a few days ago.

People strive so hard these days to "make a difference." As if every life doesn't make a difference. In science fiction movies, time travelers are always careful not to alter the course of history by impacting it in the least. Even a small impact is believed to act as a stone cast into a pond creating ever-widening ripples into the future. Those who are trying to make a difference should remember that simply by living an authentic life, each of us matters. Robbie hadn't figured this out. No one who is happy with themselves could be so miserable to everyone else and so blatantly superficial.

I ran my hand through my short hair, which had been blowing around since I'd left The Melting Pot after lunch with Greta's top down. I hadn't replaced my lipstick and my clothes looked like I'd been walking around in a dusty parking lot. Which, of course, I had. I was feeling tired, grimy and not really up to doing battle with Robbie.

"I only need a few minutes, Robbie. Since you can't get out without me moving my car, why don't you just talk to me and get it over with." The war of her emotions was plain on her face. First anger, then outrage, and finally, resignation. But she didn't have to be nice about it.

"Alright. What do you want?"

"I don't think either one of us wants to discuss this in the driveway in front of your neighbors. Why don't we go inside?"

She walked right past me and up to the front door, digging in the bucket bag for her keys. When she got to the door, opened it and stepped inside, she turned around and snapped, "Come on then. Let's get this over with. I have to be somewhere else in fifteen minutes." I hustled to get through the door before it slammed in my face.

Robbie continued walking through the house and into the dining room where she remained standing and didn't offer me a seat. "What do you *want*?" Maybe she could have been nastier. I don't know her that well.

"What I *want*, Robbie, is for you to start acting like a woman who *wants* to know who killed her father. That's what I *want*." I emphasized each of my "wants" in the same nasty tone she had used, but she wasn't fazed.

"George has been arrested already, in case you've forgotten. I'm interested in putting this behind me and going on with my life. And I don't want you pestering my mother, either. Now if there's nothing else, you're making me very late."

"Look, Robbie,“ I said as I pulled out an oak dining table chair and sat down, "neither one of us is going anywhere until I get the answers I came for. Now, you can sit down and talk to me for about ten minutes and then I'll leave, or you can keep up your little routine and we can stay here until all Florida freezes over. Your choice."

She waited several seconds before apparently concluding she'd have to throw me out bodily if she wanted to get rid of me before I was good and ready to go. She sat down, folded her hands on the table, and in what I can only assume is the best "now there, dear" manner Dr. Andrews the psychologist could muster for badly behaved patients, she said, "What is it you'd like to know?"

I resisted the urge to tell her that was more like it. Instead, I asked her something much more personal. "Tell me about your relationship with your father." She bristled again, raising her hackles, whatever hackles are.

"My relationship with my father wasn't any different when George killed him than it was when you and he were friends, Willa. He detested me. He loved boys, his sons, and my husband, but he had no use for girls or women. You know that. Is that it?" She started to rise.

"Not quite. How did you feel about him?" I watched her closely. She actually started to get a little blinky, like she had some feelings under that armadillo exterior she dressed in Chanel.

"I loved my father because he was my Dad in the same way any girl loves her daddy. But I didn't like him very much. I didn't know him well enough to like him. He saw to that. He wasn't much of a father, really. Not to me, anyway. You'd have to ask my brothers how he was to them. I'm sure he loved them very much when we were all younger." This was said with such bitterness that I involuntarily shied away from the topic. There was something more there, something under the surface that didn't make sense. But I'd have to examine it later. Her reaction to her father's misogynistic view of women was understandable maybe, but her view of his relationship with her brothers was unnecessarily poisonous.

"And how about his relationship with your husband? Did they get along?"

Her eyes widened, then she pursed her lips and pressed them together so hard white lines formed at the corners. "Yes. My husband and my father got along. They got along as well as anyone could get along with Andy. Which is to say they could be in the same room without getting into a fist fight, something George couldn't even manage."

"Only one more thing, Robbie. How about your parents? I know for a long time, there was a lot of trouble between them. How were they getting along when he died?" I was trying to sound friendly and sympathetic. From long experience, I know that you can get more from a hostile witness with sympathy than by badgering.

It didn't work. She stood up, picked up her purse and turned toward the door. "This interview is over. If you want to sit in my dining room until Chief Hathaway gets here to escort you out, feel free. But if you don't leave in the next ten seconds, I'm calling to make a formal complaint." And to emphasize her threat, she reached into the bucket bag and pulled out one of the things I imagined she kept in there in addition to the kitchen sink—her cell phone. She must have bumped her house alarm button in the process because the alarm started its loud, shrill screaming as she dialed 911.

I continued to sit and look steadily at her while she dialed. When the operator answered, Robbie said, "I'd like to report an intruder in my house. I know her name. Would you like me to tell you on this recorded line?" She looked at me meaningfully.

I could barely hear her over the noise of the house alarm and I doubted the operator could either. But, she'd effectively called my bluff. I wasn't going to be named in a recorded 911 call by Robbie Andrews when my husband was out on bail after being charged with murdering her father. I heard a siren somewhere in the distance, getting louder. It couldn't be coming in response to her call, not that quickly, and not when she hadn't even requested assistance yet. The siren was so loud now combined with the house alarm that I could barely hear myself think. She could shoot me and no one would hear it. The siren was coming this way. Even if it hadn't been sent in response to her call, it could easily be diverted here.

"Judge Willa Carson is her name," she said. "I'm afraid of her. Her husband killed General Andrews, my father, last week. Please send a car to my house. Now."

I could only hope that the 911 operator couldn't hear her either. Before she had a chance to repeat what she'd said, I grabbed her phone and hung up. I handed it back to her and then I left. Slowly. It was the wisest thing to do. Otherwise, I might have been arrested for assault. I was gripping my hands into balled fists so tightly that my short trimmed nails were biting into my palms.

No wonder her father hated her, I thought rather uncharitably. There's not much there to like. Nature or Nurture, though? It was only on my way home that I began to feel sorry for John Williamson. Of course, that was before I knew the whole story.

14

By the time I got home, ran the dogs, spent some time with my journal and a Bombay Sapphire and tonic over ice with lemon, I was feeling a little more charitable toward Robbie, but not much. I had to put it aside because I was having dinner with Jason and George and I wanted to ask George about his gun. But before that, I logged onto the Internet to check my letter to "Ask Dr. Andrews." I wasn't really entitled to an answer already because I had only sent the letter to her column, not to the paid encrypted service, but I looked anyway.

My letter wasn't in the column for today. She responded to a couple of questions about personality conflicts at work (grow up and get along), three problems with teenage rebellion (this, too, shall pass) and a question of infidelity (nobody's perfect, forgive and forget). All were interesting and much more colorful than my newspaper's Ann Landers column, but seemed irrelevant. Since I still hadn't figured out a way to use the encrypted service, I logged off.

I met George and Jason downstairs at eight o'clock. They were already seated in the dining room and looked like they'd had more than one cocktail each. I was only an hour late. They were engaged in quiet but heated conversation and they didn't see me approach.

I heard George say, "He shouldn't have sent that damn memo. I don't care what his reasons were. It was not called for. The vote was going the way he wanted it. He was just trying to manipulate the process."

Jason was just as hot. "The whole process is about manipulation, and you know it. Andrews came by Warwick's office to lobby for a yes vote. I heard he went to every one of the senators on the committee with the same plea. You can't blame Benson for playing the same game."

"But Benson was supposed to be on Andy's side. How would it look to the rest of the country to know the President was trying to torpedo his own nominee?" George responded.

"Good evening gentlemen," I said. Jason stood up and gave me a quick hug and a kiss. George stood, too, held my chair and kissed my cheek. How gallant. They were still glaring at each other, but they tried not to let me see it.

"Don't look now, but you are beginning to draw attention from the crowd. I don't know what you were discussing, but unless you want everyone in the room to witness it, you should keep your voices down." I had a smile on my face and kept my voice very quiet.

George poured me a glass of wine and Jason steered the conversation to his mother. We all talked about Kate for a while and her upcoming trip to Italy. She'd been planning it for months and it was the only thing she wanted to talk about. Jason was planning to meet her there for a few days, but mostly she would be with an old friend. A male friend none of us had met and all were curious about.

After we ordered appetizers, I took advantage of a lull in the conversation. "What were you two talking about when I came in?"

"Just politics. Nothing you'd be interested in," George said.

"It sounded interesting to me. Did I hear Jason say that Andrews visited every one of the senators on the judiciary committee the day before he died?"

Both men looked uncomfortable, but Jason was the one who answered me. "It's not something we're supposed to talk about, now that he's dead. But it's not that unusual. It's been done before."

"I didn't realize the vote on a Supreme Court nominee was a popularity contest," I said.

"It's not. But it is politics as usual. Everyone takes the Supreme Court appointments very seriously because of how long the justices serve and the impact they have on the country. No one wants to vote yes on a man they know nothing about," Jason explained.

The political process seemed like one big bartering game to me. George was the politico in our family, and I was glad to leave it that way. This time, though, it occurred to me that any of the Senators Andrews talked to the day before he died could have killed him. Who knows what was said between them?

I pondered this silently while George and Jason attempted to change the subject to the recent coup attempts in Cuba. When, not whether, Cuba would once again be open for American travel is a constant topic of conversation in Florida. Tampa is closer by water to Havana than Miami, which is partly the reason we have such a large Cuban community. Another reason is the cigar business, which was already in full swing by the time Castro came to power. Tampa's Cuban community has a lot of emotional attachment to Cuba and many say they are planning to return as soon as they're allowed to do so. At least to visit family and friends, if not to immigrate permanently.

Most Floridians believe Cuba will again be a tourist Mecca and hot vacation spot some day. The sentimental motive is a strong one, but many just want to be in on the ground floor of what they think will be a money-making operation. Key West has been planning for the increased cruise ship trade for years.

Reopening Cuba is a hot political topic, too. Senator Warwick and Jason were both very involved in lobbying for change. Jason and George could argue the merits of this issue for hours. But I wasn't as interested in Cuba as I was in General Andrews.

When I could get a word in, I asked them what memo they'd been talking about. The way they looked at each other, I could tell I wasn't supposed to have overheard this bit of information. And they didn't want to elaborate.

"It's not something I can discuss, Willa. It's supposed to be strictly cone of silence stuff," Jason said.

"You were discussing it with George. If it's so cone of silence, why does George know about it?"

George looked up desperately for our waiter and flagged him over. We all ordered desert and coffee.

"Look. I'm not going to drop this. You can tell me about it now, or I'll call Sheldon Warwick myself in the morning and ask him."

Not wanting to draw any more attention our way, George said quietly, but with more firmness than I usually accept from him, "Just leave it alone. Please. Let's have our coffee in peace."

"I'm not going to make a scene. But I am going to find out what's going on here. After we have our coffee we can go upstairs and talk about it. Or I'll find out some other way. You two can decide while I go powder my nose." I didn't really have to powder my nose, or anything else, but I wanted to give them some privacy so they could come to the conclusion that I would not be changing my mind on this.

When I got back to the table, our key lime pie had been served. Café Con Leche for me and decaffeinated Colombian for the men. We ate and drank in relative camaraderie, finishing our after dinner Tia Maria.

"Well," I said, "What's it to be? The word straight from you two tonight, or I start calling Senate Judiciary Committee members tomorrow. Your choice." With that, I rose up to leave the table. They followed me out of the dining room and up to the flat.

When we got settled in our den, neither one of them had broached the subject they knew we were there for. So I prodded them again. One last time.

"What memo were you two talking about at the dinner table before I came in tonight?"

They had apparently agreed that Jason would field my questions. The choice was curious because Jason had more of a professional obligation to keep his secrets than George did. Jason was a senate employee, aide to Warwick and on the Democrats' side.

"You know the confirmation hearings weren't going well, right?"

"Well for whom, is the relevant question."

"Senator Warwick was against the confirmation from the start. Like George, he knew Andy personally and didn't think Andy had the judicial temperament necessary for a Supreme Court Judge."

"That's one of the reasons I do like Sheldon. He has a firm grasp of the obvious," I said dryly. George and Jason both grinned.

Jason cleared his throat. "Yes. Well, Warwick tried to convince President Benson to withdraw the nomination. Warwick knew Andy was strong-willed and opinionated and, even if he had otherwise been qualified, that Andy could never do the right thing politically to get confirmed."

"Andy had been around politics a long time," George picked up. "He'd made a lot of enemies among the people who knew him. No one was looking forward to standing behind the party's man."

Jason was fidgeting, rubbing his hands together, as if to warm them, but it was over seventy degrees tonight and he had on a tropical wool jacket and tie. He wasn't cold. He cleared his throat again. "It was a very real political dilemma for Warwick and all the other Democrats. No one wanted to openly oppose the Presidential choice, but none of them wanted to or could vote for Andrews in good conscience. Warwick, as the chairman of the committee and one of the most senior Democrats on the Hill, was on the spot. The younger guys looked to him to figure out a way to finesse this."

George intervened. "And Warwick, for his part, had no intention of losing his seat over this nomination the way Illinois Senator Alan Dixon lost his over the Judge Thomas vote."

"What do you mean? Thomas was confirmed." I was confused. Clearly, my lack of political savvy was a handicap in this maze of relationships and back room dealing.

"Thomas was a controversial nominee. Some people were unhappy with the way the hearings went and the way the vote came down. Politicians paid the price with their jobs. No one wants to be in that position. It was a hot spot for all of them."

George said. "The view was that it was their fearless leader himself, President Benson, who put them all on the hot seat. Nobody liked it."

"And that's where George came in," Jason said. "Warwick gave a statement to the press. He said that the committee had been criticized in recent years for being 'too supine and deferential' to the President in the Kennedy and Souter nominations. Warwick said that under his stewardship, the Judiciary Committee would take a more active role. He said there was no presumption in favor of confirmation. Benson and Andrews were outraged. It was a plain power play. Warwick said he is the reigning Democrat, not the President. And certainly not Andrews. But Washington is all about power. Nobody gives you power. You just take it."

I was beginning to see the problem. Warwick, the Democratic senior senator from Florida, was taking on the Democratic President in his second term. The President couldn't be re-elected, but the Senator could. In recent years, the political types have been taking the position that control of Congress is more important than control of the Presidency. This is one of the reasons why.

"This is all very interesting, in a political science kind of way," I told them both. "But what does any of it have to do with George?"

George answered this time for himself. "We never wanted Andrews. We were shocked when he was selected. We wanted to defeat him and Warwick was willing to help us do that. For once, Warwick and I were both on the same side. Jason works for Warwick. We were discussing the issues." He said it like a Packers fan would be interested in the 1997 Super Bowl game where the Packers won for the first time in over twenty years.

I could buy that. The battle over Andrews' confirmation had been intense, but I hadn't realized Warwick had put all his political clout on the line. If he lost, his career would be finished. The Democrats would replace him as party leader. He would go out in disgrace. He had a personal stake now in defeating Andrews' confirmation. George would have viewed this as a gift of Trojan proportions. George knows everything about every bill that's up in every legislative session. He follows foreign and domestic policy. He was on the verge of winning a round against the Democrats with the Andrews nomination. And he loved it.

Jason was still focused. George, more savvy in the conversation game, would have let it go. Jason, the lawyer, was honed in on the question. He brought it up again himself.

"Benson feared that Warwick's behind-the-scenes opposition, supported by George's efforts, was making a difference. So, to save face, he sent a memo out to each member of the party the Friday night after the committee hearings closed. The evening Andy died. The President's memo said he had recently learned that the army had received sexual harassment complaints about Andrews. Although the complaints had been fully investigated and were unfounded, neither Andrews nor the President wanted them revealed. Andrews couldn't withdraw, but the senators could vote no on the nomination, with no hard feelings. In fact, the President said he wished they would vote 'no,' to avoid political and personal embarrassment for everyone."

"He let them all off the hook? Gave up his leverage? Why?" I was incredulous. This was not politics as I knew it was played in every arena, from the condominium board to the school board to capitol hill. George was frowning at Jason and Jason must have realized that he'd revealed too much.

"I don't know why he did it. I'm not his advisor," Jason snapped.

George picked up with his explanation. "That's what we were discussing when you came in. It would obviously be a political faux pas if the memo came to light after the vote. The President could have withdrawn the nomination when he saw it wasn't going to be confirmed. But he chose to sabotage it instead. It's a damn sneaky move, but what do you expect from a Democrat?"

And if General Andrews knew about it, it could have caused him to kill himself. Maybe it was a highly creative suicide after all, for which George could easily be framed. But, George would have a motive for murder only in the nomination itself. If this piece of information got out, George could be off the hook, and the focus could be put back on Benson and Warwick. Things were looking up.

The argument began again in force. I was tuning it out until about twenty minutes later, when the noise of it all suggested that I could tastefully throw Jason out for the night. That point came about twenty minutes later. I heard Jason say, "You and I are never going to agree on this, and it's getting late. I need to go." He was still in a huff, but the result was what I wanted.

"I'm sorry you have to leave, Jason, but it is getting late," I said, much to Jason's surprise and George's, too, for that matter. I stood up and Jason had no real alternative but to do the same. I ushered him out with a hug and a promise to see him later in the week.

George would have followed Jason out, but I asked him to wait a while. I wanted Jason to get out of the driveway before George left, and I wanted to discuss both this development and to ask him about his gun. Privately.

George insisted he needed to be going, but when I suggested a short night cap, he agreed to stay a few more minutes. We took our Grand Marnier over to the couch. "You know, maybe Andy found out about that memo." George said nothing.

"If he found out, he could have been so upset that he killed himself, George. Maybe this really was a suicide." I suggested it softly. "People are always surprised by a suicide." I repeated what I'd read in Robbie Andrews' online column, "And we never want to believe it was inevitable."

"It's possible," George said, "but I don't think it happened that way. You know the physical evidence doesn't support the suicide theory. And so far, there's no evidence that Andy did find out about the memo."

I could hear the smile in his voice. "Nice try, though. It would have been an easier answer than having me on trial for murder." He leaned over and kissed the top of my head. "I need to get going, sweetheart. It's late, and I need my beauty sleep." He got up to leave.

"George, before you go, I want us to talk about your gun. The murder weapon. I went out to the gun club yesterday, and the box is still in your locker. Why was your gun out of its box? How did it get removed from the club? And who took it?"

"Not now, Willa. It's too late to get into all that. I already discussed it with Olivia, anyway. Talk to her about it, or we can go over it later. Trust me, it's not the link from the gun club we need to worry about. Goodnight." He said as he kissed me at the door on his way out.

I locked up and went to bed with quite a lot on my mind for my subconscious to work out. Kate swears that your mind solves your problems overnight if you just remember to program the questions before you go to sleep. I sure had a lot of questions to be considered. If I woke up with the answers tomorrow, no one would be happier than I.

15

I might have had some fabulous dreams that night, but when I woke up, I couldn't remember any of them. The sunlight was streaming into the open window but the air was more than a little chilly. I stretched my arms out in either direction, there not being any reason to avoid taking up the whole bed since I was the only one in it—again.

I let the dogs go out by themselves. The hell with it. I probably wasn't going to be running any marathons any time soon, anyway. I do love running, but sometimes resistance sidetracks me just like everyone else. Besides, I wanted my coffee and I wanted it now. I needed to get it together. Since there was no trial scheduled today, I planned to make two things happen. Olivia would tell me what she'd been doing behind my back. Such as asking George about the gun when I had never authorized her to do that. And I'd go talk to Madeline Andrews. The worst that could happen is that Madeline wouldn't talk to me. If I could just avoid seeing her when her daughter was around, Madeline would be her usual gracious self.

I tackled Olivia first. She works for me, dammit. I hired her. She would answer to me, too. I thought I'd made that clear before I ever introduced her to George. I'd never have hired her if I'd known she was going to be uncontrollable. I left messages for her at all her offices, her car and her home. That I couldn't find her made me even more uneasy. Who knows what she was out there doing that I hadn't authorized?

It took me about three hours to get it together and get out the door. I drove east on Bayshore beside the five mile continuous sidewalk, where once there had been a shore line. In a gentler era, grand waterfront estates once stood, high-rise condominiums now blocked the view. Saturday's *Tribune* reported that three hundred new luxury condominiums were slated to be built with a Bayshore address. It was this kind of progress that made me happy to live on Plant Key. Owning our little island means we decide what gets built there.

I passed Tampa's newest high rise condominium, The Stovall. I haven't been in it, but the pictures I've seen in the sales literature makes it look like a reasonable abode for Donald Trump or Bill Gates. Housing is still a relative bargain in most of the areas around Tampa. Retirees come here to live in very nice (and some not so nice) mobile home parks. Young families and empty nesters will settle in Brandon and other suburbs where a nice house can still be had for less than $100,000. But people moving here from more expensive housing markets can apparently afford the newest luxury high rises such as The Stovall.

To the extent I could take my attention away from the road construction, I thought about all this on my way to the Andrews house in Thonotosassa. Is there a highway in America that isn't being repaired? I-4 is perpetually disrupted and requires drivers to keep their wits about them to avoid getting killed by out of control eighteen wheelers and tourists. My favorite bumper sticker around here reads: "Some day I'm going to retire, move to Michigan and drive slow."

This time, I was able to park near the house since there was no other car in the driveway. Andy's house had once been grand, but it had changed, gotten older along with the rest of us. Apparently, no one in the house loved gardening and the lawn service didn't do the world's best job. All the plants were overgrown. The liriope had grown as large as philodendron. Tropical plants were overcrowding every part of the walkway and nearly covered the windows. The lawn looked well trimmed, but it had bare brown patches all over it, as if it was diseased and no one bothered to plug it.

Nothing had been painted in much too long. The door hinges and hardware were rusted and the place looked almost unoccupied. An army man is often away from home, but Madeline had been living here on her own for the past ten years, waiting for Andy to come back from wherever he was posted. They stopped traveling together a long time ago. Whatever she did with herself didn't include house maintenance or gardening.

I rang the bell and eventually I could hear her shuffling toward the door, and talking to someone. "Elizabeth, Judy, Caesar, get out of the way so I can open the door."

She turned the knob, apparently without having to unlock the door first. She was out in the country, but someone had come onto her property and murdered her husband just a few days before. I would have had four locks, an alarm system and an armed guard installed by now, if I stayed here at all. It was curious that she hadn't.

She finally opened the door, seeming completely uninterested in who was standing there. "Hello, Willa. Come on in," she said, as she bent down and scooped up a long-haired cat. "Elizabeth, look who's here. It's Willa Carson. You remember Willa, don't you, Judy?" This last was directed at another cat off to her left.

Having been invited in, I wasn't going to demur, no matter how odd this all was. I pushed the door open and it squeaked loudly enough that Madeline didn't need an alarm after all. I stepped around Judy and two other cats, trying to keep them from running out the door as I came in.

"Madeline, I don't remember you owning cats," I said, trying not to sound judgmental about their behavior, or their smell, which was overwhelming. I've learned never to give people advice on how they raise their kids or their pets.

"You like cats, don't you?" she asked, as she walked on toward the interior. The house was dark and cool inside. I noticed at least six other cats lying around on the floor tile in the dim light. The litter boxes were out of sight, but definitely not well tended.

"Sure, I love cats. George is allergic, or we'd have some, too. What are their names?"

"This one," she said, stroking the cat she still held in her arms, "is Elizabeth Montgomery. Kind of looks like her, don't you think? I always thought Liz had green cat eyes. Kind of like yours." And she really did. Beautiful green cat eyes, I might add.

Madeline was going on. "On your left is Judy Garland and that's Caesar Romero. The others are Betty Grable, Jimmy Stewart and that old one over there is George Burns. I've had him forever."

I reached down to pick up Jimmy Stewart. Like his namesake, he was long and skinny and easy going. He purred immediately, and I carried him along while I followed Madeline into the living room where more cats sat on every available cushion.

"Marilyn," Madeline said to another white cat, "move over and let Willa sit down." Marilyn showed no such signs of life, so I gently pushed her aside and sat beside her, trying not to think about how much white cat hair would be on these navy wool slacks when I left here.

Madeline kept talking. "I started collecting the cats when all the children left home. A friend of mine is a breeder and she shows them. When they are past their show days, she gives them to me. They keep me busy. They have to be combed every day."

"How did you ever come up with names for all of them?" I asked as I put Jimmy Stewart down on the floor. He didn't go anywhere, just lounged at my feet. Marilyn decided that since I had taken her seat, she'd sit in my lap. Now there would be long white cat hair on my thighs as well as my rump.

"I was in Key West with Andy once and we visited Hemingway House. Hemingway loved cats. He had six-toed ones. They've kept descendants of his cats on the grounds and named them after movie stars. Andy thought that idea was so stupid, but I liked it. He didn't like my cats anyway, so I just picked names for mine the same way. None of my friends have six toes, though. They're all perfect really. And so much better company than people, don't you think?" She added as she hugged Elizabeth and Judy at the same time.

Marilyn was simultaneously kneading my leg with her front paws and purring in my lap. I don't know if she was better company than people, but it was comforting, in a quiet way.

"How long have you had these fellows?" She put Judy down and Caesar Romero jumped up in her lap. Elizabeth Montgomery just moved over a little bit for him to sit down. He was polite about it.

"My friend gave me George Burns when Andy went off to the Middle East the first time. I was so lonesome here then. He'd been traveling on short trips for years, but he hadn't been on assignment away from home since the children left. I wasn't used to so much quiet in the house and George came to keep me company. Pretty soon, we'd added Judy Garland and Caesar Romero. Then, it just seemed that our family grew by one or two members every six months or so. I think we could film an epic here with all the talent we have now, don't you?"

She was kidding. I think. I had been watching her closely since I came in, and she didn't really seem to be talking to me at all. She seemed to know who I was, and she wasn't drunk, but she was distracted, unfocused.

"Madeline," I said gently, "I'm sorry about Andy's death. I wanted you to know that."

She turned her blue eyes to me, and looked squarely into my face for several moments before blinking slowly, like one of her cats. Then she smiled. "I know you are, Willa. Just like I know George didn't kill Andy. George is a good man."

She couldn't have surprised me more if she'd said she killed Andy. Given her daughter's behavior, I'd worried that Madeline would be as nasty toward me and George as Robbie had been. That Madeline was so forgiving was typical of Madeline and probably what made her such a doormat to her husband and children all these years.

"You must miss Andy," I suggested, picking up Marilyn Monroe and attempting to move her onto the floor. This was a mistake. As soon as Marilyn got down, Cary Grant jumped up. I was about to give up and accept a cat as a part of my suit. At least Cary was black and his hair wouldn't be so obvious on my slacks.

"Miss Andy? Not really. He was never here. I hadn't spent any time with him in years." She said this lazily, without rancor. Maybe she was taking tranquilizers. Her affect was so flattened that she might have been on some substance after all.

"I guess I thought you two had been together more since you became empty nesters, but I can see that his job probably took him away quite a bit." I gently pulled all ten of Cary Grant's claws out of my left thigh, as he just as gently hooked them back in my right thigh.

"Andy had been away quite a bit, as you put it, all of our lives. After the children left home, that just reduced the number of excuses he had to make not to come back more often. Would you like a cup of tea?"

As an excuse to stand up and get away from all of these fur lap robes, I accepted. We walked into the kitchen, Madeline still carrying Caesar Romero, and a trail of cats behind me. I saw six kitchen chairs, none of them empty. Attempting to evict a cat from its sleeping place was apparently impossible. They just slept in the same place, even if I happened to be sitting there first.

Madeline got down the tea kettle and managed to fill it without putting the cat down. When she opened the cupboard to get out two lovely antique china cups and saucers of different patterns, there was another cat sitting on top of the plates on the bottom shelf. "Dean Martin," Madeline chided him, "I've been looking for you." She petted his head, but didn't ask him to move. And he didn't. She left the cabinet door open so he could see.

Madeline walked around the kitchen collecting the tea things as well as a box of what the English call biscuits and I call crackers. She set them all on a beautiful old silver tray with a silver tea service. All this she accomplished with one hand, while still holding one or another of the cats. Cats were sleeping in every available space, every cabinet she opened, on every flat surface I could see. No wonder Andy never came home. Where would he sleep?

Finally, she finished the tea service and had to put the cat down to carry the tray. "Shall we go back to the living room, or out onto the sun porch? It's lovely out this morning in the garden." She asked me as if it was my decision, but she carried the tray out toward the garden without waiting for me to answer.

When we were finally seated, after I had moved Robert Mitchum off the chair I wanted and Madeline had convinced Grace Kelly to let us put the tray down on the coffee table she was sunning herself from, I quickly picked up my cup and held it in my lap. Robert Mitchum was eyeing me from the floor right by my feet, but I could keep him off my lap if I kept it full. It was a little difficult to maneuver the cup and plate, eat the crackers and keep an eye on Robert Mitchum while investigating a murder, but I'm good at multi-tasking.

"Haven't you been lonely out here by yourself all these years, Madeline?" I asked her. I was feeling more than a little ashamed that I hadn't kept in touch with her. You never have too many friends and I'd always liked Madeline. She badly needed a human friend. I could feel myself tingle all over, like I always do when my behavior would have disappointed my mother. I could do better. Most of the time, I try. It's probably irrational for me, at my age, to feel I'm disappointing a mother who died half my life ago, but it's been with me long enough now that I know it always will be.

"Not really. I have all my cats to keep me company, and you can see it's hard to get lonely with them around. Besides, Andy and I hadn't lived like husband and wife for so long, I've felt like a widow for years. In my heart, I buried him a long time ago."

"Do you mean you've been having an affair?" I was beyond being polite with her.

"Only with Cary Grant and Robert Mitchum here." She laughed. "No. Sex has never meant that much to me, or to Andy. It's never been worth it."

"Worth what?" I wondered aloud, not getting her meaning.

"Did I ever tell you how I got Andy to marry me?" she asked. Instead of asking her why she'd wanted him to, I just shook my head.

"I was the girl next door. Andy never paid me any attention at all, but I was in love with him from the time I was five years old. I was always at his house and his parents became very dear to me." She looked dreamy, as if she was remembering her childhood's happier times.

"Albert, Andy's dad, was my special favorite. He was disabled, you know, in World War II. He operated an old country store at the crossroads of nowhere and back, and I would help him out after school. When he didn't have any customers, he'd tell me stories about our town, the war, and Andy. How he loved his son!" She bent over to offer more tea and biscuits. I took both, just to keep Robert Mitchum off me. The real Mitchum didn't have as much trouble with women, I'm sure.

"Anyway, I was determined to marry Andy and to have Albert for my dad, too. When Andy graduated from college, we had a big party back at the house. Andy had been in ROTC and was going into the army with a commission two weeks later. We had lots of liquor. I got Andy drunk and seduced him. When I turned up pregnant, he had no choice but to marry me. I always felt sorry for Robbie, though. Andy wanted a boy desperately. He was so disappointed when Robbie was born. He never got over it."

"Well, it sounds like Andy participated in the seduction, too. I wouldn't feel too badly about it." I told her.

"Actually, he didn't. Even when he was drunk, he didn't seem interested at all. I had to do all the work. And after that, we only made love because Andy wanted sons." She said this flatly, like old history, but I was appalled. Madeline was one of the most gracious, pleasant women I'd ever met. It was such a waste that she'd never been loved, except by her cats.

"So you see, Willa, I didn't really miss him all that much when he wasn't here. He was just someone else to wait on. And he treated all of us as if we were privates. We were allowed to do only what he ordered us to do. It was a relief when he left, actually. Now that he's never coming back, I can't say I'm overly sorry."

When we were here after Andy died, Madeline had played the part of the bereaved wife so beautifully. But then, she'd played the part of the army wife perfectly all these years, too. It's true you never know a marriage until you live in it.

"It was worse for the children, though," she continued without being prompted.

"Why?"

"Because I chose Andy. I chose my life. They had nothing to say about it. These happy babies, growing up with a father who hated them. I've never forgiven myself for that."

"Surely you're exaggerating," I know I sounded shocked to her, because I sounded that way to myself.

"No. Unfortunately, I'm not. It took years of alcoholism and therapy for me to deal with it all. The children never had the escape of booze. It's funny," she said with a quirky little smile in the corner of her mouth. "Andy wanted to be a 'family man' because he thought he needed it to get promoted. You can't be a single general, you know. But he didn't want a family. And now, none of his children are sorry he's dead. It's sad, isn't it?" She didn't sound sad. She sounded kind of satisfied, actually. Like she'd won, in the end.

She made it easier for me to ask her about Andy's death, though. I put the teacup on the silver tray and leaned forward, my forearms on my thighs. I was getting quite adept at cat-prevention.

"I agree with you. George didn't kill Andy. But, who did?" People seldom ask direct questions. Watch Barbara Walters some time. She never just comes out and asks the interviewee: Did you do it? And it's surprising what you learn if you ask directly.

"It's hard to say. There are so many possibilities. Whoever had the current number up, I'd guess." She said this they same way she might discuss a stranger. She'd given me the impression that her children might all be candidates for murderer of her husband, and she didn't seem at all interested in correcting that impression.

"Were you here the morning he died? Did you hear or see anything that might help me?"

"Yes, I was here. Sound asleep. I was in my room, with the windows closed, the curtains drawn. I'd taken a Valium before I went to bed. That dinner at George's was so dreadful, I wanted to be swallowed up in sleep. I actually prayed to die in the night, just so I wouldn't have to face you or anyone else ever again. Andy was always doing that to me."

"Doing what?"

"Embarrassing me in public. Not caring how I felt about what other people thought. He never cared at all. He just did whatever he wanted."

"You didn't kill him, did you Madeline?" I laughed, like I was making a joke. Some joke.

She didn't deny it right away. She took more tea, and another stale cracker onto her plate, not looking at me. I waited for her answer, sensing that something was going on here that I didn't quite understand and wasn't sure I wanted to. Finally, she said, "No. I didn't kill him. Not that I hadn't thought about it. But I didn't. If George did kill Andy, thank him for me, will you?"

16

I decided Madeline must be mentally unbalanced, and I doubted I could get much more out of her. But I pushed on anyway. "Did you see or hear anything at all that might help me, Madeline? Unlike you, I do love my husband and I'm not interested in visiting him in prison for the rest of his life."

She studied me closely for several minutes. She seemed to be weighing her thoughts, deciding what she would tell me and what she'd keep secret. Finally, her battle between discretion and dishonesty ended. "When Andy got the Supreme Court nomination, he thought he needed to make it look like he still had a marriage. It's a lifetime appointment, but he had to get confirmed first. He knew he might not get there. So, he started staying home more. He moved into the guest room, which is attached to his den. He could come and go through the outside entrance there, so I rarely saw him, but he did get mail here." She stopped at that point for a long time. Was I supposed to know something about the mail delivery, or what?

She got up and began to clean up after the tea service and we went back inside. She was still struggling with herself. What could she tell me? She wasn't going to continue unless I prodded her, so I said, "What kind of mail did he get?"

"Just the usual things at first. Magazines, bills, junk mail."

"And then, something else?" I prompted her after another long pause.

"Yes." She had picked up a hand towel and turned back to face me, still standing in front of the sink where she'd been washing the cups and saucers. "Yes. After a while, he got three or four plain business envelopes with no return address. At first I thought they were some type of advertising gimmick."

"But they weren't?"

"No. One day I did something I've never done before in my life. I opened Andy's mail. I was sure it was from a lover and I'd find out why he never wanted me. Or maybe I just wanted my suspicions confirmed. I'm not even sure anymore."

"Was it a love letter?"

"Unfortunately not."

"I don't understand. What was it, then?"

"It was a plain sheet of paper, printed from a computer. It said 'Stay away or you'll die.' In a way, I was almost glad to have my fears confirmed. It does a terrible thing to your self-esteem to be ignored for thirty-five years." Tears were slowly making their way down her face from the inside corner of each eye. No tantrums or hysterics. Just silent streams of water, dropping off her face onto her shirt. She seemed not to notice them. I was a voyeur to pain that no one should witness.

"Did you talk about the notes with Andy?"

"No. Andy and I hadn't talked about anything of consequence in years. I threw the letter away, and I didn't open any of the others. I'm sure they were all in the same vein."

"Did you tell the police about this, Madeline?"

"No. I'm telling you only because of George. I can't stand the humiliation of the world finding it all out. Please keep this to yourself, Willa. Use it in your search for Andy's killer if you must. But don't tell anyone our true story. Please." She was pleading with me for something I couldn't promise. It seemed General Andrews had more secrets than anyone I'd ever known. Or thought I'd known.

I wasn't going to get anything more from this visit but cat hair, allergies, stale crackers and weak tea, so I took my leave. Madeline had given me quite a bit to think about, though, and she knew more than she was telling. The only reason I could think of for her reticence was that she killed Andy herself or she suspected one of her children. Of what, I don't know. But that could be the only thing that would make her refuse to divulge the rest of what she knew, given everything else she'd told me. The way she felt about Andy's death, Madeline wasn't likely to be pointing the finger at anyone.

On the long drive back to Tampa from Thonotosassa, I tried to reach Olivia several times. She had left me a couple of voice mail messages, but they were completely innocuous. Giving up on talking with her personally, I just left her a message to meet me in my office this afternoon, and I went there to wait.

Again, I logged onto the Internet. Robbie's column was addictive. I'd been reading it every day since I'd first found it. Her opinions on things were harshly worded. Not much compassion there. Today's topics were consistent with the pattern I'd noticed: three or six letters on three basic topics, career advice (don't sleep with your boss, no matter what), child rearing (kids need discipline and parents need a life) and advice to the lovelorn (forget happily ever after). Because she dealt with this stuff constantly, I expected my letter to show up soon, although I had no idea how many letters she got every day.

Not long after I started reading Robbie's column, my secretary, Margaret, buzzed me and said that Olivia Holmes was here to see me without an appointment. I hadn't told Margaret or anyone else that we'd hired Olivia and I wasn't about to relieve her curiosity now. I went out to Margaret's office to get Olivia and greeted her professionally, with little warmth. I told Margaret to hold my calls and visitors, without explaining why.

Olivia was carrying her yellow leather Vuitton brief case and nothing else. Again, the comparison of her attire to Tremain's was remarkable.

She was the female version of the GQ Man, and I wondered, not for the first time, why that armor was so necessary to some women, particularly the diminutive ones. It must be a struggle to be taken seriously when you're less than five feet tall and well under a hundred pounds, not to mention beautiful. She looked like a hand-painted china doll. Perhaps the accouterments of success added stature in a way that compensated for lack of physical size in a culture where size matters and bigger is better.

When Olivia and I got into my chambers, I invited her to sit down and my tone was icy. Some ground rules had to be established. I was grateful for Olivia's help, but I was paying more for it than some luxury cars cost. Beyond that, this was my life, my case, and I was, for once, the client. I was going to control the relationship or I'd find someone else.

"Olivia," I said as I stretched out my hand from behind my desk. Standing on the platform that my predecessor had installed to raise the desk up above those mere mortals on the floor, I towered over Olivia by almost two feet. She had to tilt her head up to look at me the same way one might look at the stars at night.

"Willa," she said, just as professionally. If she felt intimidated, she didn't act like it.

"Please sit down," I motioned her to one of the ugly green client chairs opposite my desk and returned to the oversized black leather desk chair, another hold over from my predecessor. It had the effect of making me an imposing presence, a posture I've exploited more than once.

"I don't want you calling me here and leaving messages with my secretary. My desk is not private. I have law clerks, the Court Security Officer, court reporters, my staff, just about anyone can come in here and look at what's out in plain view. If you need to talk to me, leave your name and number only. I'll call you back when I can." I said this firmly, and watched her bristle. Clearly, she was used to much more deference than I was showing her. I thought she might actually quit over this, and it took a few minutes for her to decide how she wanted to handle it. "Of course," she finally said. "I didn't realize that my representation of your husband was a secret from your staff. I'll be more careful. But you should be careful, too. Secrets are impossible to keep. Two people can keep a secret only if one of them is dead." Something about the way she said it sent a chill up my spine, and I shivered involuntarily.

"There's something else," I said.

"What's the problem? If you've got something to say, why don't you just say it, so we can get to work?"

"Alright, Olivia, I will. I did not give you permission to talk to George about this investigation and I was amazed to learn from him that you had. I don't want you to do it again." I put all the sternness in my voice that I could manage.

"You're suggesting that I'm supposed to defend George for capital murder and *never* talk with him? That's a little unconventional, isn't it? There's no need for you to be jealous. George may be the last faithful husband in North America."

"I am not jealous. No, it is not unconventional to insist that someone who works for me do what I want them to do. And, no, I am not suggesting that you never speak with George, only that you do it when I've approved it. Not otherwise."

Olivia didn't respond right away. Instead, she went over to the water carafe on my desk and poured herself a glass of water, slowly and deliberately. She returned to her chair and sat down. Finally, she trusted herself to speak.

"Willa, we need to get something clear here. I've accepted this case because I wanted to. I don't need the work. And I don't need you. You are not my client. You know that. George is. When you're charged with murder, maybe you can call the shots. Now, if you want to fire me, then that's your choice. It won't make me stop working on this case and it won't keep George from talking to me if he wants to do so. Why don't you think about it a minute before you respond to me. I need to go down the hall." She put down her glass and walked out! On me! No one had left my chambers without my consent, ever. I was flabbergasted. And flummoxed. And outfoxed.

Because, of course, she was right. George was the client and even if he wasn't, he could talk with whomever he pleased. I'd known when I set my conditions that they were preposterous and not enforceable anyway. I could be laughed off the bench for even suggesting that Olivia's first duty was to me and not George. Besides, if there was anything George demonstrated lately, it was that he would do just what he wanted to do, no more and no less. So, I had no leverage. Olivia knew it before she came in here and I certainly knew it now, whether I liked it or not. I thought Olivia and I shared a common goal that would have made her acquiesce to my decisions. Wrong again.

When she returned from the restroom, Olivia had freshened her lipstick and taken a few deep breaths. We were both calmer. A response was due from me, so I said, "You're right, of course. I'd like to apologize. This is very, very upsetting to me and I was shocked when George told me last night that you had been to interview him and asked him about his gun."

She was graceful in her victory. "We have a lot of work ahead of us, Willa, and we'll get farther if we work together. It's pretty obvious that you and George are not communicating that well right now. He has taken care of you for seventeen years and he isn't about to stop doing that now just because you've decided it's time for you to take care of him. So why don't you let me handle George professionally. Just until we get this figured out?"

She was right again. If I wanted George to get out of this mess, I'd have to let Olivia do her job. I didn't like it, but I really had no choice. "The least you could do is to keep me informed of what you're doing and your progress. So we don't duplicate effort."

"And you could do the same for me." She looked at me pointedly. Olivia might look like a diminutive doll, but she was one hard woman. If I hadn't understood that before, I did now.

"Let's work together, shall we?" I asked her, and stuck out my hand. She took it and we shook on our new arrangement. Time would tell whether it would work any better or longer than the last one.

"You first," I said. And she smiled. Judges are not used to giving in gracefully.

"Okay. Let's get down to work. Can we move to your conference room?" She said as she walked through the door that connected my office to the conference room without waiting for my consent. I had no choice but to follow. She put her briefcase on my conference table and extracted a light green pasteboard file with a flexible side that expanded with the papers she carried in it. From the size of the file, it looked like she'd been doing more than just talking to George without my knowledge.

"I have conducted several witness interviews and what I've learned has shed a lot of light on what went on the night before the murder."

"Really? In what way?"

"Well, after Tory Warwick beaned you with the Waterford and George told everyone to leave, the Warwicks had a doozy of a fight on the way home. I interviewed both Tory and Sheldon separately and they told me essentially the same details. When they got back to their house in Hyde Park, about a five minute drive from Minaret, Tory went up to bed and passed out. Sheldon claims he stayed in the rest of the night and then went to bed. But there's no one who can support that." She was looking at the close shorthand notes she'd made with blue ink from a fountain pen on a white legal pad. I admire anyone who can take usable shorthand. I've wished more than once that I could do it. Usually because I'd like to take better notes myself, but it also thwarted my excellent skill at reading upside down.

"Since Andy was killed in the morning, does it matter whether the Warwicks can prove their whereabouts the evening before?"

"Let me finish. The next morning, Tory claims to have slept until eleven. Alone. And Sheldon claims to have gotten up and gone directly to the Blue Coat tournament. Again, neither one of them can support the other. Both had motive and opportunity, just like George. Of course, there's still the problem with the gun."

"Yes," I said, "Let me fill you in on that." I told her about my trip to the gun club and what I'd figured out from George's logs.

"I could have saved you some time there," Olivia responded. "I asked George about it."

"So did I. He wouldn't tell me." I was peeved and she ignored it.

"Actually, George's explanation is quite simple, as most truthful explanations are. He shot the gun every Wednesday at the gun club, as you discovered. The last time he shot it, Peter, George's Matre d', was with him. George had to leave, but Peter wanted to stay longer and keep shooting, so George left the gun with Peter, who took it with him when he left the club that day. For a lot of scheduling reasons, Peter never gave it back."

This actually made perfect sense. Peter and George often shot together. Peter, too, had been in the military and liked to keep handguns. George is not only fond of Peter, but Peter is very responsible. George would view loaning Peter his gun as a friendly gesture, no more. And it also explained why George didn't tell anyone about his gun. He wouldn't want Peter to be suspected of murder just because he'd borrowed the gun.

"So how did the gun get from Peter to the killer?" I asked her.

"I don't know that yet. I haven't been able to interview Peter privately. But I will and I'd appreciate it if you'd let me do it my way. In other words, don't ask him yourself just now, alright? George wants Peter shielded. Peter has talked with George about this and George says Peter's answer to the question is simple, too. But I told George I wanted to hear it from Peter directly and I don't want him to repeat it to you first." She must have seen my resistence to this, because she said, "If you won't agree to this, Willa, I'll stop reporting to you right now. I won't have you interfering where I think I can do better. It's my call. You decide right now whether you'll be working with me or not."

What choice did I have? I agreed. But if Peter just happened to tell me, or if I could get George to tell me first, that wouldn't violate my word to Olivia at all. Did I mention that when I was in private practice, I was a very creative lawyer?

I told Olivia about my interviews with Madeline Andrews and Robbie Andrews. I also told her about my work with "Ask Dr. Andrews" while she took lengthy and skilled shorthand notes I couldn't read right side up. I didn't tell Olivia about seeing John Williamson and Tremain at The Melting Pot because at the time, I didn't think it was relevant. When I finished reporting on my progress, I asked her if she'd done anything else.

"I've done a lot of things, actually. But what I think you'll be most interested in is my interview with Robbie Andrews' husband, John Williamson." With this, she smiled in a self-satisfied way that made me want to slap her and hug her at the same time. John had been there at the Andrews table for dinner and would probably have a good idea about what happened afterward. And he'd have been easier to ask than General Andrews' widow, even if I'd thought about it while I was talking to her, which I hadn't.

I used to watch that old "Colombo" television series where the detective kept going back, asking questions again and again. I thought, as the audience was probably supposed to think, "why can't this guy just ask everything at one time?" Because you just can't think of everything all at one time, that's why. No matter how clever you think you are.

"Ok. You're very good and I'm sorry I got mad at you. What did John Williamson have to say?" We smiled at each other then, friends again, storm over.

"John's a very interesting guy. I'd never met him until now and I caught him at his office unexpectedly, otherwise I doubt he'd have consented to talk to me." She looked satisfied with herself again, even though I couldn't imagine very many men declining any request from

Olivia for long. Not only was she beautiful and so petite men would want to help her, but she was persistent. John never had a chance.

"He said there was one hell of a row among the Andrews clan after George threw them all out of the restaurant, too. They started before they left the dining room and continued into the parking lot. As luck would have it, they'd all ridden over together in a limousine, so they were able to keep up the fighting until the car dropped John and Robbie off in New Suburb Beautiful."

"What was the fight about?"

"That's the interesting part. It seems Madeline Andrews is a long-time alcoholic. Did you know that?" she asked me.

"I knew Madeline had had some problems over the years. Hers has not been an easy life," I told her.

"Right. Well, she's in a twelve-step program now and she was at the point where she was supposed to forgive everyone and ask forgiveness in return. So she scheduled the birthday dinner for Andy, strong-armed the kids into coming, and set it all up as a surprise to him. Apparently he was surprised, but not too thrilled, so there was quite a bit of tension before the fight in the restaurant."

"I can believe that. From what I've seen of the family, it was a tinder box waiting for a small spark anyway."

"Right again. The fight was one of those really nasty ones that dredges up old grudges and involves a lot of screaming. John said by the time he and Robbie got out of the car, she was in a fit of rage and crying. Of course that meant their part of the fight didn't end, either."

Having had a small taste of Robbie Andrews myself, I could believe that. She was vicious to me and she wouldn't quit until she'd drawn blood.

Olivia continued. "The best part, for our purposes, is that these two went to bed separately and mad, too. And they woke up separately with no one to confirm what they did the rest of the night or in the morning."

This was another bonus. What Olivia was doing was collecting enough evidence to create reasonable doubt as to whether George had committed the crime in the hope that we could take it to Jasper, the State's Attorney, and persuade him to drop the charges before taking the matter to the grand jury for an indictment. It seemed to me she had now identified eight other people with motive and opportunity to shoot General Andrews besides George. Things were looking up.

Olivia opened her briefcase and took out a couple of sheets of paper, handing them to me over the table.

"What's this?" I asked her as I began to scan the closely typed pages. I needed my reading glasses, and I was looking around for them when she saved me the trouble.

"It's the autopsy report on General Andrews. I got it from Ben Hathaway this morning when I went over there to discuss the case. It wasn't ready when he let you look at the file initially."

I'd found my reading glasses by this time and started to read down the first page. The autopsy was unremarkable, except for the damage to the brain and the skull done by the bullet. Andy had the expected levels of deterioration of a human body in his age and socio-economic circumstances. The cause of death was pretty obvious.

The time of death wasn't quite so easy. The report considered rigor mortis (the rigidity that comes and goes shortly after death), livor mortis (the discoloration of the skin caused by the settling of the red cells of the blood due to gravity) and algor mortis, (the gradual cooling of the body). Andy was still in full rigor when they found him. That meant he'd been dead at least two hours and less than forty-eight. Of course, we knew he'd been dead less than two days because we'd seen him the night before. Sometimes, science is not the only answer. Which is a good thing for all us non-scientific types.

The blood had settled in Andy's feet and buttocks, consistent with his sitting position. Again, the livor mortis pointed to the time of death at least two hours earlier.

Andy's body temperature, measured at the scene, was low enough that the medical examiner felt confident he'd been dead at least six hours when they found him. All of which is a fancy way of saying he died well before time for the Blue Coat Golf Tournament. Knew that, too.

At the bottom of the first page, I hadn't learned anything I hadn't known before, and I was impatient with Olivia's drama. She could sense it, but said nothing. I flipped to the second page. Much of this I'd already learned from the police file, except the notation in the third paragraph where it said that the bullet, once they removed it from Andy's head, had tiny strands of gray wool fabric embedded in the tip, possibly from a jacket or heavy sweater. The conclusion was that the bullet had passed though a wool jacket or sweater on its way to Andy's head. Find the fabric and whoever was wearing it was the killer.

I grudgingly gave her the praise she was due. "Well, Olivia, I guess you do have a right to be pleased with yourself. You've gotten some real evidence for us to work with."

"There's a problem with it, though. It's not that helpful of itself, but it did tell us that we should be looking for a gray wool jacket or sweater. Like most business men, I assume George has several gray wool jackets?" She asked me, with a natural arch to both eyebrows that any woman would admire. She noticed my preoccupation with the report when I didn't respond right away.

"Of course he does. That's not the curious thing. The curious thing is why Ben Hathaway hasn't asked to see any of them," I told her.

"Ah, yes. That is the curious thing." She waited like a comedienne to deliver the punch line. "And why do you think that is?"

I finally looked up at her, giving her the full attention she craved. "Why?"

"Because they're afraid they won't find it." She was almost rubbing her hands with glee, like an Oz munchkin after a great rib dinner. "I asked Ben Hathaway if he planned to request a search warrant for George's closet. What do you think he said?"

"I give up."

"He said, maybe later. Then I asked him if he wanted me to look first. He said he'd appreciate that."

"I don't get it. Why do you want to do his job for him?"

"Think about it, Willa. If we look for a grey wool jacket with a hole in it and we find it, I have an ethical obligation to turn it over to the police. So do you. Otherwise, we'd be obstructing justice. Hathaway wins. But if we don't find it, he doesn't have to report a negative result after obtaining a search warrant, and his prime suspect is still his prime suspect. Hathaway wins again." She laid it out for me as if she was explaining the strategy behind a major league playoff.

"I understand all of that, Olivia. What I don't understand is why we would want to help Ben Hathaway keep George under suspicion of murder for a second longer than necessary. You're supposed to be representing us, remember? If Ben Hathaway looks like a fool, that's just fine by me." I rose up to pull off my robe and hang it on the back of the door to my private bathroom. I picked up my purse and said to Olivia, "Let's go search my husband's closets."

We took separate cars back to Plant Key and I was definitely not practicing my mindfulness during the drive. I was trying to decide whether to tell Olivia that George had moved out. She probably wouldn't be able to tell just by looking at his closets, because he'd only taken a few things with him when he'd moved to the club. But the point of looking at his jackets was not to find an incriminating one. To do that, we'd have to look at them all, and some were at the Club with George.

I arrived just moments before Olivia and we both parked in valet at the entrance to Minaret. Thankfully, there were no reporters out front and we were able to go upstairs without incident. After I let us into the flat and got Harry and Bess calmed down and out the back door, Olivia and I went into George's dressing room.

When we remodeled the house, we took one of the bedrooms and made it into two dressing rooms with walk in closets: His and Mine.

George's closet was meticulous. He had his suits hanging the same way you'd find them displayed at Brooks Brothers, each on wooden hangers and all facing in the same direction, colors grouped together, followed by sports coats. Shirts were boxed and neatly stacked in cubby holes. Ties were hanging on racks between the suits and shirts. Casual clothes separated from the dress clothes by a row of drawers for underwear, hose and the carefully pressed and stacked monogrammed linen handkerchiefs George carried every day. Just standing in his closet bothered me. It was so George. I missed his steady presence.

"Help yourself," I told Olivia. "I'll go make us a cold drink." I left her in George's closet so I wouldn't have to watch her look. George didn't shoot Andy, so there would not have been a hole in any of his grey jackets to find. But if he had done it, George would never have left the evidence in his closet. I assumed Olivia had already thought this through, but I wasn't going to help her with it.

She came out of the closet empty handed about ten minutes later. She was smiling and shaking her head, amused by George's closet or what she didn't find there.

"George is a real find, you know," she said. "That closet is a wonder to behold. Because the curiosity is killing you, I'll just tell you that I didn't find any holes in any of his seven grey jackets." She followed me out to the veranda, sat in George's chair, and waited while I lit my Partagas.

"Now what?" I asked her.

"Now, I'll tell Ben Hathaway I've looked for a grey wool jacket with a hole in it and found nothing. He'll not get his search warrant. You'll be spared the inconvenience and insult of a search. Believe me, after the police searched that closet, it wouldn't look anything like it does now."

She reached into her pocket, removed and ate three shortbread wafers shaped like Mickey Mouse. She ate the ears off first, just like the child she resembled in size. She didn't offer me one, and I didn't ask her to. This was the third time I'd seen her do this. I refused to ask her why.

We talked about the contents of the police file for a while. Both of us had seen it before, except for the autopsy report we'd gotten today. Much of the evidence didn't really point to anything, except for the gun. I showed her the gun logs and inventory George kept, which corroborated his story about when he last shot the murder weapon, although not that he had loaned it to Peter, as he'd told Olivia. I kept nothing from her. It was a relief to let someone else share the load, even though I wasn't sure her small shoulders could handle the burden. I trusted her. What else could I do?

I had invited my husband to dinner again tonight. I wanted to talk about the case and the evidence with him and find out what his real views on the issues were. Olivia was right that George would continue to view it as his duty to protect me and my office from scandal. But judges have been involved in all sorts of behavior that was much worse than being married to a man accused of murder. One of my colleagues on the state court bench had defeated an impeachment attempt after being accused of pointing a gun at a law clerk and threatening to blow his head off. And while I was practicing law in Detroit, a judge was accused of taking bribes for fixing traffic tickets, an offense clearly depicted on a video tape "sting." He was tried and acquitted and returned to the bench. Judges are people, too.

So George was being overly protective. As usual. And depriving the investigative team of some of its best potential strategic thinking. We needed him. It was that simple and I planned to make him see that tonight.

George arrived for dinner carrying a small box beautifully wrapped with a big pink bow. He was casually dressed in his usual Florida uniform of well pressed khaki slacks, a teal golf shirt and highly polished, brown Cole Haan woven loafers. No socks. When he hugged and kissed me, he smelled wonderfully like the combination of Irish Spring soap and Old Spice deodorant he uses. I had really missed him and I was very glad he had come home. Maybe he'd stay the night. Harry and Bess were acting like they hadn't seen him in years and he rolled around on the floor with them while I mixed drinks and asked for permission to open my gift.

The present was a retired Herrend wild goose in purple fishnet to add to Aunt Minnie's zoo. I had no idea where he'd been able to find it. The purple color is only available for special trunk shows and there hadn't been one in Tampa for a couple of years. When I asked him where he got it, he just winked and said "I've got my sources." Over the years, George has learned that the smaller the box, the more successful the present. Remember Pavlov: reward behavior you want repeated. I put the goose up on the mantel out of the reach of wagging tails and thanked him properly.

We spent the evening the way we would have before all this craziness had begun. And after dinner, over Tia Maria and coffee in the den, I said, "George, Olivia has uncovered some other suspects who have stronger motives than you. We need to analyze the evidence and figure out what to do."

George sat his drink down on Aunt Minnie's highly polished mahogany table. On a coaster, of course. "Honey, listen to me. I have been talking with Olivia pretty regularly. I know what she's found. I don't want to spend my time with you talking about this. I know it will all get resolved and it will be fine. Have a little faith." He seemed amused. George just refuses to deal with anything he doesn't want to deal with. His arrest fell into that category.

"Well at least tell me what Peter did with your gun. How did it get out to the Andrews' house?"

"Peter didn't do anything with the gun, Willa. He didn't give it to anyone and he didn't kill Andy with it. Let it go. I have to leave now." He got up and walked out the door, just that fast. I was left alone with another night of furious journaling, unanswered questions and too much room in the flat.

The morning promised to be another Chamber of Commerce day. High, light clouds in a clear-blue sky with just a gentle breeze. The kind of day when the locals wore long pants and long sleeves, and the tourists went to the beach. The forecast called for a high of seventy-six, and a twenty percent chance of rain. In contrast, the high in Detroit was to be twenty-seven degrees. Have I mentioned lately how much I love living in Florida?

I ran along the Bayshore today instead of around the island. The days of an endorphin producing run on the Bayshore are limited by threatening progress. The wind was stronger here and had actually managed to whip up a few choppy waves on the shallow water. The light clouds prevented reflection of the sun's clear blue, so the water looked gray and stormy. It was clear enough to see the Big Bend Power Station in the distance and to remind me how long it had been since I'd gone to see the manatees that gathered there.

I wanted a long run to clear my head. Besides, people-watching on the Bayshore is more interesting than the exercise. I watched as two men passed each other, running in different directions. Each raised a high five to the other. "What's up, stud?" The westbound runner shouted. "How ya doin, cool?" The eastbound one cried back. Neither looked studlike nor cool to me. Bodies of every shape, size and description were clothed in outfits similarly interesting. Handkerchiefs around shaved heads, striped shirts with plaid shorts on males; females in full war paint, dressed as if they were making a Jane Fonda workout video. The number of infants sleeping in jogging strollers being pushed by adults on roller blades was surpassed only by middle-aged men with headphones. In short, a typical day on the Bayshore.

By the time I completed my morning routine, my plan was formed. Jason was staying with his mother, Kate, while he was in town so it was a simple matter for me to track him down in a location where he couldn't avoid me and at least make arrangements to talk with him. I called Kate's house and he answered the phone. Luck was on my side.

"Hello, Jason. How are you today?"

He was wary of me because he knew I wanted something. Jason and I are close, but we don't talk often. In truth, I wondered more than once how well we knew each other any more. When I was growing up in his household, he was already off to college. He'd come home on weekends, but we didn't spend a lot of time together. I'm really closer to our younger brother, Mark. But Jason is someone I've always felt a bond with, and I think he felt the same with me.

"I'm fine, Willa. Kate's not here right now. Can I tell her you called?"

"Yes, but I really called to talk to you. I need about thirty minutes of your time. Today."

"I don't have time for you today, unfortunately. How about tomorrow?"

"No. I need to see you today. I'll be there in ten minutes." I hung up the phone, picked up my keys and headed out. He might not stick around to talk to me, but I'd cross that bridge when and if we came to it.

I pulled around the corner of Kate's house on Oregon. The driveway faces Watrous, with a straight shot to the double garage. I blocked both exits. If Jason parked on the empty side of the garage and was still there, he'd have to wait for me now. I walked up to the back door and opened it, walking into Kate's kitchen. She always leaves the door unlocked, no matter how many times George and I tell her not to. If Jason had left, he'd have locked it. He must be here.

I went through the house calling him and finally found him sitting at the small desk in the television room that Kate uses to do her household bookkeeping. He was on the phone, gestured me to sit down and turned back to his call.

"I know, Sheldon. There isn't much I can do about it right now. The local police are investigating, they've made an arrest, the ball's in their court." He waited for Senator Warwick to finish talking.

"It's not an army matter. The General was retired and the murder was not on army property. This is a civilian investigation. You have a lot more influence in the civilian world than I do. Why don't you use some of it if you want to know what's going on?" Jason didn't sound too deferential to his boss. Maybe nerves were fraying just a little under pressure. The senator must have felt the same way, because Jason signed off shortly after that by promising to meet with his boss later today.

Then, he turned to me and said, in the same exasperated tone, "Now what can I do for *you*?" I thought maybe a little mood altering was in order before I began my inquisition, so I suggested that we go out to the kitchen and I'd make coffee. He must have wanted the break, too, because he agreed.

I filled the Italian espresso coffee pot with Cuban coffee and water and set out cups, spoons and sweetener while I heated the milk in the microwave. During this process, neither of us said anything, but Jason sat at the table with his shoes off, in well-worn jeans and a faded, once red T-shirt with "I Survived The Honolulu Marathon" emblazoned on the front in now-cracked purple letters.

"Did you?" I asked him.

"Did I what?"

"Survive the Honolulu marathon?"

He smiled and gave up the pout. "No. But I survived the girl I was dating at the time who did. She gave me the shirt and I refused to give it back when she left me."

"Sort of like the one who gets left keeps the ring?"

He laughed. "Something like that." And the ice was broken. I, for one, was glad. I hate personal conflict in my life. It was one of the reasons I was so upset over George leaving the house. I deal with conflict in my professional capacity every day of the year. I don't want it anywhere near my personal life. Usually, I just refuse to engage.

I finished up the coffee ritual and we sat down with a mug full each. "Ok. What is it?" He asked me.

"Jason, I need to know why the President appointed Andy to the Supreme Court. It doesn't make any sense to me. There are hundreds, if not thousands, of well-qualified jurists for the court. Andy never even practiced law. He was a hothead who was used to giving orders that other people followed. I don't believe he could write a well-reasoned legal opinion. And he certainly didn't have a judicial temperament, as we say. Benson had to know that. So, what gives?"

"Everybody on the hill is asking the same question and has been ever since this all started," he said, trying to deflect the question.

"You're more of a politician than I gave you credit for."

"What do you mean?"

"Look. Sheldon Warwick has been your boss for ten years. I know you're friends. He is the chairman of the Judiciary Committee, the reigning Democrat on the hill and a personal friend of both the President and the General. Don't tell me Warwick doesn't know the answer to this question and don't tell me he didn't discuss it with you." I sat my cup down hard enough to splash caramel colored liquid all over the table. I ignored it. So did he.

"Assuming that's all true, it would be a breach of confidence for me to tell you. I can't do that. If you want to know, you'll have to ask Warwick yourself."

"So, he does know?"

Jason laughed ruefully, shaking his head in defeat. "Look, Willa, I love you. I love George. But I can't tell you anything."

"Come on, Jason. We're talking about my *life* here." I was pleading now, and he knew it. He considered for a long time. How much loyalty did he have, and to whom? Hard facts make hard choices.

"Alright. I can't tell you what I know without permission from Warwick, which I'll ask him for. In the meantime, I'll give you a hint, that will point you in the right direction if you won't tell anyone where you got it." He was asking me now to trust him. Did I?

"I'll accept that for now. If I have to breach that confidence, I'll tell you first. Fair enough?"

After thinking about it some more, he finally nodded. "Fair enough, I guess, if it doesn't get me fired. If this thing blows up, I'll be without a job anyway. So, here's your hint. Ask George's lawyer what happened to her brother."

Now, I was totally confused. What could Olivia's brother have to do with Andy's appointment? She'd told me she believed Andy killed her brother, but I thought she was being a little dramatic and she obviously had no proof or she would have had Andy prosecuted at the time. And that happened years ago.

"Jason, are you trying to jerk me around here? Because I really don't have the time to go off chasing wild theories. My husband is days away from being indicted for murder. You haven't forgotten that, have you?" I was more than a little nasty with him and he seemed to step back a little.

"Just ask Olivia." He said.

"Olivia already told me. It's the reason she's taken George's case. She thinks General Andrews killed her brother. So what?"

"No, Willa. So *why*?"

17

I'd planned to finish out my interviews with the Andrews family while Andy's two sons were still in town. As long as I was getting nowhere fast, I might just as well complete the trip today.

When I left Jason, I turned toward town. The Andrews twins were staying at the Harbor Island Hotel, so I would try there first. I had Greta's top down and when I drove over the Harbor Island bridge I could smell the night jasmine blooms. I'd never smelled such sweetness from another flower. It's true: paradise does smell better than the rust belt.

I parked Greta myself in the underground garage and walked up the stairs to the entrance to the hotel. Florida waterfront hotels put the lobby and registration desk on the second floor. You have to go up an escalator to get your bags to the front desk. It's so inconvenient that it probably increases tips to the bellmen by at least fifty percent. But that's not the reason for it. The real reason is hurricanes. If we had one, something that hasn't happened here since the 1920s, Harbor Island would be under water. The second floor reception desk, where all the computer equipment is, is an attempt to protect the major operations of the hotel from flood damage.

Someone asked me once if I'm afraid of hurricanes. I figure that as far as natural disasters go, they're about the best because you know they're coming. Tornadoes and earthquakes are unpredictable, floods last longer and do more damage and we all know my views on snow storms. In the past five years, hurricanes have killed fewer people than any other type of major weather disaster. I'll take hurricanes any day. You might get a new house out of the insurance company and at least you don't have to shovel them.

At the front desk, I asked for Bobby or Randy Andrews. True to all security measures now in place in public buildings for us paranoid Americans, the clerk told me "I'll ring his room for you and you can take the call on that white courtesy phone over there." Bobby was in. He said he'd meet me in the lounge on the outside deck in ten minutes, so I went out. By the time the waitress had brought my Perrier with lime, Bobby had reached my table. I stood and shook hands with him. He sat down in the chair directly across from me, not the one that faced the water. Somehow, he didn't strike me as the kind of guy I wanted to hug. In fact, I was so wary of the Andrews clan by now, I didn't really even want to shake hands with him.

Bobby had always been the serious one. He was shy and quiet as a teenager, which he'd been the last time I'd had a conversation with him. The intervening years didn't seem to have changed his Gary Cooper approach to conversation any. The only small talk was of the "nice to see you again" type that takes about thirty seconds. Then, he was waiting for me to say something. In truth, so was I. I started in a direction that I was fairly sure he wouldn't have anticipated.

"Bobby, did you know Thomas Holmes?" I asked him.

"Sure. I knew Thomas. He was in my class at West Point. Why?"

"Do you know how he died?"

"Yes. He was killed in a training accident. He was out in the field on maneuvers and someone had live ammunition in their gun. It was investigated. No one was ever charged. I don't think they could find the gun that shot him. Why do you ask? That was a long time ago."

"Was your dad there at the time?" His eyes widened and he looked at me with wariness that hadn't been there before.

"Yes," he said slowly. "Andy was there. But he was a General. He wasn't in the field with Thomas."

"But couldn't he have put the live ammunition in one of the guns so that Thomas would get shot?"

He was shaking his head. "I don't see how. How could he know where Thomas would be, who would be in a position to kill him and what gun he would have? I don't think that's possible, Willa. Really. I'm willing to believe a lot of bad things about my father, but I don't see how he could have killed Thomas Holmes."

I let him think about it for a while. Then I said, "Let me put it this way. If Andy had *wanted* to have Thomas Holmes killed in that training exercise, could he have arranged it?"

He considered the question. "I suppose so," he said thoughtfully. "A four star general can arrange just about anything. Hell, I don't know. Maybe he did do it. But why would he bother?"

"Bobby, you said you and Thomas were at West Point together. How well did you know him?"

"Pretty well. It's a fairly small group. I knew President Benson's son, Charles, too. We all hung out together. My brother, Randy, and Sheldon Warwick's son. That was early days of the Benson Presidency. We'd get invited to the White House. It was all pretty cool, really, for army kids."

"Charles Benson and Shelley Warwick were in the army?"

"Shelley was. Charles was just at West Point. You know, a special exercise for the President's kid. He was kind of a behavior problem even before his dad got elected. After they got into the White House, he was quite a handful. As a favor to the President, Senator Warwick and Dad arranged for Charles to join us at West Point for a year. That's all."

That's all? That's all? Charles Benson, Shelley Warwick, Thomas Holmes and both of General Andrews sons were friends, hung out together at the White House. And Charles Benson was a juvenile delinquent. I knew I was getting warmer. The little hairs on the back of my neck were tingling.

"Are you still friends with Charles Benson?" I asked him.

"No. Something happened with Thomas and Charles and the President told us we couldn't hang with Charles any more. Shelley was a little older than us and had left West Point already by then. Randy and I didn't mind. Charles was kind of a pain anyway, always getting into stuff and we'd get into serious trouble for it. It wasn't worth it. Our Dad was a General, but Charles' Dad was the President. We had more clout with regular army guys, you know?" He smiled.

"How about Thomas. Did he mind being banished from Charles' company?"

"Actually, he did, now that you mention it. Thomas really liked Charles, you know? Shelley, Randy and I were just being his friend because the General said we had to. But Thomas and Charles were really close. Inseparable in some ways. Thomas was pissed when the 'hands off' order came down from Dad. Thomas said he wasn't going to do it. He said the army couldn't order him to abandon his friends; the General's reach didn't go that far. But it did."

"What happened?"

"The next week, Thomas got orders to maneuvers in Korea. He was killed there a few months later. I never saw him again." Bobby said this as if he was just putting it together in his mind. I could see the gears meshing, see him adding two plus two and coming up with what I had come to believe was the only possible four.

"Still think Andy didn't kill Thomas?" I asked him.

"But why? It doesn't make sense. Oh, Andy was capable of killing. He'd done it a lot in Viet Nam and other places. But why kill Thomas? He'd already sent Thomas half way around the world to separate him from Charles. That would have been enough, even for Andy. It was the army way."

Based on Jason's hint, I now figured Olivia was right. General Andrews did kill Thomas Holmes, directly or indirectly. But why? And how was it related to the General's death? That, I still didn't know.

Those people who tell you that they just know what to say when the time comes to say it infuriate me. I've never been able to do that. I usually plan out most conversations in my head well in advance. Some of them I actually get to use. This time, my imagination had failed me. So I used the direct approach, my usual fallback.

I sat up straighter in my chair and looked directly at Bobby, resisting the urge to clear my throat first just as a delay tactic. "I guess you've heard that George has been charged with murdering your dad."

He actually smiled. Not a happy smile. Just one of those lines of the mouth that turn up on one side to let me know he found the statement mildly amusing. He nodded, but he didn't say anything. He wasn't going to help me communicate with him in the least.

I started again. "George didn't kill the General." I said, with as much conviction as I felt in my heart, which was considerable. He nodded.

"You knew that?"

"Sure."

"How did you know?"

"I know George."

"What do you mean?"

He studied me for a while, and I thought he was going to ignore the question. Instead, he said, "George has too much to lose. Besides, he would've had to have take a number and stand in line for the privilege."

"What do you mean?" I felt like a parrot.

He straightened himself in the chair, put his forearms on the small round glass table between us and leaned toward me, as if he didn't want to be overheard, even though we were the only ones on the patio. "Andy wasn't a very nice guy. You know that. He had a lot of enemies, public and private. It's not really a surprise that someone killed him, is it? Isn't it more of a surprise that someone didn't do it years ago?"

"I know he had a lot of public enemies, but I don't think any of them would have taken the trouble to try to make his death look like a suicide. What I'm interested in are the private ones."

"Most homicides are committed by family members or someone close to the victim, now aren't they?"

"You think one of your family killed Andy?"

"I think all of us would have had good reason to. If motive and opportunity count for anything, it makes sense, don't you agree?"

"Yes. I do. But you know much more about the motives than I do. Why don't you fill me in."

"Dad," he emphasized the word with such vindictiveness that I struggled not to recoil from him. He looked like he might actually spit. His hands were gripping his highball glass and I could now sense that it wasn't his first of the day. Many drinkers get quieter when intoxicated, and Bobby had all the signs. Just how much in control was he?

"Dad loved all of us. Especially me and Randy. Why would we want to kill him?" Again, he emphasized "especially" in a vicious way, like he was giving me a clue, trying to communicate something without saying anything specific. He looked directly at me, almost challenging me to understand. He'd been thinking about this for some time. He'd decided to tell someone and I just happened to be in the right place at the right time. I'm always lucky that way.

I leaned back and took a look at him again. He was tall, lean, strong and good looking. He'd been like that since he was about nine or ten years old. He and his brother were as different from his sister in body type as they were in temperament, goals and life achievements. Neither of the sons had ever married. Nor were they now in any kind of long term relationships.

Sometimes, I'm quicker to catch on than others. But it took me another few minutes. "Are you saying Andy abused you?"

"Not sexually. He did manage to draw the line there. With his own sons, anyway. But psychologically. Emotionally. Yes. Every day. It was emotional torture. He was so happy that we were just like him. He just *loved* us so much, see? He'd punish us because he *loved* us, he said. He'd threaten us, freeze us out, keep his nose in every second of our personal lives because he *loved* us, you know? I think now that he was trying to change us, to force us to be different. I think he hated us and what we were. He wanted us to be different. Straight. If it was possible, he probably would have succeeded. We definitely hated him. But it didn't change us."

When he saw that I finally understood, he relaxed a little. He sat back in his chair and turned toward the water, extending his legs out in front of him and crossing them at the ankles. He was sunning himself. He closed his eyes and dropped his head back, slouching further in the chair. Neither of us said anything for so long he might have fallen asleep. My mind was so busy twirling around the possibilities that I wanted to write it all down before I forgot any of it. I kept forcing my attention back to him. When I had just about decided he wasn't going to talk to me ever again, he began to speak, without changing his position in any way. His voice was low and I had to strain to hear him.

"Andy figured out we were his personal property when we were both about ten. When we were just figuring ourselves out. When we needed him the most. He spent all his free time *raising* us up right. Sexual orientation is nature, not nurture. Andy was on us all the time to be different. To change. Mom saw it. So did Robbie. That was when Mom really started drinking heavy and Robbie just started getting heavy. She was a pretty girl before that, you know? But it was weird that she just got so jealous of us. We would have happily traded places with her.

"The only break we got was when he was away. We began to pray for him to go. As soon as we could get away to military school, we went. No matter how hard it would be for us there, it was the only place he'd let us go. This was long before the days of 'don't ask; don't tell.' We were out of home like a shot. And we rarely came back."

"Why'd you come back now?"

He sighed. "You get older. You try to forgive and forget. You recognize that he has no power over you anymore. You know that you are what you were born to be. Your other family members have to be forgiven, too. Anger eats you up, you know? It destroys your life. You try to get past it."

"Did you? Get past it?"

"Before he died, you mean?"

"Yes."

"No. I tried. I was in therapy for years. So was Randy. I think we both managed to go on with our lives. But the anger was still there. It's such a betrayal, you know? We wanted to be like him. We were him. He was off protecting the *country*, for God's sake, and he couldn't take care of his own family." For some reason, the venom was no longer apparent in his words. It was almost like he was reminiscing about someone else. The pain in his face was impossible to watch. I turned toward the water myself.

"Did you kill him, Bobby?" I wanted him to say yes. I would have forgiven him if he'd done it, and the State's Attorney would do the right thing. It would have tied the whole thing up with a neat bow and let George and me go on with our lives. I was just so tired of the whole thing. I wanted my life back.

"I'm sorry to say I didn't. I wanted to. I tried to make myself do it. I knew some of it he was born with. And so were we. The bond was still there, somehow. No matter how much I hated him for the way he'd treated me and Randy, our whole family, he was still my father. I wish I'd killed him, Willa. But I didn't. And Randy didn't either. God forgive us." Just like his mother, silent tears began to slowly slide out of his eyes and down his face. I reached over and touched his arm, thanked him for helping me, and took my leave. I paid the bar bill on the way out and asked the waitress not to disturb him for a while.

Then, I called Olivia from my cell phone. I briefed her on my interview with Bobby Andrews and she told me she planned to talk to Randy Andrews today to ask him about the night before the murder.

It was time to compare notes and to find out whatever I could about Olivia's brother. I needed to know why Andrews killed Thomas Holmes.

Jason told me that Thomas was connected to Andy's Supreme Court Appointment, and I had to find out how. No time like the present.

"Olivia, was Thomas gay?" I asked this softly, for I didn't want to offend her. Someone told me once that a lawyer gets so close to her clients because they go through the crucible of trial together and share things no other two humans share. Maybe so. Trust didn't come easily to me, and I had come to trust Olivia. That's when you lose your objectivity. When you begin to trust someone. You invest too much of yourself when you trust. Olivia's motives for murdering Andy were as strong, or stronger, than everyone else's. What real evidence did I have that she hadn't done it? Just her word. Was that enough?

"Olivia? Did you hear me? I need to know whether Thomas was gay." I thought the question impertinent, and I was sure she did, too. But I was discerning a pattern in General Andrews life that was disturbing. His secrets seemed to be consuming him in the days before his death. His views on gays in the military were well recorded. He was brutal to his own sons because they were gay, but he didn't have them discharged from the army. He could have. If Thomas Holmes was gay, it would explain what Olivia had said was Andy's enmity toward Thomas. Think how he would have treated other soldiers. He must have made Thomas's life a living hell.

Being gay in the army years ago would have been a dangerous matter. The U. S. Military's "Don't Ask/Don't Tell" policy says gays can serve in the military if they keep their sexual orientation to themselves and do not engage in homosexual acts. If they do, they can be honorably discharged. Like so many compromises, this one between gay-rights advocates and those flatly opposed to gays in the military, was unsatisfactory to both sides. There are those that feel the "don't ask/don't tell" policy violates the First Amendment. A federal judge held the policy unconstitutional. And the policy is particularly ironic when you remember that it is the military's job to uphold the Constitution, which protects free speech. The bigger problem is controlling behavior. Hate crimes are rampant in the civilian world. No matter what the army's policies are, hate crimes would still occur there, too.

Olivia answered my question. "I don't know if he was or not. He was actually quite homophobic. Men would hit on him all the time. It would make him furious. I always wondered about the ferocity of his responses. When guys hit on me, a simple "no" is usually sufficient. Thomas would blow a gasket. But after he died, several male friends came to the funeral that I thought were probably gay. I wondered if he'd lived a secret life all those years. I'll probably never know now, and I'm not sure it matters. My parents need to believe in him as the all American hero, killed in the line of duty as an honorable soldier. I guess after I couldn't get President Benson to help me prosecute Andrews for Thomas's death, I decided to leave it at that."

"But what if he was gay, and he'd been having an affair? He could have been court martialed, couldn't he?" I pressed her, and her anger flared immediately.

"I don't see what that could possibly have to do with you. Why don't you just leave it alone." She snapped at me, and I was tempted to let it go. Something so painful might mean nothing now. Or it might mean everything.

"Don't you see, Olivia?" I asked her, as gently as I could. "If Thomas was having a homosexual affair, it might explain his death."

She was still unconvinced. "How so?"

"What if he was having an affair and General Andrews found out? How would Andrews have reacted to that?" I asked her. She already believed Andrews had killed her brother. Now she had a motive for the murder. It made sense, and she knew it, even if it could never be proved.

"How is this related to George's situation?" she finally asked me, deflated. "George isn't gay, or in the military. Why would it matter to George if Andy killed Thomas for his homosexual experiences?"

"It wouldn't. But remember, George didn't kill Andy. What we have to do is to find out who it did matter to." I explained patiently.

"Why would anyone kill Andrews over Thomas?" She was so confused by the possibility of a motive for her brother's murder she wasn't thinking with her usual razor-sharp clarity.

"I'm not saying Andrews was murdered because of Thomas. But, if he killed Thomas, he probably killed others. Maybe the murderer cared about one of them enough to seek revenge."

"Or maybe Thomas being gay, if he was, had nothing to do with Andy having him killed," she said.

"True. But then, why kill him? We're back to that," I told her.

We agreed to meet back at Minaret and compare notes. I called Jerry Benton, an openly gay member of the City Counsel and asked him to join us. When he arrived, we settled in the den.

Jerry told us that the American political climate on gays was conservative. Same-sex marriage had been rejected in the U.S. Congress several times. Job discrimination against gays is not illegal. Even the president, a liberal by all accounts, signed the latest bill against gay rights. Poll after poll shows the vast majority of Americans believe homosexuals should be free to earn a living, but lawmakers were unwilling to allow legislation against gay discrimination. Politicians want people to be able to refuse to hire or promote gays if they want to do so. Moral and religious beliefs against homosexuality are viewed by many as paramount to anti-discrimination laws.

I told Jerry and Olivia about some of the evidence in the *Newton* case I was trying in my courtroom right now. I'd read that some polls say eighty-seven percent of Americans who know someone who is gay favor equal rights for gays; only sixty-five percent favor equal rights of those who don't know any gays. Even in ignorance, most Americans are more tolerant of almost everything than politicians or, certainly, the military.

Jerry said, "Yes. The country's almost pathological support of children and families, aided by political rhetoric from both parties, is at the center of much of the hysteria."

Olivia added, "Didn't I see where the Hawaii Supreme Court all but declared the state's ban on gay marriages unconstitutional?"

Jerry nodded. "Vermont, too. Nevertheless, legal battles over the raising of children by biological or adoptive parents, where one is abusive and the other gay, continue. It's all designed to incite strong feelings. One guy was quoted as comparing same-sex couples to convicted felons. Felons in prison can marry; law abiding gay couples cannot."

Again, I recalled the *Newton* case. I said, "Psychologists will testify that a family unit with a married mother and father gives a child the best environment in which to develop. Others testify that gay couples make good parents, particularly where the choice is loving gay couples or foster care."

"Why does it matter, in this day and age of living together out of wedlock by couples of all persuasions?" Olivia asked.

Jerry said, "It comes down to several major issues: spousal benefits—health insurance, pension plans, inheritance rights—are denied gay couples, even those in long-term relationships; certain states-rights activists want to avoid being required to recognize same sex marriages allowed in other states but outlawed here; and that ever-present issue—whether such unions would weaken the 'traditional family,' whatever that is." He sounded disgusted by the whole thing and I could see why.

Finally, Jerry added, "As you well know from your trial, it's all complicated by the issue of 'coming out.' There are those gays who are just braver than others, more secure. And there are those who believe that honesty promotes understanding. Actually, October 11 is National Coming Out Day, and has been since 1988."

I said, "I know. That's one problem in my trial."

Jerry's political astuteness was valuable once again. "Actually, the politics of being gay is getting easier all the time, mostly because homosexuals are regular voters. For a time, candidates from both parties were willing to take campaign contributions from gays, but that was as far as it went."

Olivia contributed, "But I saw several of the Republican candidates in the last election talking about 'inclusiveness' didn't I? What does that mean if not some understanding of the issue?"

Jerry looked at his watch. "Unfortunately, I have a meeting I'm going to be late for up in North Tampa. But for your purposes, just understand that talk is cheap. Sure, both parties are talking about 'inclusiveness,' but where it counts, in legislation and policy matters that would make a real difference to the daily lives of gays, opposing things like gay adoption or excluding 'sexual orientation' from hate crime laws, most of the politicians are either not interested or openly opposed."

After Jerry left, I said, "I think, though, that the Andrews murder has to be somewhat about politics. Otherwise, why didn't someone kill him a long time ago? Andrews' views on gays in the military have been out there for years."

Olivia and I discussed every angle of it for another couple of hours and decided that it made as much sense as any of the other motives we'd already uncovered. The list of suspects was now longer than three pages. I wasn't sure if this was helping George or not. Being one of many possible murderers had to be enough to establish reasonable doubt at the trial, but would it be enough to get the charges dismissed? I had to hope so. I didn't think State's Attorney Jasper, even though he had been an Andrews supporter and was a staunch Democrat, would want to take this to trial and lose.

I had to bet on being able to convince Jasper to look at other alternatives. Time was getting short. George's grand jury had been convened. It wouldn't be long now before an indictment would be returned and we'd be careening down a path I, for one, wanted to avoid. There would be no middle ground. Either he dropped the charges or he went to trial. George would never plead guilty. To anything.

The one significant thing Olivia had done since we'd last talked was to interview Peter about George's gun. His explanation was so simple that I was once again impressed by how small things can completely change your life. Peter had brought George's gun to Minaret because he didn't have a locker at the gun club and he had no key to George's locker. He put the gun in the top drawer of Aunt Minnie's sideboard in the foyer so he could give it to George. But, with George being gone so much and Peter being so busy when George was around, Peter just never thought about the gun when he had time to give it back.

Peter was overwhelmed with remorse when George's gun turned out to be the murder weapon, of course. He offered to quit right on the spot. George told him just to wait and see. George had instructed Olivia not to share the information with the police and I agreed. For now. But I would be having a talk with George and Peter when this was all over. Without Peter's carelessness, none of this would be happening.

Later, I recognized what she'd said that I missed in this conversation. Sometimes, I'm so busy being clever that I forget to follow up. This one would have saved me a lot of time if I'd been listening. But I was too focused on Thomas Holmes and I knew where to go for answers.

My relationship with Sheldon Warwick was purely professional, even though Jason has been working with him for years. He was one of Florida's two senators long before George and I moved here. He'd had to support my nomination as a U.S. District Court Judge and to steer me through the confirmation process, which he had done smoothly and expeditiously.

We traveled in the same social circles and had a number of common friends. His wife, Victoria, is a casual friend of Kate's. And, of course, they ate at George's from time to time when they were in town. Otherwise, I seldom had any dealings with either of the Warwicks. I didn't even know they had a son until Bobby Andrews told me.

So I didn't know them well enough to arrive at their Bayshore mansion unannounced. They probably wouldn't let me in. So, I called first. I'd reached Tory, the Senator's wife, who said sure, I could come by for a drink before they went out to the symphony this evening.

When I got there about six-thirty, the maid showed me in to the drawing room where Senator Warwick stood with a two-onion martini, dressed in his tuxedo, waiting for his wife to come downstairs. He offered me a drink and I accepted a glass of white wine. He didn't ask me to sit down, so we stood by the bar and talked like two guests at a cocktail party.

When I thought it was about as appropriate a time as I was going to get, I said, "Senator."

"Call me Sheldon."

"Sheldon," I started over, "I want to talk to you about General Andrews."

"That's not a subject I'm prepared to discuss with you, Willa. Not now or ever. Choose something else." He said. Firmly, but not with belligerence. The voice of a man in control. One who gets his way. Always.

"Unfortunately, Sheldon, that is the only subject I need to talk to you about right now. Short of throwing me out, and since your wife knows I'm here you'll have to explain that to her, you'll need to hear me. And if you throw me out, I'll find another way to talk to you. So, it'd be easier for both of us if we just did this now."

He drained his martini glass and poured himself another without responding. He didn't change the onions. I forged ahead. "I want to know why President Benson appointed General Andrews to the Supreme Court."

"Maybe he thought Andy was the best man for the job."

"We both know that's not true and it's not the answer, either. It has something to do with Thomas Holmes. And his murder." I was watching Sheldon closely. He'd played poker in politics for a long time and he didn't give anything away.

"Who is Thomas Holmes?" he asked me.

I shook my head. "Won't work, Sheldon. You knew Thomas Holmes because he was at West Point with your son. You also know how and why he died and that President Benson wanted Thomas Holmes' death kept quiet. If you let me keep digging around, I'll find out from someone else. And maybe take you down in the process."

"My wife will be here any minute." He looked toward the staircase, willing Tory to appear. He called up, "Victoria, Willa's here and we've got to get going. Come on down, dear."

"Nice try, Senator. Now you've got about three minutes to tell me what I want to know. Because otherwise, when I leave here, I'm going straight to Frank Bendler at NewsChannel 8, tell him what I know so far and let him investigate. Which will it be?"

He thought about it for a little while. We heard Tory call down that she'd be with us shortly. He wanted to call my bluff, I knew. Finally, he said, "Thomas Holmes was a bad influence on Charles Benson. He supplied Charles with drugs and was trying to lead him into that life, which Charles wasn't sure about, but Thomas was pushing. When the President told Thomas to leave Charles alone and never to bring drugs to Charles again, Thomas refused on both counts. President Benson discussed it with me and I suggested he ask Andy to arrange for Thomas's transfer overseas. Andy did that."

I had surmised much of this. I didn't know about the drugs, but I'd thought it was something like that. "And how did he get killed, Senator?"

"That really was just an accident. A stupid accident. I know that Olivia woman thinks Andy killed her brother, but that is just not true. There was a full inquiry. That's all it was."

"I don't believe you. I think the General killed Thomas or had him killed. And I think you and President Benson knew about it. Maybe you were both involved in it."

"I don't really care what you think, actually," he said. "And you might keep in mind that there's a law against slander."

Tory Warwick picked that moment to walk into the room. "Hello, Willa dear," she said as she gave me a small southern hug and kissed her husband on the cheek.

"Tory, you've taken so long to get ready that we're going to have to go or they won't seat us. Willa, I'm sorry we have to rush. It's been a pleasure." He called the maid to show me out and I was on the front porch with the door closed behind me before I knew what happened. I'd just been given "the bum's rush."

18

Usually, when I go to the beach I just go home to Plant Key. We have a great beach and it's private. But I felt the need to drive with the wind rushing at me and to take a really long walk along the sand. I wanted to hear the Gulf pounding in big waves, the noise to silence my distracting thoughts. I left the Warwick's house and sped over Gandy Boulevard and across the Gandy Bridge as quickly as I dared. This drive used to be fairly quick, but in the last few years Gandy has become almost as progress-choked as Dale Mabry. And progress means traffic.

I made all the lights. It might have taken me less than fifteen minutes to make it onto I-275 south. I wasn't really checking the time. I opened up Greta's engine on the freeway and when I looked down at my speedometer again, I was traveling over a hundred miles an hour. The freeway was not crowded and I could weave in and out of legally moving cars. In no time I was driving toward St. Pete Beach and Treasure Island. The speed and the wind still hadn't blown away all the ugliness I'd heard. It was dancing around in my head when I parked the car, put two quarters in the perpetually ravenous meter, picked up my journal and walked toward the water.

There were a lot of condos in this area, but I was mostly oblivious to the other people on the beach. It was a little cold for bathing suits, but there were a number of tourists laying on the sand, turning blue. It amazes me that people will do what they came for regardless of the weather. Vacations are like that, I guess. This is the time they intended to spend at the beach and, by God, Herbert, I'm going back with a tan, even if it means enduring goose bumps to get it.

I can't tell you what I thought about while I walked, but when I became conscious again, I found myself near Sunset Beach. One of Kate's bridge-club friends has a condo here, and I was walking at the water's edge in front of her complex when she spotted me. It's hard to go anywhere without running into someone you know here. People from Miami, Chicago, Boston and Los Angeles don't understand this, but it's true. Everyone knows everyone. The local joke is that if you want to have an affair, you have to go out of town.

Dottie came waving a handkerchief toward me, calling my name. She was only about twenty feet ahead of me when I finally saw her. Of course, I had to stop and make small talk for a while, but my mind was so preoccupied that I wasn't really paying attention. My "ums" didn't seem to deter her. Dottie can talk for thirty minutes to a wrong number. Finally, she took my monosyllabic responses for disinterest, but misinterpreted the cause. Dottie is what Kate calls a little ditzy. It's true she's not a genius, and she's more involved in her bridge-club than world events, but she's a sweet soul and I often think the world could use more like her. There's not a mean or ugly bone in her body. It's just that she's so flighty.

"Are you and George getting along alright, Dear?" she said, putting her arm around my waist and walking along with me.

"What?"

"I said are you having trouble with George?"

"Oh. No." I must have sounded less than grateful for her sympathy. She drew away from me.

"Aren't you upset about his arrest?"

"Not really." And I wasn't, not at that moment anyway. I wasn't even thinking about George. I was thinking about Andy, Madeline, Robbie, Bobby and Randy, and how pathetic they all were. I was thinking about how horrible growing up in that household must have been and whether that would be enough to make me kill my father. I thought about Olivia and Thomas and his parents and how sad their life was. I thought about how hard it would be to be gay in the old army. Maybe the new one, too. And how much harder Andy had made it. George, for the first time since all this started, was not uppermost in my mind. I almost asked her: George who?

I thought the whole sordid story could use a fresh eye and decided to talk to Dottie about it. I made up some hypothetical reason for bringing it up. And I didn't tell her the real names of the players. I tried to make it sound like it was one of my cases I was working on. I just wanted to see if I'd lost my objectivity on this thing. Maybe George wasn't uppermost in my mind, but I had started this investigation because the thing was so close to home for me. Maybe I was looking too hard, and in the wrong places.

Dottie listened politely. Then she said something that, for some reason, just had never occurred to me before. "So you mean the father was gay?" I stopped in my tracks, and Dottie kept going. It took her a few steps to realize I wasn't next to her anymore. She turned around and looked at me. Clearly, she thought I'd lost my mind.

"What did you say?"

"I just asked if the father was gay. We get a lot of gays here on the beach you know. There's a large gay community in Tampa. They're all so nice to us. In fact, you know that general who was killed a few weeks ago? He was gay. He used to come here with his boyfriends. Of course, we all just acted like we didn't recognize him. We didn't want to be rude. But we knew who he was."

"General Andrews came here with men?"

"Not men, sweetie. Boyfriends. Cute ones, too. My neighbor across the hall, he'd sometimes let the General use his place."

"Dottie, did the General bring any particular boyfriend around?"

"Not at first. Only the last few times."

"What did he look like?"

"Tall, dark and handsome, of course. Just like the rest of them. Rugged looking. But he had this cute little widow's peak in the front," she was gesturing with her thumb and forefinger near her hairline. "You just never know."

"How many times did they come here together?"

"Goodness, Willa, I don't know. I don't spy on my neighbors." I knew, of course, that was exactly what she did, but I didn't let on.

"Of course not. I just thought you might have heard something, that's all."

"Why, Willa! I'm surprised at you. With all your troubles, I wouldn't think you'd want to be gossiping about someone else." She scolded me. "Well, maybe this will just take your mind off your troubles for today." She patted my arm again. "Now let's see. I guess I saw them here together a dozen times or so since my neighbor went back to New York for the summer. He's a snow bird, you know. A decorator. He decorated one of the Kennedy's apartments. Actually, I think it was that sweet Caroline and her husband."

I thought I might scream if she didn't get to the point. At least, the point I was interested in. "Is that right?"

"Yes. Anyway, I think the General first came to stay when Jeffrey left. And it seems to me that he was here, on and off, for most of the summer. In and out, I mean. Actually, I was about to report him to the condo board because we're not supposed to sublease. I wanted to sublease last year when I went on that Hong Kong cruise, remember? The one I took Lydia on?" She was looking at me as if I was supposed to remember this.

"Sure," I said. "They wouldn't let you sublease." Dottie didn't need much encouraging to rattle on forever about the vacation and never get back to the issue.

She looked annoyed at me for interrupting her again. "Right. So, I was just a little peeved about the General being in Jeffrey's place so much and bringing that young man with him. Jack, I think his name was. And I was discussing it with Lydia. We were both about to complain, but that young Jack, he was just such a charmer. He talked us out of it. He said they weren't really subleasing from Jeffrey, they were just using his place occasionally. Of course, I didn't know he was the General then. I didn't recognize him. Lydia said she knew who he was all along, but I don't think she did. She's always claiming to know more than she does. You know people like that, don't you?"

I tried counting to ten while smiling and nodding. I was so preoccupied, I nearly missed Dottie's final bombshell. Not that she recognized it as a bombshell, of course. Dottie could be hit on the head with a bowling ball and not realize what had happened. I tuned in at the very end of the story.

"So Lydia said maybe they'd had a fight or something. But I just didn't think that could be true because we would have known about it with them being right across the hall and all. There had to be some other reason they stopped coming here. Maybe just because Jeffrey got home."

"What?"

"Haven't you been listening?"

I rushed in so she wouldn't repeat the whole thing again. "Sure, but what does Jeffrey being home have to do with it?"

"Well, Jeffrey's place only has one bedroom. If he was back home for the winter, they wouldn't have had anywhere to sleep. So they must have had to use some other place. It didn't necessarily mean they'd broke up, does it? That Lydia always jumps to conclusions like that. Just because she's divorced, she thinks everyone else has to be miserable. For instance, she just can't stand the fact that my Arthur and I were so happy until he died. She believes I've been making that up." Dottie was wounded by this idea, but I couldn't deal with one more story from her. Besides, she'd already given me so much to think about that I had to go.

I pried myself from her grasp as quickly as I could, without giving away how much what she had told me meant. She hadn't told the police or the media what she knew so far. I could only hope she'd remain in happy oblivion for a while longer.

19

All the way home, I kept the facts in my head. I noticed nothing as I raced toward my study. When I got there, I sat at my desk with my journal and wrote down everything I'd learned today. It took me over two hours.

I had given each of the local suspects a page in my journal and listed what I learned about them as I learned it. I decided to go back over my notes now with the benefit of a strong drink to lubricate and elucidate my thinking. I began by listing everyone who I knew had a motive and opportunity to commit the murder, including some nut from one of the fringe groups opposed to General Andrews' nomination. I still thought that would be the strongest and first choice. My list included General Andrew's three children, Robbie, Bobby and Randy. In good conscience, I had to include his wife, Madeline, although I didn't really think she'd shot him. I had to include Olivia because the same motivations that made her want to defend Andrews' killer had to give her a strong reason to kill Andrews herself. Andrews' son-in-law, John Williamson, had to be near the top of the list now, if Dottie was right. And probably lovers Andrews' had had over the years, but I didn't know who they were. Or at least, if I knew them personally, I couldn't identify them.

I also had to include President Benson, Senator Warwick, his wife Tory and, to show how scrupulously fair I was, Jason Austin. I wouldn't explore whether I would let Jason be tried for murder if it meant I could have my husband back. The potential losses there were just more than I was interested in examining right now. I refused to write George's name down at all. George was a political scapegoat, nothing more. I knew that and I was certain anyone with half a brain knew that. But I had to accept, in my less impaired moments, that at least State Attorney Jasper disagreed with me: he had authorized George's arrest and expected an indictment shortly.

I wrote down all the motives and opportunities for each of the suspects. I was only trying to come up with enough reasonable doubt to convince Jasper not to indict George. After that, I was more than happy to let someone else solve this murder. All I wanted to do was to save my life as I knew it. Which meant George had to be exonerated. Fully. It was the only way he'd come home.

I made my lists, refilled my drink twice, and got lost in the minutiae of the investigation thus far. There were two issues that I still had to resolve. How did George's gun get to the crime scene and where did that grey jacket fiber come from? And where the hell was George when all this was happening, anyway?

I've discovered that this relaxing and letting the subconscious communicate with you is a good idea. I was, quite honestly, more than a little looped when I tugged at a memory in the back of my brain and it just floated up on a sea of Bombay Sapphire right into my journal through my blue flair felt tip. I doubt it had much to do with the tonic.

When I'd finished, I was so exhausted, and it was so late, that I just let the dogs out by themselves, left the door open so they could come back in, and collapsed on my bed. I was asleep in less than five minutes.

While I slept, my dreams were full of cats, beach houses, crashing waves, young boys and good-looking young men. Okay. That last may have been a reflection on the emptiness of my bed. I tossed and turned and woke up several times with heart palpitations, sweating. What was my subconscious mind trying to tell me? I told myself I'd think about it in the morning as I turned over and fell back to sleep, exhausted. But when I woke up with a jerk at four o'clock in the morning, I gave up.

I stepped over a sleeping Harry and Bess and went into the kitchen in my yellow cotton Donna Karan night shirt. It's more than a little indecent, even thought it covers my arms and everything else to just above the knee. I said it was cotton, I didn't say it was thick cotton. Not that it mattered. Harry and Bess were asleep and there wasn't anyone else here but me.

I put on the Cuban coffee. While I scalded the milk, the coffee filled the kitchen with that heavenly aroma only fresh brewed coffee can give you. It's too bad they haven't figured out how to get that smell into television commercials. Watching someone else supposedly enjoying the aroma isn't nearly as powerful as actually experiencing it. And it's no wonder Saudi Arabian women are allowed to divorce their husbands if the husband refuses to give them coffee. That should be the law in all civilized countries.

The coffee and the milk finished about the same time. I pulled down a large mug that George had given me a couple of years ago, poured the milk through a strainer and then added coffee to the right color. If you're going to get up at 4 o'clock in the morning and drink coffee, you might as well make a special occasion out of it. I turned off the burner and put the pot back on it.

I took the coffee into the den. It was a little chilly with the windows open and the night air coming in. I indulged myself further with a small fire. It's a gas log system, so it's easy. I know it's not a real fire, but it's a lot less work. Then I selected some quiet piano music and turned on the stereo with the volume down. I wanted Harry and Bess to sleep a little longer. I wasn't worried about them having bags under their eyes or anything, I just wanted total peace and quiet. Unlike me, they are bundles of energy when they wake up. Of course, I don't usually wake them at this hour, so who knows?

During my fitful sleep, I had worked much of the scenario for General Andrews' murder out in my head. I was still having trouble with one very big piece of the puzzle. How did George's gun get to be the murder weapon? George told Olivia that he'd loaned the gun to Peter who brought it home from the gun club. What I didn't know was how the killer got it from where Peter put it in Aunt Minnie's sideboard.

George had loaned the gun to Peter a week before. Peter put it in the sideboard two days before the murder and forgot about it. He hadn't checked for it at any time after that and it had turned up at the scene of the murder.

So the question was, in that two days, who had access to the gun? The answer included George, me and Peter. It also included everyone who worked at the restaurant and everyone who'd been here in that time frame. But most of those people had no motive to kill Andy beyond the political one. Except George, and I'd eliminated him from the start. So we were back to all the names on my list. Every one of them was in the restaurant the night before Andy was killed. Except Olivia. Or was she there, too, and I just didn't know her then?

So, which one of the suspects with motive and opportunity had taken the gun? The gun could have been taken the very night of the murder. I went over each suspect carefully, but none of them could be easily eliminated. I closed my eyes and visualized everyone at the restaurant that night. It was easy to do. That night was indelibly imprinted on my brain forever. It seemed I could see all the tables in the dining room; recreate the argument between the Warwicks and Andy; see Tory Warwick hurling the glass toward me and even feel its solid weight against my forehead. I raised my hand to the place where the lump had come up the next day. All traces gone. What a shame inside wounds don't heal as quickly as visible ones.

Okay. Just for starters, I considered that the gun was taken sometime before that night. Then, the possibilities were endless and I got nowhere. So, I decided to consider that someone in the room took it that very night. I looked at each of them closely. What were they wearing? The gun was too big to conceal in a pants pocket, but it could have been tucked into a man's waistband. Or it could have easily been slipped into a handbag. Which one of the women had a handbag big enough to hold it? Victoria Warwick never carried one, so that left her out.

I was so startled when it hit me that I nearly spilled my coffee. Of course! Now I remembered it. One of those large, open feedbag types. The kind you could fit the kitchen sink in. But, had I seen it that night? Did she have it then?

I refilled my coffee and sat there until the dogs woke up at their usual hour, planning how I would make her tell me the truth. Nothing but a confession would satisfy me. Considering my previous failures with confessions, you'd think I would have learned my lesson. Hubris, thy name is lack of sleep.

An early morning walk on the beach with the dogs might make me feel a little more like normal. The dogs were bounding ahead of me, running in and out of the surf. They wanted to play fetch, so I threw a stick for them for a while. By the time we were done, all three of us were thoroughly soaked. I rinsed them off and put them in their kennel to dry. Then I slugged myself up the stairs and into the shower and went back to bed. I'd worry about it later. Later, I'd get some answers. When I woke up again, I went back at it from another angle.

I'd almost given up looking for a response to my letter, even though I had gotten a feel for Robbie's style and her answers were pretty canned as well as increasingly harsh. Today, she had the usual questions on the usual topics. Are people who use the Internet less imaginative and experienced than letter writers? Or do they really lead such dreary lives? Takes one to know one. Here I was writing a letter to an online therapist. Might be time to cancel my online service.

In any event, today's column had three letters about workplace issues involving sexual misconduct of one kind or another. The child rearing queries were about sexual abuse. And the lovelorn letters were about sexual dysfunction. Except for mine. Mine was the only letter of the day that wasn't about sex, but Robbie's answer was. "You can't have a sexual relationship with a man who is in jail," she wrote. "If he's convicted, divorce him or resign yourself to infidelity."

Interesting take on the whole thing, Robbie. No chance he really was innocent, hmmm? Guilty conscience?

Whenever I'm looking for someone in Tampa with old money on Saturday, I start with the Old Meeting House. The Old Meeting house on Howard in the district some clever marketer with a sense of humor has now called "SoHo," meaning "South Howard," is a page out of history. It was a diner in the fifties and they still make their own ice cream. To say it is reasonably priced is like saying it snows in North Dakota. Have you ever noticed that people with old money so rarely spend it, while those who've made their money more recently seem to have a much better time? Sure enough, I found Warwick there, politickin' as they call it in these parts.

For meeting with the masses, Warwick dressed the part. He had on an old pair of khaki pants that looked like they'd need a patch any day now. The required beat-up Topsiders with no socks and a cloth belt with small fish on it that was ragged around the edges finished the bottom half. His golf shirt was a faded navy blue that had a few speckles of paint on it, just for effect. I wondered if he got these clothes from his gardener. He certainly couldn't have worn these clothes out in his years in Washington.

Warwick was surrounded by several Tampa movers and shakers, all of whom were dressed exactly as fashionably as he was, but they wore their own clothes. They dress this way to be comfortable and because they're not trying to impress anyone. The difference between these folks and Sheldon Warwick is that they are all genuine. I took a seat at the counter and ordered a grilled tomato and cheese sandwich and a fountain coke. I knew they all recognized me, but this was not a gathering where women would be welcome or accepted. They didn't want to be rude, so they just acted like they didn't know I was there. Once acknowledged, the southern gentlemen's code of honor would require them to include me. And be polite about it. After I'd finished my sandwich, it sounded like Warwick was about to get up and leave. As he did, I followed him out to the parking lot and interrupted him as he tried to get into his fifteen-year-old Volvo. Another sign of old money is to buy your cars by the pound and never replace them while they still run.

"Sheldon," I called to him. He turned around.

"Oh, Willa. How nice to see you." He smiled for the crowds, or at least any crowds he thought might be looking. He held out his hand and took mine for the same reason. There was no warmth there.

"That's funny, Sheldon. I didn't have the impression you'd want to see me again so soon after our last chat."

"You exaggerate, Willa. You always have." He turned to unlock his car door. "I do need to be going, though. Have a good day." Before he could step into the car, I moved closer to him and took off my sunglasses.

"Sheldon, I'm sure you know I'm not going to let this rest. Olivia told me that you have no alibi for the time of Andy's murder. Unless you give me a good reason not to, I'm planning to put you on my list of suspects and give State Attorney Jasper another dose of reasonable doubt about indicting George." As I said, I've always been a fan of the direct approach.

This time, Sheldon took off his sunglasses. His were five hundred dollar Ferragamos. I guess when he got dressed for his burger with the boys he must have neglected to borrow his gardener's old aviators. "Look, Willa, I've indulged you because you're Jason's sister and George's wife. But don't push your luck. There is nothing you could tell Jasper that would make him look at me as a suspect. Beyond that, I had no reason to kill Andy. As for my alibi, I don't have one because I don't need one. But I do have an appointment. If you're looking for a plausible alternative to George as murderer, you might consider your lawyer. She had more of a motive to kill Andy than I did." He tried to get into his car again and I took the door handle, refusing to let him pull it closed without making a scene.

"You're a political animal," I said. "You have been all your life. Andy was making you look bad, ruining your first confirmation hearings, disgracing you before your constituents. He exposed your lack of real political clout for all the world to see. Men have killed for less. I think Jasper will look into it if I ask him to. Think about that, Sheldon. You've had a long and successful political career. I'm sure you wouldn't want to be indicted in your last term."

He slammed the door, started the engine and backed out of the driveway, leaving me standing there holding nothing but the air and a fingernail broken down below the quick.

Another talk with Jason was now a necessity. He was the only one I could really discuss all this with and I knew so much now I believed he would be more open with me. I called Jason and asked him to meet me at the Club. It was the lunch hour, so George should have been at the restaurant.

Jason walked into the small private dining room about twenty minutes later. We ordered appetizers and drinks, talking family matters for a while. Our brother Mark's return to Tampa, our sister Carly's relationship with a local plaintiff's lawyer of questionable character, Kate's impending trip to Italy.

It was pleasant to sit and talk with Jason about ordinary things. We hadn't had much contact in the past twelve years. He'd been living in Washington, D.C., but he was often out of the country on business for Senator Warwick or helping him campaign in election years. Jason wanted to be secretary of state some day. He had high political aspirations and he was thinking of running for Senator Warwick's seat when the senator retired. I have to say I would have been proud to have Jason in the Senate, but it was a waste of his considerable talent. I've already recorded my view of the political process and everyone involved in it.

"Jason, I took your advice and investigated Thomas Holmes' death."

"I know. Warwick told me."

I smiled. "What did he say about our interviews?"

Jason smiled, too. "That you are just another impossible woman and it's too bad you already have a lifetime appointment. He said he can't get rid of you, but he won't support you for advancement to the Court of Appeals, either." Jason took a sip of his bourbon and water. "Sorry."

"Actually, unlike almost everyone I know, I don't have any aspirations to higher office. So it's not much of a hardship. Besides, if what I think is going on is actually going on, I'm not too sure Senator Warwick will be in a position to make a difference to my career if I should change my mind about that."

He looked troubled, now. It's always whose ox is getting gored, isn't it? Jason wanted Warwick to stay in the senate for another term and then retire while endorsing Jason to replace him. If Warwick couldn't do that, Jason would have to change his career plans. Jason has had his life planned out in concrete progressive steps since he was ten years old. He wouldn't be too happy about anything that upset the applecart at this stage of his career. He'd worked too long and too hard to get where he was.

Which made me look at him a little more closely, too. Wasn't he just a little too satisfied to have George accused of murder? Not that he wanted or expected George to be convicted. But if George was arrested and the police were no longer investigating, that gave Jason as well as his boss a little more breathing room, didn't it?

"So, what did you find out that made Sheldon so upset?" Jason still sounded like there wasn't any possible way that I could be a problem for Senator Warwick. Maybe that's what made me decide to shake him up a little.

"I found out that President Benson asked General Andrews to get Thomas Holmes out of Charles Benson's life and shut him up. Permanently. And Sheldon Warwick not only knew about that, he arranged it." I said this as if it were a fact, not just a few well-placed guesses on my part. Judges don't actually lie. I just stretched the evidence a little. Jason wasn't likely to repeat it anyway.

Jason almost choked on the ice that he'd just started to chew. Kate always told us that chewing ice was bad for your teeth. She didn't say anything about breathing. It looked like the Heimlich maneuver would be required for a short while, but the fortunate thing is that ice melts. Jason just choked and coughed and eventually, got himself straightened up.

"Willa, you are barking up the wrong tree there," he said, once he could talk again.

"Maybe you better straighten me out, then, because unless I get some other information, this is the story I'm going to State Attorney Jasper with. And Frank Bendler. I've only recently discovered what a powerful thing public opinion is. I want my husband out from under suspicion and back in my home. You can help me accomplish that or not. Your choice."

Jason is a tough political animal and I was counting on that to get him to help me. He was finally coming to see that he had no real choice unless he wanted to make a new life plan. "I didn't mean to suggest that Thomas Holmes was murdered. His death really was an accident, just as the army said."

"If you believe that, then why did you steer me in that direction?"

"Don't you believe it?"

"No. But answer my question," I said.

"Because you wanted to know why President Benson appointed Andy to the Supreme Court. Andy was no more qualified for that job than I am. Maybe less. But Andy wanted the job. He hadn't really wanted to retire from the Joint Chiefs. The army was all he knew and he loved it. He'd have stayed forever."

"Then why didn't he?"

"Because they made him leave." Jason took a deep breath and got up and poured himself another bourbon and water from the drink cart. He stood there with his back to me and drank a few sips of it before he walked back to the table. He put the drink down and put his hands in the pockets of his khakis. I recognized the stalling tactics that precede information one doesn't want to disclose. I just waited. It wasn't my turn. He took another drink.

"You've already figured out that Andy was gay?"

I nodded. No use denying this now.

"It's mostly irrelevant to the world today in most circles, but in the army? Well, you know what the status of the world is there." He took another drink. At this rate, he'd be pie-eyed before he finished. I sipped my white wine spritzer. Slowly. I wanted to have my full attention on the facts.

"Yes, Jason. I know. And Andy knew, too." I said.

"Sure, he did. Just being gay wouldn't have been a big problem if he'd kept it to himself. But he couldn't do it. He had to make advances to other army personnel. Even if they were willing participants, Andy was so senior and had so much rank that you'd never know for sure. And some weren't consenting. At least, that's what they said when they filed sexual harassment complaints against him. One particularly nasty event came to the Senator's attention. Sheldon went to President Benson and they told Andy he had to retire. If any of the complaints were made public, they'd ruin his career anyway. Andy had no choice but to step down."

"Except?"

"Except he wasn't going to go quietly. He told Sheldon and the President that he would only retire if the President agreed to nominate him to the Supreme Court when the next vacancy came up. President Benson refused and Sheldon refused to support him in the confirmation hearings." Jason sat down and took a few more gulps. I continued to wait.

"And that's when Andy told them both that if they didn't make sure he got on the Court, he would make sure the world knew about Charles

Benson's drug use and how they'd all handled Thomas Holmes. Because it touched Sheldon personally, too. His son, Shelley, had been a part of that crowd."

"What did Benson say?"

"What choice did he have? Charles has straightened his life around. He's married now. Got a couple of kids. You know, a man will do a lot of things to protect his kids. He said he'd think about it, but Sheldon knew he'd do it. And Sheldon was glad. We were all hoping there wouldn't be another vacancy before Benson's term finishes out next year so Rumpelstiltskin wouldn't get the King's first born sons. But then Miller announced his retirement and there you have it." Jason drained the glass and sat there, saying nothing, waiting for me to respond.

Now I knew why Andy had been appointed to the Supreme Court and I felt certain that appointment was related to his death, even though I still believed he would not have been confirmed anyway. The confirmation hearings were too controversial and after President Benson issued his midnight memo telling the Democratic senators they could vote no without being disloyal to the chief, there was little chance of the confirmation.

"Jason, we both know George didn't kill Andy. I want you to help me find out who did. I'm playing beat the clock here. Once the State's Attorney gets a grand jury indictment any day now, there will be no turning back. There will be a trial. I don't want that, George doesn't want that, and I can't believe you want it, either."

"I'd like to help you, Willa, I really would. You know I love George as much as everyone else does. I know he didn't kill Andy. But I don't know who did."

"If you knew, would you tell me?"

"I'm not sure. I guess that would depend on who did it." Jason was nothing if not honest. As much as it pissed me off, it also made me believe him. Go figure.

20

When I got home, I fell into a deep coma which lasted until about six-thirty that night when Harry and Bess decided it was time for me to get up. I took a shower and dealt with the dogs, called down to the kitchen and ordered up some dinner. The special was plank roasted salmon with snow peas and lemon caper sauce. It certainly sounded better than any of the science experiments growing in my refrigerator.

While I waited for dinner to come up, I fixed myself a Sapphire and tonic with a wedge of lemon, not lime, picked up the newspapers and took everything out to the veranda to read and enjoy my first Partagas of the day. The sun had long since set and I had to turn the lights on, but fighting the bugs was preferable to being inside another minute. After a few sips of the Sapphire, it was a lot better than sitting inside. Sometime after dinner, I went back to bed.

Saturday and Sunday were uneventful. I would have done something, if I could think of something to do. Olivia was out of town, I guess George was busy with the restaurant, I couldn't reach Kate and I just needed to recharge my batteries. I didn't hear from George all day Saturday, which caused me alternating bouts of anger and anxiety. I tried to work through them with exercise and journaling, but I guess I was just too close to my own musings.

By Saturday night, I'd ordered dinner up and settled in with a good book, trying to distract myself while I figured out how to fix this whole mess, when I heard a knock at the door and went to collect my meal. I was pleasantly surprised to see it was dinner for two. And the waiter who delivered it was a certain tall dark and handsome man I knew quite well. I can't remember ever being so glad to see him.

A long time later, I was heating up the dinner in the microwave while George poured Stag's Leap Cabernet into Aunt Minnie's Bacarrat goblets. We were eating in the kitchen. By the time we finished dinner, it was late and I didn't want to spoil the mood by talking about the case, so I seduced my husband for the second time that night and persuaded him to sleep in his own bed. Harry and Bess joined us and we were all dead to the world until the rooster crowed at six o'clock. Figuratively, of course. We don't have any roosters. We live in the city.

Sunday was more of the same. I spent the day with the dogs in introspection. George invited me to dinner Sunday night, but he refused to discuss anything "unpleasant" as he called it. He came up for a night cap, but left around eleven. I was actually looking forward to the trial the next day because it signified that everyone was getting back to business, but I was about a half hour late taking the bench Monday morning. The jurors had all arrived and the litigants were set up in the courtroom. I had my Court Security Officer go in and tell them they could take a short coffee break and I'd be ready to begin at nine-thirty. No one dares to question a federal court judge's trial schedule. But I felt guilty anyway.

Olivia had left several messages at my office, each with a more demanding sound. The last one said she'd be over to see me at three. She left no number to return the call, so I had no choice but to wait for her.

I looked at the rest of my pink message slips, quickly reviewed my notes from the last trial day, put on my robe and walked slowly into the courtroom. I hope they thought it was a stately entrance and the day would go smoothly, but that would be too much to ask for.

During a jury trial, some judges literally sleep through the evidence. The jury decides the facts, so paying close attention isn't all that essential. I usually try to pay attention anyway, just so I won't be bored. Today, it was a real struggle. The testimony was long and tedious. There were few evidentiary arguments. Even the jury was bored.

Why do people still go to law school? If every student was required to sit through a month long trial before they took the LSAT, I guarantee law school admissions would be down at least fifty percent. The rest of the applicants are just masochists.

After the lunch recess, the gallery was full of reporters. I recognized at least two from each newspaper as well as the local and network news stations. It had been a long time since I'd had a Dateline reporter in my courtroom. And I saw Frank Bendler in the back. Whatever was expected, it was big news.

Before we brought the jury back, I called counsel to the bench. "What's up?" I asked them both simultaneously, covering up my microphone with my hand so the question and answer wouldn't be broadcast at six and eleven.

"I have no idea, Judge," Newton said. I believed him. We were still in the middle of the plaintiff's case.

I turned to Tremain. "Well?"

"Me neither." He looked me right in the eye. I wish I was a better judge of liars. I was pretty sure this was a whopper, but aside from public flogging, I had no idea how to get it out of him.

"In my chambers. Both of you. Alone." I looked up and said, "The court will stand in recess for ten minutes." Both lawyers followed me back, leaving the goslings twittering around at the defense table. I signaled the court reporter to remain in the courtroom. This would be off the record.

When we were all seated, I turned to both of them. "I know you've got something up your sleeve here. I don't know what it is, and I'm not continuing this trial until I find out. So, you can tell me now, or you can all go home until you do tell me. Your choice."

Tremain looked uncomfortable, thinking it over. Newton looked merely curious. I'd entered a gag order in the case, and besides, if Tremain had already spilled the beans to the press they wouldn't be here en masse to find out what the story was. So I had to figure he'd just hinted that there'd be big news today. He'd have to send them all home, in which case they might not come back, or he'd have to tell me what he had planned and risk ruining his show. It took him a while to decide.

"Mr. Newton plans to present the Court with a motion this afternoon for an injunction preventing us from publishing his tennis club membership list."

"Why do you want to use his tennis club list?" I asked.

"Because I have a witness, a member of the club, who will testify that the club is all gay."

Newton said, "And the names of the people on it include men who are not publicly 'out,' Judge. This is outrageous. Only a first rate scandal rag like this Defendant would ever consider such a thing! It's just not done!"

I rubbed the throbbing that had started between my eyes. I didn't have the mental acuity to deal with this issue today. I doubted I ever would.

I turned to Tremain,

"Putting aside for the moment how you got the list if it's so top secret, why is it relevant to this trial?"

"Because Mr. Newton's name is on it, your honor. It's an all-gay club and he's a long-term member. It establishes our truth defense."

I thought about it, the wheels turning ever so slowly in the process, and it seemed he was right. At least it was evidence of the truth of the matter, clearly relevant.

"What's your response to that?" I asked Newton.

Now he was the one who looked uncomfortable. "Judge, the prejudice of this document is unfair. If you allow him to publish this list, even tell that the tennis club is not just a men's club, as everyone believes, but a gay men's club, a number of innocent people will be irreparably harmed, including me."

I considered the matter for what I like to think was longer than it would have taken me if I'd been a little more with it. "Let me get this straight, you should pardon the pun. What exactly are the issues here? In short sentences, please."

Newton started. "Judge, this list is information that is completely unrelated to any legitimate purpose. Its only value is to justify public curiosity about people who are not even parties to this case. If you disclose this list, everyone on it will be thrust unwillingly into the full glare of public bigotry, with no corresponding benefit to the public." Good point. I looked at Tremain for his response.

"Mr. Newton has alleged two things in this case. The first is that whether or not he is gay is a private fact which *The Review* should not have printed in any event. The second is that he is not gay and the article is defamatory as untrue. This list is evidence of the truth of the 'Mr. Tampa' article. Beyond that, whether Mr. Newton is gay is newsworthy, and the list goes to our defense. This is a question of fact and it can only be determined by the jury's informed weighing of the competing interests involved. 'Mr. Tampa' had this list at the time the article was printed. If we are precluded from using the list, the policy you'll be espousing is that the media should always skirt trouble by completely avoiding any possibly sensitive area. Surely, that is a chilling effect on the First Amendment." Another good point.

"Look, the only way I'm going to be able to resolve this is to look at the list, and your briefs. I presume you both have law on this subject?"

"Yes, Judge," they said in chorus.

"Ok. What we're going to do is to go back out there. I'm going to put an innocuous statement on the record and call the jury in and dismiss them for the day. You're going to submit your briefs and the list, and I'll consider it. You'll get my ruling tomorrow morning. Between now and then, if one word of this appears anywhere outside these four walls, you two will be spending some quality time together in close quarters, do you understand?"

So that's what we did. Not surprisingly, they both had briefs prepared already. When I got the paperwork from them, I recessed for the day.

I spent the next couple of hours trying not to worry about what Olivia might have to say, whether it would be good or bad news, what she'd think of my news and my conclusions. On the theory that the best defense is a good offense, I decided to call the CJ and take my frustrations out on him. Unfortunately, it was too late to catch him. I had to smile when I thought of his reaction to getting my message when he came in tomorrow at the crack of dawn.

I reviewed my mail, most of which had been previously screened by my secretary or my law clerks. Usually, what I got were motions, briefs and exhibits, letters inviting me to speak at one bar function or another, invitations to conferences, professional journals, and so on. The mail that has been piling up on my desk was more of the same. By the time Olivia called to say she'd meet me at a little restaurant in Ybor City, I'd reduced my in box by half and filled my trash can over capacity. Do lawyers create paper the same way sanders create dust? That must be true if my daily trash is any indication of reality.

Ybor City is a unique enclave in Tampa and a good example of the fickle nature of popularity. The area began as a cigar manufacturing community populated with Cuban expatriates. Cigars eventually went out of vogue and the community declined. In the late 1980s, the area was rediscovered and turned into a thriving night time destination. Teens cruised Seventh Avenue under the canopies of twinkle lights until the residents finally insisted on a curfew and an anti-cruising ordinance.

Night life doesn't start in Ybor until ten o'clock and it carries on until the wee hours, getting progressively more wild and loud. My golf partner, Mitch Crosby, told me about a client he represented who actually got shot while cruising the bars and didn't even know it happened. There was so much noise in the bar, no one heard the gunshot. She was so drunk, she didn't feel her missing tiny phalange until two bars later. The case had to be abandoned because she couldn't even identify which bar she'd been shot in, let alone who shot her. At least she had a vacation story to tell that would top most of the others for the folks back home in Fargo.

I met Olivia at a trendy place called Bernini where patrons can smoke cigars during dinner in the upstairs dining room. Bernini reminds me of a few places that I have a fondness for, like the Gotham Grill, in New York City. It's got a huge bumble bee for a door handle, but other than that, it's well decorated in a way that is not Tampa. The food is good, too.

Olivia was waiting for me on the lower level with two glasses of Chardonnay at a corner table in the back. After greetings and small talk, I asked her where she'd been over the weekend.

"You don't own my time, Willa. I needed a break. You probably did, too."

"I did need a break. And I got a lot of rest, which I also needed. But I needed to talk to you, too."

"Well, I'm here now. What did you want?"

"I wanted to ask you whether you killed General Andrews?" The hell with her. I'd wanted nothing of the kind, but I'm a Federal Court judge. I don't have to put up with this attitude.

"Okay. Calm down. I'm sorry I didn't call you back. I was indisposed. It won't happen again. Don't get your panties in a wad." She smiled, trying to cajole me into a nicer tone at least.

I was placated, a little. "Okay. I accept your apology." No reason to be too obsequious just because I'd made my point.

"But it's a good question, anyway. Did you kill him? Like a lot of other people, I'm finding out, you certainly had good reason to." I was no longer belligerent, but I needed to watch her reaction when she answered the question. Of course, I'd temporarily forgotten the defense lawyer's creed, "deny, deny, deny."

Olivia looked me right in the eye, unwavering as she'd done hundreds of times to juries, witnesses and convicted felons. "I did not kill General Andrews. And I know you don't believe I did. If I was going to kill him, I would have done it a long time ago. And if I had killed him, I would just let George take the rap for it because that would relieve me of any possibility of conviction. No. I didn't kill him."

"Do you have an alibi?" I asked her.

She looked at me through narrowed eyes and then relented. "As it happens, I do. I was in Tallahassee. With the governor and about five hundred other lawyers. At a conference. Feel free to check."

She must have wanted to kill him. I think I would have wanted to, in her shoes. "Why didn't you kill him?"

She looked away, sipped her wine and began to review the menu for her lunch order. Olivia signaled the waiter, a tall, thin man with the smallish grey glasses that are popular with the twenty- somethings these days. We both ordered salads and decided to share the excellent fried calamari.

"Look, Willa, this is totally non-productive. Why don't we just bring each other up to date and get back to work. My psyche isn't at issue here. I don't owe you any explanations for my actions. You can believe I killed Andrews or not. You can investigate me or not. But you and I need to work on getting George cleared before that indictment comes down this week and we're running out of time. Why don't we concentrate on that?"

So, for the remainder of the lunch, we did. Since she'd been "recharging" over the weekend, she didn't have much to report. I told her what I wanted her to know. We noodled for a while and then went our separate ways. I had a lot of work to do tonight and I needed to get started.

Once I finished my after-work routine, I got out the pending motions for the Newton trial. The parties were expecting an answer in the morning.

I started with the list of club members itself. I pretty well understood the legal arguments and I knew that it was mostly a matter of judicial discretion. What that means is, as usual, the judge can do whatever she wants. This sounds easier than it actually is. Have you ever tried to figure out what you want? So, I decided to start with the list.

The title of the document was simply, "The Men's Tennis Club Membership List." It was four pages of names, all men. The addresses included San Francisco and Key West, but also Indianapolis, Kansas City and other Bible Belt areas. Some of the names I recognized and was surprised to see. There was a married actor, several lawyers and doctors, a recently divorced state governor running for congress, and more than one law enforcement officer. Just for good measure, there were a few military men. Indeed, all occupational groups seemed to be represented.

The list wasn't arranged in any particular order that I could discern. It wasn't obviously alphabetical, regional, or occupational. It was two single-spaced columns containing names, job titles, business and home addresses and telephone numbers. There was a double space between each listing, as if the list was used to print mailing labels. Clearly, there was plenty of ammunition here to ruin more than a few lives.

I read the first two columns carefully, feeling like a voyeur. This list was a private matter. It was true that many of the men on it were public figures who, for the most part, were not protected by libel laws, even if their names were erroneously placed. But the potential destruction from making such sensitive information public without the knowledge or consent of the participants was overwhelming and offensive, to say the least.

After a while, I realized that I was reading a list of partners. A casual reader, without knowledge of the secret these men shared, might think it was a list of tennis partners. Perhaps that was the idea. My eye continued to travel down the second page and I saw more and more names I recognized. By the time I got to the third page, I had almost stopped registering the information. And it was then that I saw it. On the third page, near the bottom. Both names together. A. Randall "Andy" Andrews and John "Jack" Williamson. So that was why Tremain had been lunching with Jack. He wanted Jack to testify about the list. Would Jack do that? Had he tired of living in the closet? Or, was it some sort of revenge against Robbie? Could Jack really want more sorrow heaped on the Andrews family? And I knew not only what my decision would be, but how I would resolve my personal problem as well.

I knew, but I wasn't happy about it. The whole thing sickened me. Andy wasn't murdered because he was gay, although I was pretty sure he just narrowly missed being killed for having an affair with his daughter's husband. What a despicable man he'd grown to be in the years since we'd known him. George thought Andy had become mentally unstable and that much was clear. But nominating such a man to the Supreme Court was morally corrupt, regardless of why it was done. The trouble was, at this point there was nothing to be served by bringing it all into the public's awareness. Andy was already dead. Society couldn't execute him again.

My mother, or George, or what Kate calls my "spine", or maybe even my subconscious had already decided this matter before I ever even knew it existed. What people do with their personal lives is not going to be the subject of dinner table conversation in Tampa because of any decision that I make. Newton had made some valid points about privacy in his trial. And maybe if Andy was still alive, the public would have a right to know he was gay before he was put on the Supreme Court for life. But he was already dead now. Secrets are corrosive, but even if I do behave like Mighty Mouse sometimes, I know I can't change the world. The older I get, the more I understand the benefits of just being kind.

The list was not going to be made public. I don't know where Tremain got it, but the private lives of consenting adults were going to stay private in this trial. I also reviewed my journal and accepted that I had reached the point where I could no longer put it off. One last issue had to be worked out. I slept soundly the sleep that comes with making what I believed in my heart was the right decision.

When we reconvened Tuesday morning and I announced my ruling on the list, there was a great gnashing of teeth at the defense table. Both parties allowed as how they had reached a conditional settlement overnight and agreed to a voluntary dismissal. Neither of the litigants offered the reason for the decision and the terms of the settlement were not disclosed. Newton's sexual identity was never proved, but neither was the item retracted by *The Review,* and I got to cross the case off my docket, improving my statistics. I turned my attention to more important matters.

21

I'd had a while to think about how I would handle the denouement. It seemed to make the most sense to do it alone. I couldn't do it in my chambers, the place I felt safest in the world. Since the Oklahoma City bombing, Federal courthouses are guarded like the Crown Jewels. It would be next to impossible to get a gun, knife or other deadly instrument in here. But I could never get the killer to go for it. So I had to go there.

I went over my props and my dialogue. I thought I had worked out all the possible snags. Even the knotty little problem of proving what I was sure I'd hear had been gone over carefully. At exactly six o'clock, I left my office. It took Greta and me about twenty minutes to get to Jetton street. The house was closed up tight, just like the last time. The uninitiated might think no one was home, but I knew better. I parked down the street and waited until the pretty, Cuban assistant left. Then, I got out and walked up to the front door.

I didn't bother to ring the bell. I now knew it didn't work. I just turned the knob. Locking the door is a habit and we only think we do it most of the time. Actually, burglary is easy because people don't always lock their doors and windows.

I wasn't looking to steal anything and I wasn't breaking any laws. Not really. After all, I was a family friend. At one time, anyway.

I heard the sound of computer keys clicking and followed them down the hallway to the third door on the right, facing the back of the house. The door was open. I could see her sitting at the keyboard. She was concentrating intently on the screen and didn't sense me standing there for quite a while. It gave me a chance to look around the room. The window was closed and the drapes drawn so as not to have the light reflecting off the computer screen. When I saw the couch, I had to laugh. Even an online psychologist has to have a couch, I guess. There were two end tables and the only light was from the two small table lamps.

The computer desk, a tall bookcase and the very large chair she was sitting in completed the furnishings. Not much room for a physical struggle. Not that I thought there would be one. Anyway, I could take her. Right. She outweighed me by a hundred pounds. I was just hoping she didn't get the opportunity to bowl me over.

Finally, Robbie looked up. She was startled. "Did Juanita let you in?" If she had, she'd be looking for a new job tomorrow.

"No. I knocked, no one answered and I let myself in."

"I guess I'll have to talk to her about keeping the doors locked, then. I'm working. And I said all I've got to say to you already. Please show yourself out." She turned back to her screen. I guess she intended to ignore me so I'd go away.

"I'm not leaving, Robbie, until you talk to me. You can do it now or ten years from now. But we are going to talk." She looked at me with such contempt that I nearly lost my resolve. For a while, she continued to ignore me, but eventually, she got tired of staring at the screen and pretending to work. She finally turned around and got up. Even standing, she was a good foot shorter than I am.

"What do you want?"

"May I sit down?"

"No. You don't have anything to say to me that you need to sit down for."

"Alright. I'll say this standing up." I leaned my side against the left door jamb and propped my right arm against the right jamb, effectively blocking her exit, unless she wanted to knock me down. "I've discovered that your husband and your father were having an affair. I know who killed Andy."

I watched her closely. She was controlled. She was trying to decide how to handle it. That she was deciding told me more than any instant reaction would have. She knew about the affair. And she'd known for some time. This was no surprise to her. It made me wonder who she'd told about it. She didn't seem the type to keep a secret.

Secrets were something I knew a thing or two about. I had my own secrets, which I guarded carefully. But they were the tame variety, just privacy issues, really, that a woman in public life has to be vigilant about. Over the years, I've learned that most people have secrets of one kind or another. And the lengths they'll go to protect them are farther than one might think.

"That's preposterous. If you're through slandering my husband and my father, you can leave now. You'll hear from our lawyer." She came toward me and I think she really expected me to let her through the door. I refused to put my arm down and she stopped before she ran into it.

"Is there something else? Surely you don't want to continue with this?" She was still forceful, belligerent.

"Yes. I do. Don't you want to know who killed your father?" I asked her softly. I didn't need to get into a shouting match with her. Besides, if you're quiet, sometimes they listen. It worked.

"Of course I do. But why would I believe you? You just lied to me and I already know you can't be trusted. Just get out." She was coming toward me again. I stood up from my slouching position and filled the door way as completely as I could. Since she couldn't step through unless I moved, she stopped about two inches from my face.

"I think I understand why you killed him, Robbie. He was a mean, vicious and vindictive man. He never loved you. He stole, in the end, the only thing you ever thought you had: Jack. Under the circumstances, I might have killed him, too." I'm sure I couldn't actually kill anyone, but I had learned to lie so easily. It's simple to have principles and values when you live in a safe world, surrounded by people who love you and take care of you. Many of us never put those principles to the test. Based on my experiences lately, I wished I never had. I liked what I thought my life had been much better than what I've learned we're all really like. I resented the whole damn situation for making me learn that lesson.

As I confronted Robbie, I became so filled with anger that I was tempted to hurt her. I was shaking with the barely suppressed rage. I wanted her to try to brush past me, to give me an excuse to hit her. She had turned my entire life inside out and upside down. I wasn't too motivated by compassion for what her life had been like. Fortunately for both of us, she just sat back down and cried. I found her pathetic, the situation abominable. And, I really believed, in that moment, that a jury might have excused her if she'd done more. My anger evaporated like dry ice.

Andy wasn't just a lousy husband and a lousy father. He had never loved Robbie and he had taken from her everyone she ever thought had loved her: her mother, her brothers and ultimately her husband. How much was a human supposed to withstand? A colleague told me once that men are animals, civility just barely keeping their hostility under the surface. I'd scoffed at the time. Life is just one big learning experience, isn't it?

"I didn't kill my father, Willa." She sat down heavily in the chair across from me. "Not that I didn't want to. I would have. I went out there the night he died. To kill him. I even took George's gun with me. Only, I didn't know it was George's gun until later."

"How did you get George's gun?" At last, the thing I really came here to confirm.

"I just took it. I opened the sideboard at the restaurant and there it was. I picked it up and put it in my purse. I wanted to see if I could get away with it. And I did." Of course, she did. George would never expect a guest to steal from him. No one at Minaret would expect it. Stealing is just not done.

"Why had you decided to kill Andy that night?"

"You already know the reason. His affair with Jack. It had been going on for years. Even when we lived in Colorado. Jack only wanted to move here to be near Dad."

"How long had you known?"

"A long time. I'd tried everything. I'd threatened Jack, argued, pleaded. I'd pled with Dad, too."

"Sent threatening letters?"

Her eyes widened, then narrowed. "I told you to stay away from my mother," the snarling Robbie had resurfaced. It was hard to feel pity for this one.

I ignored her change of mood. "So, why that night? If you'd known about the affair for years, why kill him now?"

She sighed and her shoulders drooped. "You already know we were all arguing that night?" I nodded.

"We were fighting over my threats to tell the world about Andy being gay. The family was outraged with me. Families keep a lot of secrets, Willa, for a lot of dysfunctional reasons. When the limo dropped us off at home, Jack told me he loved Dad. More than me. And if I told the world Andy was gay, they'd just be free to be together. And he said they would. I could live with a bisexual husband. The only way to keep him was to eliminate the competition."

"What happened when you got to Andy's house?" I asked her.

"I went around to the door to his den. He was getting ready to go fishing. I knocked and he looked up and waved me in. I took George's gun out of my purse and went in pointing it at him. I had every intention of killing him. I wanted him dead. I'm glad he's dead. But I wanted to tell him what I thought of him first. That's where I made my mistake." She'd started to shake remembering the confrontation. Her face suffused red and her mouth was tight with white lines on either side of her pursed lips. Her emotional state was volatile and unpredictable.

"I told him to leave my husband alone. I told him he was a lying, despicable person and a worse father. I said everything to him I've ever wanted to say. Everything I'd said in therapy for years. And you know what he did?" She was enraged again now. Her memory of the confrontation taking on a life of its own. She had relived this humiliating scene at least a hundred times.

"What did he do?"

"He laughed. He refused to talk to me. He said, 'Put the gun on the desk and go home, Robbie.' Just dismissed me! Went back to his fishing tackle! I wanted to shoot him. I wanted to. I really did." She started to cry, then. Huge, wrenching, uncontrollable sobs.

"What did you do with the gun?" I needed to know. This was perhaps the most important part of her story to me.

"I put it on the desk, like he said. I left the suicide note I'd written for him there, too. I just left. I didn't do anything to him at all." The psychic cost of not following through on her desire to kill her father might have been more than Robbie could cope with. She might kill herself instead, I thought. I couldn't leave her alone like this because I had no idea what she might do.

While I was trying to think what to do next, she pushed right past me. I had my guard down. Here I was feeling empathy for her and she was intent on getting away from me. She ran quickly down the hallway and out the front door before I realized what she had in mind. By the time I got out after her, she was in her car with the door locked, backing down the driveway.

I ran after her, pounded on the window, shouted for her to stop the car. She ignored me, tears still streaming down her large, round cheeks and pouring from her red nose. She backed out into the street. I ran down the block and tripped on one of our damned uneven sidewalks. I got up, limping and holding the bleeding scrapes on my arms, pulled out my key and jumped into Greta. Robbie took off and Greta sped after her.

Robbie knew her neighborhood streets better than I did. She made a quick left turn and then a right. By the time I got to the intersection, I had lost sight of her. I had no idea where she went. I pounded my hand on the steering wheel and said a very unjudicial, not to mention unladylike, word. It didn't help me find her.

Except that I was afraid I'd pushed her so far that she'd hurt herself, maybe it didn't matter. I now knew what I needed to finish this, once and for all.

I became aware of Bob Seger singing on the radio. "*Make it calmly and serene. The famous final scene.*" I was ready now. For this, I didn't want to catch him at home. I'd asked Jason where I could find the senator this afternoon and, to his credit, Jason had told me. Conveniently, Senator Warwick was playing golf at Great Oaks. Alone.

I asked the starter where I could find Senator Warwick. Playing alone, the Senator would be making pretty good time. I picked up a couple of clubs, took them out to one of the carts and drove off to the ninth tee, which was a little distance from the Clubhouse.

I saw Sheldon Warwick on the fairway of the ninth hole, just in the middle of his back swing on what was probably his second shot. The ninth hole is a straight par three. The idea is to keep you playing, so your last hole or your last hole on the first nine should be a fairly easy one. The Senator was a good enough golfer to get on the green in one from the tee. He must have missed his drive. Something on his mind, maybe.

As he was walking back to his cart, his second shot having landed on the green where the first one should have been, I drove up to Warwick and stopped. "Hello, Senator. Mind if I join you on the tenth tee? The starter sent me out here since you're alone." I'd had so much lying practice during this investigation I found myself doing it now without so much as a twinge. This wasn't a character trait I'd wanted to develop and I vowed to work on it as soon as my husband was no longer a murder suspect.

"Is there any way I could stop you?" Warwick asked. He was a fast learner, anyway.

We drove both carts, me following him, up to the ninth green. He took his putter and I followed him without a club, just to watch. I won't say I was making him nervous, but it took him three putts to put in a six-footer. Neither of us said anything.

When we got to the tenth tee, I took out the driver I'd borrowed from the pro shop and put the ball on the tee. I hadn't hit a golf ball since the day of the Blue Coat. Usually, I take some warm up shots, but I wasn't here to impress anybody. I hit the ball a respectable 150 yards, straight. Warwick took his time and hit the ball a little further. As we walked back to the carts, I said, "Sheldon, I need you to know that I've figured out who killed General Andrews."

"Have you now?" He said, as he got into his cart and headed off toward my ball, which was about twenty yards from his. Apparently he was unwilling to get out in front of me on the fairway. Wise man. But he didn't get out of his cart, either, and after I hit the ball another 150 yards, he sped off, leaving me standing there.

I got up to him when he was walking back after his second shot, pulled between him and his cart and got out. "I think here's the time for us to talk about this and get it over with."

"Willa, for God's sake. First you invite yourself to join my game. Then you get in the way. And now you want to hold up that foursome behind us, too? Aren't you being just a little childish?" He stepped around my cart and got into his. As he'd done before, he sped away and stopped at my ball in the fairway. His ball had made it to the green. "Hit the ball, Willa. We'll talk at the green where we're not making a public spectacle of ourselves." I hate it when men act so condescending to me. Who the hell did he think he was anyway?

When we got up to the green, he putted his ball in first. Then he stood by waiting for me. He said, "It was just a matter of time before someone killed Andy. He had cheated death a hundred times and there were at least that many people who would have liked to kill him. If he'd been the first one out of his limousine the last Friday of the hearings, he'd have been shot instead of John Hamilton right then. What difference does it make now who did it and when?" I put my ball down in two and we drove separately to the eleventh tee.

Again, Warwick arrived before me. I had beat him on the last hole, but he went first anyway. "It makes a difference to me, Sheldon."

"Why? You know it wasn't George. He's not worried about it. Jasper will never be able to convict him. Let it alone. Justice has already been done."

"Not good enough. I don't want my husband to go through a trial or risk conviction. I want my life back." I hit the ball, taking a cue from my friend Dr. Marilee Aymes who pictures the heads of her enemies as the ball. It worked. This time, my drive was much longer than his. Who'd have thought not having enemies was a golf handicap all these years? We rejoined at his ball and I didn't tell him how I'd hit mine so much farther.

"How'd you get George's gun?" I asked him as he hit his second shot about a hundred yards off to the right. The fairway dog-legged to the left. Not his day. Next we met at my ball.

As he watched my second shot, he said, "I didn't 'get' George's gun. Andy had it. I think Robbie brought it with her when she meant to kill him. He laughed about it. He said she'd never done anything right in her life. She couldn't even hold on to her husband. I picked the gun up off his desk and put it in my jacket pocket before we walked out to his fishing boat."

We'd both need another fairway shot on this par five hole, so once again, we met at my ball. This time, his was just a short distance away. We both got out of our carts, me with my five iron and him with his seven. I set up and hit. He hit a few seconds later. Both shots landed on the green, although he was closer to the pin.

"Why'd you shoot him, Sheldon, if all you had to do was wait and let some anti-abortion nut do it for you? Or one of his kids or lovers? Why get your hands dirty? It's the end of your career, you know." He sank his put and it was my turn.

"Timing, Willa, timing. If Andy could have been confirmed and gotten on the Court, he'd have been satisfied only until the next scandal, when he'd be right back asking for more favors. But his confirmation was not going to happen. Mostly because of his own belligerence and foolhardiness. He made it impossible to support him, even if I'd wanted to. When I told him that night that I was voting against him, he threatened to frame me for the murder of Thomas Holmes. Which, of course, I had nothing to do with. Except that I kept quiet about it after I found out he killed Thomas. Andy made a pass at Thomas, but Thomas wasn't gay and he had an immediate, visceral, irrational response. He had a gun in his hand and threatened Andy with it. Andy was quicker. He shot Thomas and then he covered it up. I swear, I didn't know. But, when the other sexual harassment complaints came out in the President's memo that night, I went to talk to Andy, to try to persuade him to decline his nomination. He wouldn't hear of it. He was raging, irrational. We argued. He told me about Thomas. He said he'd tell the world that I had asked him to kill Thomas to keep him away from my son. I know he would have done it, too. He laughed when I said I'd kill him first. He laughed at me. Me. *Andy was laughing at me.* Can you imagine? So I shot him. End of story." He could have been discussing his last appearance on *Meet The Nation*. When did politicians become their own law?

I sank my putt in three again. Good thing I wasn't betting on this game. "You didn't take the gun out of your pocket because you didn't want to wake Madeline?" I asked him.

"Something like that," he laughed. "Of course, you won't ever be able to repeat any of this. Even to free your precious George. You have no corroborating evidence and I'll deny it all."

"Where's that beautiful grey cashmere jacket I saw you in the night before Andy died, Sheldon? The one that must have a very inconvenient bullet hole in the pocket?"

He laughed again and I felt a little of what Robbie felt when she confronted her father. "The trash truck picks up in our neighborhood on Saturday morning, Willa. Isn't that convenient?"

I remembered a trash truck behind me as I sat at the curb after the golf tournament that Saturday. That's when I first heard about Andy's death on the radio. "Then I'll testify," I said.

"I doubt it," he replied, smugly.

"And how are you going to stop me? Shoot me, too, right here on the golf course? That would be a little awkward wouldn't it?" I learned another lesson at this point. It's best not to be sarcastic to a murderer in a golf cart when you're on foot.

Instead of answering me, his cart sped off toward the clubhouse. By the time I caught up with him, he'd left his cart with the bag boys and gone into the men's locker room. I couldn't very well chase him in there, so I just leaned up against the wall near the entrance and waited.

After a while, he came out. With the mayor, the CJ and two other pols. They nodded at me, said hello, and went on out to their cars. Jason drove up in a Mercedes sedan, Warwick got in and Jason waved as they drove off toward the airport.

By the time I found Greta and followed them, both Warwick and Jason had gotten on the Senator's private plane and were taxiing down the runway, probably on their way to Washington.

I'm not sure how a woman looks with her tail between her legs, but that's exactly how I felt. I fished around in my bag for my cell phone and dialed Chief Hathaway. He wasn't in. Why is it you can never find a cop when you need one?

I had no choice but to go home and reconnoiter, as they say. What a mess.

22

When I got home, George was there. I decided to come clean and tell him the whole story, including my confrontation with Warwick, the botched attempt I'd made to get a confession out of Robbie and that I now did not know where she was. He was, as always a lot of help. "Call Ben Hathaway," he suggested.

Since I had already done that and left a message for Hathaway to call me back, I ran the dogs to clear my head.

I found George reading the paper on the veranda with his Glenfiddich in his hand. He suggested I take a shower and he'd make me a Sapphire and tonic. Like I said, he's always a lot of help.

When I joined him for a drink and lit my cigar, he casually mentioned that Ben Hathaway had called and was on his way over. I was sitting there with my hair wet, no makeup on, in my nightgown. Great. Hathaway knocked at the door and George went to let him in while I put on a robe.

I could hear George leading Ben into the living room and offering him a drink. Always the consummate host, even to a man who has accused him of murder. When they made my husband, they definitely broke the mold. We only have one chair big enough for Chief Hathaway to sit in, so every time he comes here, we have to sit in the living room. They sat, drinks in hand, talking like the old friends they were until I walked into the room. George got up, as he always does when a woman walks in and Ben, not to be outdone, heaved his bulk out of the chair. I'm sure he expected me to excuse him from the courtesy. He'd have to think again. It would be a long time before I excused Ben Hathaway for anything.

"Good evening, Ben," I said, not shaking his hand but taking my customary seat near George on the sofa. George had made me a fresh Sapphire and tonic, but I needed a clear head for this conversation. I had already warned George that I would do all the talking. I didn't want him making any admissions we'd have to deal with at trial if this didn't go the way I wanted it to go.

Hathaway sat back down with a thump. I wondered how long that chair would last. Aunt Minnie's mother had owned it, but it wouldn't survive until the next generation lived at Minaret if Hathaway continued to visit us.

"Well, Willa, suppose you tell me what you've been up to. I understand you have some theories about who killed General Andrews. Besides George, here, I mean." He turned his head and winked! And George actually laughed. Men are so impossible.

I gritted my teeth and drew my bathrobe together. It was hard to maintain my judicial dignity with wet hair and no clothes on. I had decided to share almost everything I knew, but I would not tell Hathaway about the Men's Tennis Club. I didn't need to tell him to get the point across. After all, I had Dottie's eyewitness account of the "love nest," and I didn't really need to disclose the tennis club list. And Robbie had confirmed her husband's affair.

I ended with a description of my encounters with Robbie and Warwick this afternoon. He raised his eyebrows a few times during the telling, but maintained his silence until the end.

"It's amazing what kind of mischief people will get into. I can't believe none of his enemies got him. Why does it always have to be a friend or a member of the family?"

"Let's not speak ill of the dead, Ben," George admonished. "Andy was a good man once. Life dealt him some harsh blows." I was about to interrupt when George held up his hand to stop me. "I know, he did some despicable things. But judgment is not for us to make, Willa. That's someone else's job."

"Actually, George, I am a judge and I make judgments all the time. Forgiveness may be divine. I'm not." I turned to Ben Hathaway and suggested that he might want to get started looking for Robbie and Sheldon Warwick before they came here and killed one of us.

"I hardly think that's likely," Ben said.

"You didn't think either one of them had killed Andy, either. You'll forgive me if I don't agree with you." He had the grace to nod in acquiescence before he got up to go.

"He's out of the jurisdiction now, Willa. And he's right that we have no evidence to connect him to the murder. You've seen the forensics, just as I have. He'll deny the murder and you will testify against him, pitting your credibility against his. When the true, despicable nature of Andy's character comes out, it will only tarnish Andy's reputation further and hurt his family. Is that what you want?" Of course, he was right.

"No, Ben. I don't want to hurt Madeline and her family any more than they've already suffered. But I want George out of trouble and I want his name cleared. How are you going to do that if you don't arrest Warwick?"

"I'll talk to the State's Attorney, tell him the truth. He'll need some political favors from Warwick one day, if he doesn't owe some already. He'll make sure the grand jury doesn't return an indictment against George and the investigation will remain open, the case unsolved. Will that do it for you?"

It wasn't perfect, but it would solve most of our problems. "It doesn't clear George's name, though. I want you to release a statement saying that George's gun had been stolen from him and you have not been able to find the thief. I want you to say George is no longer a suspect and you made a mistake. I want you to say you're sorry."

Ben sighed. "Ok, Willa. I'll do that. This afternoon."

George said, "That'll be fine, Chief. We appreciate your help."

Ben got up to go. "I'm really sorry for all the trouble this has caused you," he said, in our general direction. "You understand I had no choice but to arrest George. I knew the real killer would turn up sooner or later." I resisted the urge to throw something at him as he left the room.

Epilogue

It wasn't easy to tell Olivia about what had happened to Thomas. She'd already expected the worst and she'd gotten most of it right. I think telling her about Thomas's real relationship with Charles Benson, Shelley Warwick and their drug use was the right thing to do, but I'm not really sure. Before I told her, she thought her brother was a wonderful young man who had been murdered by a cold hearted General. Tarnishing the image of the dead in the name of honesty may not always be the right choice.

The charges against George were dismissed after we explained the facts of life to State Attorney Jasper. He'd never have gotten a conviction at trial and he didn't want to face the public humiliation. Whether he owed Warwick any political favors was a question I didn't want answered. What Jasper did with the information we gave him was not for us to decide.

After the charges were dropped, George and I had several long conversations about the investigation and the events leading up to his arrest. He told me where he had been the night before and the morning of the murder. Infuriating to me was that Robbie Andrews had been telling the truth. George did meet with President Benson, Senator Warwick and Jason to discuss how to defeat the confirmation and the President's sabotaging memo. As much as I ignored George's interest in politics, I was still interested in meeting the leader of the free world.

George said I wouldn't like President Benson anyway, but he was projecting more than a little there.

Jason continued to work for Sheldon Warwick because he claimed Warwick was going to retire and endorse him for the next senate race. I doubted anything Warwick said could be relied on and I was sorry to hear that Jason's ambition was as great as I had feared. Ambition is like electricity: it can be helpful or destructive. It looked like Jason was going down the destructive path, but he wouldn't listen to me or to George when we tried to talk to him about it. All we could do was hope for the best.

George moved back into our house and things pretty much returned to normal between us. By normal I mean we went back to our usual routines. We ate together, slept together and were our joint best friends. But our relationship had changed. Neither George nor I were the people I thought we were. I think he felt the same way. It would be some time before we found our way around each other again. Now, picking up the pieces and reassembling our life would take some time. As Kate said, a seventeen-year marriage can still hold some surprises.

THE END